CRAVEN'S WAR
RUNNING THE GAUNTLET

NICK S. THOMAS

Copyright © 2023 Nick S. Thomas

All rights reserved.

ISBN: 979-8327215030

PROLOGUE

The campaign of 1812 offered a huge opportunity for the Anglo Portuguese army, but also enormous risks with several French armies of a similar size still operating across Spain. After many weeks of tedious but clever manoeuvres, one of those armies commanded by Marshal Marmont was encouraged into making battle with dire consequences for the fifty thousand-strong force. The French army was scattered and suffered horrific casualties at Salamanca with many more taken prisoner in a decisive victory for Wellington which few believed possible, for this was not a defensive victory as he had become known for.

With Marshal Marmont defeated, the path to Madrid appeared open, a prize and chance to liberate the city, which had been a principal aim following the battle of Talavera three years previously. This was the second chance so many believed they would never get.

On the army marches into the unknown, but with hope in

their hearts and triumph in the eyes of the world. Yet the battle of Salamanca was only the first step in driving the French out of Spain, for there was so much more work to be done.

CHAPTER 1

"You see that, Paget!" Craven roared enthusiastically as he pointed to a road sign directing them to Madrid.

It was the jewel in the crown that had evaded them years before, and for a long time it felt like a goal so far out of reach that they may never get another chance at liberating the city. It was the capital and seat of power of King Joseph, the brother of Bonaparte the Emperor himself had installed.

"Will he stand and fight, Sir?"

"Who?"

"King Joseph?"

Craven burst out into laughter.

"That puppet with only a handful men? He will fly from that city well before we are in sight of it."

Joseph had little respect in Spain, not from the Spanish, the Anglo Portuguese army, or even many of the French soldiers deployed there. But the fact remained he was the most senior appointed Frenchman in the country and a figurehead which to topple would send shockwaves throughout Europe and all the way back to Napoleon himself.

"Do you think Napoleon will finally come and face us, Sir?"

"Oh, no, he is far too busy waging his own war into Russia."

"Will he succeed, do you think?"

"With the greatest army ever assembled, it can only be a great triumph or spectacular disaster."

"Then I pray for the latter, for I cannot imagine what Napoleon might achieve with his grand army if he marched upon us. We could be swept away like we were nothing, all the way back to England, and then have to defend our own borders from his unrelenting march."

"Indeed, it has been the fear in England for many years now, and yet here we are, resisting Napoleon's forces in distant lands, and if we continue to fight and win like we did at Salamanca, then we chip away at Napoleon's Empire."

"But is it enough?"

Craven shrugged as he honestly had no idea. The echo of musket fire in the distance caused him to halt their advance. Sporadic fire continued. It sounded as though a small skirmish had broken out not far from them.

"How far is that?" Craven asked Moxy, knowing he could judge the distance by the sound of the shots better than anyone.

"A little over a mile," he replied quickly.

He peered around to see there was no one else rushing to help, and they were well ahead of the main army, though Major Spring and several of his staff came galloping towards them.

"Must be a few stragglers causing a ruckus. Get in and help, Major!" he cried out to Craven.

His timing seemed a little too convenient, but Craven welcomed a little excitement in an otherwise monotonous march.

"Riders with me!"

He took off towards the sound of the action. He didn't wait to see if the others would follow him as he had no doubt of it. He trusted in his comrades wholeheartedly in a way he never had in his previous life. It was a refreshing feeling to know that so many dependable soldiers and friends had his back. They galloped on with some speed and knew it would be only a matter of minutes before they were at their destination and joining the fray. Few shots could be loaded and fired in that time. But they were all acutely aware of how quickly a situation could change in close quarters if a fight reached bayonet and sword range, or even the threat of it, for many soldiers fled at the sight of a cavalry or a bayonet charge.

Shots continued to echo out ahead of them, and they could smell the putrid powder smoke wafting across the open ground before them, with the action unfolding in a valley below the natural shelf in the ground ahead. Craven led twenty mounted soldiers. It was a perfectly adequate troop for scouting duties but hardly a formidable fighting force, and he had no idea what sort of trouble they were about to run in to. He couldn't imagine it could be much, for the French army was in flight after the mauling they had endured at Salamanca.

Craven led them forward over the crest to find two horses with empty saddles, both the mounts of British officers from the looks of the equipment fixed to their saddles. Beyond them a small battle was raging where three carts had sought shelter among the remnants of a burnt-out farmhouse and outbuildings. Several French cavalrymen lay dead on the approach, their horses fleeing into the distance, whilst more Frenchmen fired on at the defences with their carbines. A few dozen others still in their saddles rallied for another attack. British soldiers fought from behind and atop the full waggons whilst others had sought refuge among the stone ruins where they loaded and fired from open windows and doorways.

"Make ready!" Craven took his rifle from his back.

Paget was stunned that he had not charged in with sword in hand, but also glad he had not, for they did not want to come between the fire of both sides. The French cavalry were starting their advance to make another rush on the defences and had not even noticed the arrival of Craven and the others. The skirmish and near continuous sporadic fire had entirely concealed their approach.

"Present!" Craven cried.

Even his roar went unnoticed in the chaos below.

"Fire!"

Their volley ripped into the French cavalry, knocking many out of the saddle and causing their advance to waver as they slowed in a state of confusion. Craven quickly slung his rifle onto his back and drew out his sabre, the very same sword Le Marchant had gifted him. It now meant more to him than ever, following the tragic death of the General during his most successful feat in the field of battle at Salamanca.

"Charge!" he cried out as if he were himself a cavalryman.

A British officer fighting from the ruins raced out in jubilation to see their rescuers with his own eyes. He grabbed hold of a riderless French horse and leapt onto it to join in the push as Craven's small force darted down the gentle slope. The French cavalry quickly fled, and the British officer's path intersected with Craven's as they soared on after the enemy. They could see the French cavalry regrouping ahead of them as if the fight was over, and that they could be on their way in a more orderly fashion, but Craven's force descended upon them relentlessly.

The Frenchmen made an advance towards them in an attempt to break the charge, but it would not be stopped, and the two sides crashed into one another. Craven beat one of their blades aside before hacking at it. He barely needed to put any force into the blow, for the speed of his horse powered the cut more powerfully than he ever could. The blow cut deeply, and he soon wheeled around to continue on in the melee as the clash of cold steel rang out, a far more welcoming sensation than the acrid sulphur fumes from black powder weaponry.

His next blow cleaved through a French sabre, breaking it in half. The officer wielding the remnants threw up his hands in surrender with the others quickly following suit, causing them all to become prisoners with few casualties.

"Round them up, Mr Paget! And those horses, too. They will be most useful to us!"

Craven sheathed his sword and watched the enemy throw down their arms. It was a satisfying sight as he had no desire for needless killing, and not even Charlie seemed disappointed by the lack of bloodshed. Though Birback was quick to riffle through their possessions, which he at least did without doing them harm. The horses were slight and underfed, as the French were clearly short on both animals and feed.

"I say, Sir, what time you have!" roared the officer excitedly who had ridden on beside them from the makeshift defences among the ruins and carts.

He looked to be of a similar age to Paget but was a few inches taller and stronger built. Yet he carried the same boyish enthusiasm which Paget so often exuded even after years of campaigning. He wore the typical uniform of an infantry officer much like Paget and carried the same sword. Craven's keen eye quickly spotted the makers markings in the spine of the man's blade. J J Runkel it read. A common German import blade which a great many British swords were fitted with, especially officers' swords, which were hilted up and sold by such a wide variety of cutlers and furniture makers of varying quality. But a Runkel blade had Craven's respect. They were common but of robust quality. He wondered if the sword was a wise choice by the young man or simply a lucky coincidence. For a great many young officers who had purchased their swords from a tailor's shop were not so lucky.

"Buncy?" Paget rode up beside them.

"Is your work not done?" Craven asked angrily, having given Paget orders just moments before.

"It is," snapped Paget.

He pointed back towards the enemy where he had delegated the work to others, just as an officer should, with Matthys now in charge of the prisoners. A better guardian could not be asked for, and so Craven could not argue with him.

"BP?" asked the officer in surprise, referring to Paget's initials.

The young officer almost looked like he could be related to Paget as if he was the bigger brother, and they spoke to one another with such fondness and familiarity even with only the briefest encounter.

"You know one another?" Craven enquired exhaustively, as if he was about to endure a long-winded story.

"We most certainly do. For we went to school together," smiled Paget. "Major James Craven, Richard Bunce, or Buncy as I have long known him."

"That will be Captain Buncy," smiled the officer.

His uniform was as well-kept as Paget's always was, but Craven knew there was a reason for it in Paget's case. He bought new at every opportunity and so he never looked like he had been on campaign for long. Craven wondered what this Captain's reasons were. He showed no signs of wear and tear. No visible scars or signs of serious hardship. His face and body were a little more filled out than Paget who could still be mistaken for a teenager due to his stature.

"Major Craven, it is an honour, for I am familiar with some of your exploits and today I got to witness them with my own eyes, bravo!"

"Captain already?" asked Paget in amazement.

"Promotion is quick in war. I thought you to be a Major by now," jabbed Bunce in a friendly fashion.

"We do things a little differently in the Salford Rifles," replied Craven defensively.

"It is true, the Major was only promoted as such most recently and it was quite the struggle to make him accept it," replied Paget.

"Why the devil for? What better to achieve than promotion if not glory?"

Craven smiled.

"That is funny for you, Sir?" Bunce asked in a curious manner.

"It is, for you remind me of Mr Paget when we first met."

"Is that a compliment?" smiled Bunce.

"No," replied Craven abruptly.

Bunce looked a little put out but said nothing, and the silence which followed drew all of their attention to several riders approaching at speed. It was Major Spring who approached with a great smile on his face as he drew up before them.

"Good show, Major!"

But Craven looked suspicious.

"You knew there would be a battle here today, didn't you?"

"Major, I cannot predict the future," he replied defensively.

"No, but you can set things in motion to collide with one another."

Spring smiled as he all but recognised his guilt in the set up.

"I see you have already met Captain Bunce?"

"I have," replied Craven suspiciously.

"Sir, I have orders to report to Wellington," insisted Bunce.

"So that he may inform you of your transfer, which I will now deliver to save us all the time." Spring pulled out some papers from a satchel and handed them to the captain. Bunce quickly unfolded them with great anticipation and curiosity.

"It says I am to transfer to the…Salford Rifles…" he declared in disbelief.

"Absolutely not," snapped Craven angrily.

"Craven, you have recently lost a good officer in Captain Hawkshaw. Wellington felt that you could do with a capable replacement."

"No," replied Craven sternly.

"This is not a matter for debate, Major."

"I decide who serves in the Salfords!"

"But you also answer to Wellington, and these orders come directly from his Lordship, and you will follow them."

Craven looked back and forth irritably. Even Paget looked a little put out, as it would place his old friend above him in seniority despite all the years of good service he had given. But Craven finally nodded in agreement, knowing he was in no position to fight against the transfer.

"Can I have a word, Major?"

"I will be on my way, and so you can speak for as long as you wish to follow me."

Spring turned about and went on. Craven quickly caught up.

"Why are you doing this to me? Is Wellington offloading another problem child on me?"

"I think we can all agree that Mr Paget is a most formidable asset and soldier to have under your command."

"He is now, but do you know how long it has taken to mould that boy into a soldier?"

"Bunce is a year Paget's senior and not new to Spain. This will be good for you Major."

"There is no way I am getting out of this, is there?"

"None at all. These are Wellington's orders, and you will follow them if you want to remain in charge of the Salford Rifles.

You may operate far outside of the normal confines of command, but never forget that you do answer to him. Look, the remnants of the army we fought at Salamanca retreats North, and in doing so opens the road to Madrid and a great many of French positions. Wellington has ordered advances on Tordesillas, Zamora, Tora, and Benavente. It is all hands on deck, Major, and you have been given a fine young and strong officer with which to press on forward with."

Craven groaned.

"Can he at least fight?"

Spring smiled as Craven had clearly given up the struggle, and he stopped to turn back. He watched as the carts that had taken shelter among the ruins were dragged back out onto the road, and the soldiers took charge of the French prisoners to lead them on. Craven went back to his comrades with their newest recruit who he did not know what to make of.

"Did you request this appointment?" Craven demanded of him bluntly.

"I did not, Sir."

"Can you fight?"

"I can, Sir."

"Prove it." Craven gestured towards Matthys who took out a pair of singlesticks from the back of his saddle.

"Paget, let's see what he is made of," ordered Craven.

The Lieutenant leapt from his horse and removed his sword belt in readiness, but Bunce hesitated and did not know how to react.

"Have you not fenced or cudgel played before?" Craven asked.

Bunce stuttered and hesitated as he was clearly well out of

his comfort zone.

"We fenced foil many times," insisted Paget.

Craven nodded in appreciation as he turned back to Bunce.

"And now you are a Captain in the British army, and so you must know how to cut?"

"Sir...I..." bumbled Bunce.

"Captain, you have been signed over to me, and I am therefore your commanding officer. Every soldier who fights under my command must not just know how to fight; they must be damn good at it. All of our lives depend upon it. For we do not sit about barracks and play soldier, we do the soldiering. We could encounter the enemy tomorrow or even again today, and I want to know if you are up to the task."

"Was my bravery in the face of the enemy today not enough evidence?"

"That you are not a coward is certain, but I have not yet seen you use a sword."

"Are they of great use in this war, Sir?" Bunce has doubt in his voice, as if he were questioning Craven's motivations to put so much emphasis on the art of fencing.

"If you have to ask that question, then you don't understand what we do at all."

Bunce looked around for some support, but he found none, as they had all been subjected to hard singlestick contests to keep them sharp and forever improving. And they all looked upon him now with judgemental expressions, which soon pressured him into accepting the situation. He climbed down from the saddle, looking rather sheepish and humbled as he took off his sword belt and took up a singlestick.

"I will call you to guard, and you will not begin until I say so. You will stop after any smart blow and break distance until I order you to continue. Is that clear?"

"Yes, Sir."

There was a shakiness in his voice, as he felt the pressure of the audience and the expectations placed upon him. Paget paced up closely so that they could speak quietly and privately.

"Do not fear. For this is not punishment but training. The Major means well."

"Are you sure?"

"Very much so," smiled Paget as he turned back to put some distance between them in their starting positions.

"Do not go easy on your old friend, Mr Paget, or I shall have Birback take over your duties to ensure the Captain is tested properly."

"Yes, Sir!" replied Paget as eager to please as ever.

Birback smiled at the threat, for he loved his name being used to strike fear into the hearts of men.

"Ready?"

The two officers saluted one another with their single sticks.

"Guard!"

They did as ordered.

"Begin!"

Paget advanced at a steady and confident pace, launching a snappy beat against Bunce's stick, which caused it to fly out of his hands and onto the ground. Paget looked as surprised as Bunce. He had only expected it to create an opening and not be such a dramatic disarm. Laughter followed from many who were watching.

"You score nothing without landing a blow," insisted Craven to Paget.

But Paget would not strike his unarmed friend, and he backed away to give him space to pick up the singlestick.

"You are better than this, Buncy. Let's see the battler I once knew!"

He picked up the stick and came to guard once more and into distance. Paget attempted to batter his stick once again merely to test that he had learnt from his first mistake. Bunce avoided the beat completely with a quick disengage under the beat and snapped a quick strike towards Paget's head. It caused him to have to use every bit of his lightning-fast reactions to pull back and defend himself. Craven smiled a little but tried to hide it. He could see the Captain had some skills and some speed, but he did not want to go easy on him. For he had spoken the truth when he insisted that each soldier's fighting prowess was vital to the safety and success of them all.

The clash of sticks echoed out as Paget and Bunce went back and forth. Paget was not pushing him as hard as he could, but enough to test him as was needed. Enough to show he had skill without risking embarrassment before his new comrades. Craven was happy with that. For Paget was both fair and compassionate whilst getting the job done. A blow was soon landed on Bunce, and Craven ordered them to restart, but it was clear Bunce was quickly relaxing into the situation and getting better with every exchange of blows. Paget landed another three and was getting quite cocky and playful when he launched a long range and low cut towards Bunce's lead knee. Bunce quickly and instinctively drew his leg back, causing Paget's stick to find nothing but air as his own wheeled about in a great big but fast parade, crashing down onto the top of Paget's head.

"Ooh!" cried several whilst others cheered.

Paget staggered a little as the blow had rattled his brain, and he looked a little out of sorts for a few seconds. He reached for the top of his head to find it was cut and a lump had formed, but he soon recovered and smiled.

"Good one!" he cried out.

A cheer rang out as the two shook hands as friends.

"Well, Sir, will that do?" Bunce asked.

"It will, for now," smiled Craven.

"Is there anything else I should know, Sir?"

"Have the back of every soldier who you serve with. We fight for one another. Oh, and if you come across a Major Bouchard, kill him. For there will be a great reward for you."

"Kill him, Sir?" Bunce was amazed at the suggestion.

"Major Craven has put a warrant out for his death," replied Paget.

"Is that so?" he asked with doubt and a little concern, though he clearly did not want to rock the boat further and said nothing.

"Welcome to the Salford Rifles," declared Craven.

CHAPTER 2

Charlie watched Paget and Bunce riding alongside each other ahead of her. They were deep in conversation and dead to the world as they made up for lost time, seemingly picking up where they left off as the best of friends.

"Does it bother you, that a man occupies his time?" Vicenta asked, who rode beside her.

"If I were threatened by another man I would kill him," she replied confidently.

But Vicenta smirked, knowing it was only a half truth. Yes, Charlie was quite willing to kill, but she was not entirely happy with the latest man to join them.

"Why does he bother you so?" Vicenta seemingly bypassed Charlie's denial, and it worked as Charlie sighed and finally gave an honest answer.

"Captain Bunce represents all that Paget was before we came to know him. Before he become one of us. He has changed much over the years."

"And you fear his old ways returning?"

"I do," groaned Charlie.

"Was Paget a good man before you knew him?"

"In his own way, yes," she admitted.

"Then there is nothing for you to worry about. You have trusted him with your life many times, and you should trust him now."

Charlie took a deep breath in relief, but she also looked a little sheepish as if disappointed in herself.

"Do not feel bad for these feelings. For we in Spain are not afraid of our emotions. They run deep within our blood and speak to the honesty in our hearts," explained Vicenta compassionately.

Charlie relaxed as she exhaled and welcomed the thoughts.

"Captain Bunce was appointed to be here. But you, you ride with us after all this time? Why?"

"Look where we are and what we are doing. We march on Madrid to free my people and my country."

"De Rosas fights the French, too. You could have gone back to him?"

"Yes, he does, and it is a noble effort. My countrymen fight the French far and wide in the same manner, and it weakens the enemy, but it will not defeat them. We might kill more French soldiers in the guerrilla war than Wellington ever could, but until the French armies are beaten in open battle, my country will not be free. I ride with Craven because that is where I can do the most for my country, for he is both a fighting man and an honest one."

Charlie laughed.

"What is so amusing?" she demanded angrily as if Craven's honour was being called into question.

"He was not always the man you know today. And I only saw the tail end of what he used to be when we first met. It is fair to say he has always been a fighting man, but an honest one? Far from it."

"That is the man he used to be. Were you the same before wearing that uniform?"

Charlie shook her head as she thought back to the life she used to have. The happy life of a soldier's wife and a mother before the retreat to Corunna. It felt like a lifetime ago, and indeed she was not at all recognisable compared to who she was back then. The uniform was merely the outer skin hiding all the bitterness and anger she felt inside ever since donning it for the first time. And yet she realised she was as different again now as that time, and it made her smile a little, realising she was getting a little of her old self back.

"Do you think it is a good thing, bringing in this stranger among us?" Charlie looked to Bunce and turned from her personal concerns to the wider issue of the Salford Rifles and what was best for them all.

"We were all strangers here once. I have no reason to trust that man yet, but I will give him a chance to prove he is worthy of being here."

"You are better than this at me. Accepting change, I mean," noted Charlie.

"In the times we live it is the way the people of Spain must be. We make the most of the changes we see before our eyes."

They looked back at Quicks and Nooth deep in friendly conversation as they rode beside one another on their newly acquired French horses. Not so long ago they were the freshest faces in the Salford Rifles, and yet they had been through so much together with those who had been there from the start.

"What do you make of him?" Craven asked Matthys as they led the column forward with only Moxy and Ellis well ahead of them as scouts.

"The new Captain?"

"Yes," Craven was seething. He did not much appreciate such a senior soldier being thrust upon them without any choice in the matter.

"I have faith in Paget's assessment of a man, and so I think he will do just fine. But it might take him some time to settle into the way you command and the way we all conduct ourselves."

"Because we are not like the rest of the army?"

"Precisely, and he would not be the first officer to butt heads with the way you command."

Craven smiled as that was certainly true.

"If he can fight and be depended upon, then that will do."

"And Mr Paget?"

"What of him?"

"An old friend is now superior to him in his own regiment after all he has achieved. That young man has fought more battles than most soldiers ever would in thirty years of service."

"If Paget was so concerned with promotion, he would have left us a long time ago. For this is not the place for it."

"I don't think that ambition left his mind, but I think he stays for other reasons."

Craven looked back to Charlie and knew the two were still close.

"Yes, she can have quite the influence," he admitted.

"I was referring to you. Paget looks up to you more than anyone. He forsook his father to defend you, even when you were beyond defendable."

"And lost so much in the process. Was I really worth it?"

"He thinks so, and so do I. You have come a long way since the gladiator's stage and the gambling tables of England, and look at what we have achieved together. Each of us quite imperfect, and yet together we are a force far stronger than anyone would imagine."

"Bunce will not like the way we do things, that much is clear."

"Any officer stepping in among us would be the same, but give him time, he will come around."

"Always so full of wisdom, we should get you a commission, for you certainly deserve it."

"I am flattered, but I am quite fine where I am. Orders might come from officers, but never forget that it is Sergeants that keep the British army moving forward. What would I gain with a commission?"

"More pay?"

"I do not need more than I am provided."

"There is really no price which could buy you and your loyalty? Or disloyalty to others?"

"I am here for the people, not for myself. Although I will admit it is not without a selfish part, for I get a great deal of satisfaction from what I do."

Craven looked back to Paget and Bunce once more to see they were still deep in conversation, laughing and chatting amongst themselves.

"So, this warrant for a French officer's death, is that real?" Bunce turned to an issue that had weighed on his mind since he had first heard it.

"It is."

"And you will go along with it? You would go through with it?"

"Bouchard is a truly awful man who has not conducted himself with honour. He has terrorised men and women, not just soldiers. He has tried to assassinate Major Craven more than once. He is a spy and a monster."

"But are you?"

"What do you mean?"

"Men have done awful things since the dawn of time, but do we want to join them in their depravity merely for a sense of revenge?"

"This is not revenge."

"Is it not? Authorised murder of a serving officer in the army of the enemy by any means necessary?"

"You do not understand what Bouchard has done. The warrant is not justice for what he has done, but to stop him from doing it all again in the future."

Bunce groaned uncomfortably but said nothing.

"What? What is it?"

Bunce looked out of sorts and uncomfortable about saying anything further.

"Out with it, we will not have secrets here," insisted Paget.

"You have changed, and I would not have expected this from you from all the time we spent together."

"Yes, I have changed. I was a naive young man in those days. I thought I knew the world and that I knew everything, but these past years have opened my eyes."

"And your morals, too?"

"Real life is not so simple as we had imagined."

"I have to admit that I am disappointed."

Paget initially looked put out, but as he looked around to the friends all around him, he decided to fight back.

"A few months of proper soldiering and you will feel different," he retorted.

"I have seen what real soldiering looks like. For I have served beside some of the finest officers in Wellington's army, here in Spain against the French."

Paget shrugged.

"All I can ask if that you give Major Craven a chance, because without him, I fear Wellington would never have gotten this far."

Neither said another word as the conversation had soured so much that a cold silence now followed. It did not go unnoticed by Charlie who had watched their renewed friendship with curiosity and a little concern. Craven noticed it, too.

"Why is it do you think that Wellington puts that man among us? Why now after all these years without interference? Another young man with family connections that he is hoping to palm off on us like he did with Paget?" he asked Matthys.

"Perhaps, but we are a very different outfit today than when we first came to Lord Wellington's attentions, and Wellington sees everything."

"Then why? Does he mean to toughen the young man up by having him march with us? Or is he here to temper or spy upon us?"

"I cannot pretend to understand the motivations, but a

capable fighting officer is a welcome asset I should say."

"Is he? A capable fighter?"

"You saw him. He is not you, nor Paget, but perfectly capable even before any training which we might bestow upon him."

"Do you think he would take it?"

"He is not the enemy, and so why do you treat him so?"

"Because I do not understand why he is here and I do not yet trust him," replied Craven honestly.

"Then give him a chance to gain it, and for now, trust in Paget's judgement if nothing else."

Craven caught a glimpse of movement in the distance ahead and stopped to take out his spyglass.

"What is it?"

But he could see even with his naked eye that a small group of cavalry was moving at speed with some urgency.

"KGL," replied Craven, referring the dragoons of the King's German Legion, who had earned a lofty reputation for their dependable service among Wellington's army.

"They move with purpose," replied Matthys as Paget and Bunce moved up beside them to see for themselves.

Twenty KGL dragoons were in flight and riding North, which was of concern, for the advance towards Madrid was Southeasterly. So far there had been little resistance to Wellington's march toward Madrid, but now they were just ten miles away, and nobody knew whether the enemy would stand and fight or flee without a contest.

"Are those men of the army's advance guard?" Paget asked, for if they were running Northward, it was of a grave concern.

Craven followed along the road to where they were heading to find a village occupied by British cavalry, many of which had stopped to rest and water their horses, whilst Portuguese cavalry were continuing through the town. The twenty KGL approached them at speed and only stopped to relay news for a brief moment before continuing on.

"What is this? What is happening here, Sir?" asked Paget.

The Portuguese cavalry squadrons went on in the direction that the KGL troopers had fled from. They were a far more formidable force, totalling three regiments of dragoons and supported by four cannons.

"There must be trouble ahead," insisted Bunce.

"I don't like this at all." Craven continued to survey the scene, "On me!"

He led his mounted force up to a better vantage point from where they might get a better understanding of what was unfolding before them. And soon enough they could see the French cavalry squadrons advancing North, and the Portuguese were heading right for them.

"Sir, look!" Paget cried.

Beyond the French squadrons many more cavalrymen were riding to join those at the front. The Portuguese cavalrymen soon noticed it as they quickly wheeled about and began to flee.

"Cowards," muttered Bunce.

But the French force advancing on them was far superior and so few held it against them.

"This is what those men of the KGL were warning them of, and still they went forward?" Paget pondered.

"Yes, one would say that is rather brave," replied Ferreira

in support of his countrymen.

But it was a scene of complete chaos as they were powerless to act. They watched from a distance as the marauding French cavalry overran the British cannons and captured three of the four. They continued their pursuit of the Portuguese cavalry as they fled towards the village to the North just as the twenty KGL troopers had.

"What do we do, Sir?"

"The enemy march on that village." He pointed to the North where so many troops were still resting idle, "Come on!"

He turned away and galloped on for the village, knowing he could at least get there before the enemy did. They rode on at the gallop, pushing their mounts as hard as they could, for they all knew the troops occupying the village ahead was Wellington's advance guard and was vital to the advance on Madrid.

"Why now, Sir? Does the enemy mean to defend Madrid?"

"That or merely slow us down, for we would be there before nightfall if we were not opposed!"

They raced towards the village and made it before the fleeing Portuguese cavalry regiments who vanished within the village without any attempt to turn back and fight the enemy. The seriousness of the situation had clearly begun to dawn on those stopping to rest at the Spanish village. Though it was not enough time for many of the KGL dragoons to saddle their horses and be ready to fight in the manner in which they were accustomed. Some KGL light infantry were forming up at the main road entrance of the village. They were bolstered by many of the dragoons who had no choice but to take up their carbines and pistols and fight alongside the infantry. Others poured into nearby houses to take up defensive positions.

"On me!"

Craven led his mounted troops to the flank from where they might fire upon the enemy whilst still being able to charge them down on horseback if need be. It was a makeshift and desperate defence that none of them had been expecting. Craven took out his map to quickly study the situation. He could see they were at the village of Las Rozas, and the next settlement along the road from where the French had come was Majadahonda, just two miles on the road South.

The French cavalry soon arrived and rushed upon them as they attempted to batter their way into the village. A volley rang out from those at the entrance, and Craven's riflemen fired their own volley. It was enough to shake the French cavalry, and they began to waver as a number of the KGL now in their saddles came forward, supported by the Portuguese cavalry. They stormed forward, and Craven drew out his sword and led his force forward to join them in a combined cavalry charge. The last time he had drawn this broad curved sabre he had imagined himself as a cavalryman, but now he rode alongside the dragoons in a real cavalry charge. It was impossible not to feel the magnitude of what it was to charge among hundreds of horsemen. But the enemy cavalry did not stand to face them, and it was their turn to run, just as the KGL scouts and Portuguese regiments had done in the face of such odds.

"We've got 'em!"

Bunce excitedly circled his sword about his head as if he were indeed a charging cavalryman. Craven could not think lesser of him for it, for he had felt the same himself on more than a few memorable occasions. They galloped on as they chased the enemy back to Majadahonda, but there they found far greater French opposition, as the tables were turned once more. French infantry and guns opened fire upon the combined German, Portuguese, and British advance. The French cavalry that had been chased away were wheeling about to reform and were joined by further squadrons of cavalry. Volleys of musket fire erupted, and the three French cannons roared.

"Hold firm, boys!" Craven roared.

"Look, Sir!" Paget cried.

To their horror they watched as the three Portuguese cavalry regiments turned and fled without ever having crossed swords with the enemy, but none was more broken hearted than Ferreira. It had taken the Portuguese Captain many years to have trust and faith in the soldiers of his home country, and he could see the reputation they had all fought hard to build be washed away as furious KGL troopers cried out furiously for assistance. The French cavalry loomed down upon them once more as the KGL and mounted infantry of the Salford Rifles threw caution to the wind and rode in to face their attacks in spite of the cowardly Portuguese cavalry. Ferreira was the first to meet with the enemy as if he had something to prove and cleft one man's head in two with a ferocious blow. The clash of hundreds of cold steel blades rang out in what was music to Craven's ears, but they had only traded a few blows when they realised how vastly outnumbered they were without the Portuguese regiments by their side.

"Fall back! Fall back!"

Craven did not want to see his comrades fall needlessly, but Ferreira kept hacking away angrily against the enemy without any concern for his own skin. He fought like a wild animal, but in doing so exposed himself to a great many of the enemy. He was about to be run through by a French cavalryman when Paget used Augustus to force his way through several troopers and run Ferreira's would-be killer through his body. Ferreira realised what had happened in that moment, and it was truly sobering for him.

"Come on, Sir. It is not your honour which is lost here today!" Paget insisted compassionately.

Ferreira nodded in agreement as he did not want to die there. They hacked away against the enemy's swords as they made their retreat North. The KGL and Salford rifles had broken free with only a few soldiers lost, but many were hacked and bloody from the effects of the French sabres. They rode on furiously towards Las Rozas hoping the defences had been improved as the enemy now advanced with a far larger force.

"Sir, this is…" declared Paget as they rode.

"Bad, yes, I know!"

They could all sense what a humiliating disaster they were potentially facing as the village came into view. They could see a great many of the houses bristling with muskets and wheeled to the flank to give a clear view of the French cavalry in pursuit. A great volley erupted from the edge of the village and struck down many of the Frenchmen. A second volley soon rang out. The volley's disordered the French cavalry that their charge was halted entirely, and once again the KGL dragoons saw their chance for a little revenge and quickly reformed. Ferreira was the first of the Salfords to ride out to assist them.

Together, the KGL dragoons and mounted Salford Rifles stormed towards the French cavalry and crashed into them, causing a devastating rout as they hacked at the enemy and took many more prisoners. Finally, the fighting came to a close as the enemy withdrew. Cheers rang out from those defending the village of Las Rozas, but it had been a close thing and almost a disaster. British heavy cavalry approached along the road, sealing the French fate for certain as they called off their attack.

Craven first looked to Ferreira and the Portuguese comrades he had by his side. There was shame in their faces as if they had failed the army.

"Will you say something, Sir?" Paget pressed, eager for him to say a few kind words, and Ferreira was eager to hear them as he could find no words to console his comrades.

"See to the wounded and see that the dead are buried. We rest here for the night."

"But, Sir?"

"I will see to it," he growled in response. For he did not want to pour salt into Ferreira's open wounds so publicly.

The modest village was quickly occupied by the troops who had defended it and so many more who had arrived afterward, but Craven was glad to stay on the outskirts where they might have a little peace. Fires were soon lit in the open ground to the South of the village where they had battled with the enemy earlier that day. Craven finally found the right time and opportunity to go to his Portuguese friend, a man he had known longer than all but a handful of his oldest friends from his days in England before sailing out to Portugal.

"They are not you," he insisted as he stepped up beside Ferreira at the fireside.

"But I will be seen like them in the eyes of many."

"I would have words with any man who would dare

suggest such a thing."

"I know you would," smiled Ferreira.

"Then let it be."

But Ferreira shook his head.

"I can't, because it hurts here." He placed his hand before his heart, "I never thought I would feel pride in the soldiers of my country, but against all the odds it happened. That was one of the greatest days of my life, but it also made me care in a way I never thought I would, and so this now feels, it feels…"

"Like a betrayal?"

"Yes. Englishmen and Germans would fight here, and my countrymen would not? For shame."

"Yes, for shame indeed," roared a very familiar voice as Wellington himself walked up beside them.

"Lord Wellington, Sir," replied Craven humbly.

"Relax, gentlemen, you have had quite the day, and I do not wish to burden it further."

"Yes, Sir."

"I hear you rode with the KGL and charged the enemy twice over, is that correct?"

"Yes, Sir."

"And you, too, Captain?"

Ferreira was stunned to be addressed directly.

"Yes, Sir."

"Then there is courage left in the men of Portugal. Good."

"You see, proud people," replied Marshal Beresford who came up beside Wellington, the British commander of the Portuguese Army.

"Tell them what you told me, Beresford," ordered Wellington.

"I have ordered that they should not again mount a horse or wear a sword till they may, by coming near the enemy, and have an opportunity of redeeming their credit. Till then, hanging their swords on their saddles, they lead their horses, marching themselves. The Portuguese have a good deal of feeling and pride, and it is the only way to work on them."

"What do you say to that, Craven?"

"A fair treatment, but I am not sure we can afford to lose our cavalry at a time such as this."

Wellington nodded in agreement as he went on, "They must be disciplined, but as for sending the cavalry to the rear that is impossible at the present. We have still a good deal upon our hands, and we are worse provided with cavalry than our neighbours. A body commanded by such a man as D'Urban, even though they will not fight, are better than none. In fact, they behaved infamously, and they must not be employed again alone, or with our cavalry, who gallop too fast for them."

It was a lesser punishment, but it still cut Ferreira deeply.

"You do not agree, Captain?" Wellington asked him.

"No, Sir, I only wish these horrid events had not come to pass," he replied proudly.

"A devil of an affair indeed, but redemption can come with time and work. For now, the reputation of the Portuguese soldier has been struck down many notches, and the army will not be pleased with your compatriots. Show them another way. You inspired your countrymen once, and I know you can do it again."

"Yes, Sir."

With those words he left in what felt like a surreal experience.

"There can be redemption, but you need not look for it. For you fought like a lion today," declared Craven.

"And yet I feel shame."

"Look how far you have come. From a man who did not care for crossing swords or facing the enemy to one who feels responsible for the actions of all of his countrymen. If Matthys was here, he would tell you how proud he is of the man you have become, and so am I."

But Matthys was there lurking in the shadows beyond and listening to every word, and it brought a smile to his face. He felt proud of the man Craven had become that he could share such words of compassion. Paget came up beside him to look upon Craven and Ferreira.

"Is there something we should say or do, do you think?" he asked quietly.

"All that needs to be said and done has been," replied Matthys proudly.

CRAVEN'S WAR – RUNNING THE GAUNTLET

CHAPTER 3

"The day has finally come, hasn't it, Sir?" Paget asked as they rode on the next day.

"Short of any more near fatal disasters, it has," admitted Craven.

Local people were gathering at the villages and farms on their approach to the capital city and welcomed them as liberators.

"The French attack yesterday, it could never have stopped this army for any time, could it?"

"No."

"Then why? Why risk all those French soldiers?"

"One last chance to embarrass Wellington? Or more likely merely buying a little time to evacuate the city."

"You do not think we will be opposed?"

"I shouldn't think so. For with the army we defeated at Salamanca having gone North, there will not be enough

Frenchmen to make a resistance against us."

"No more surprises today then, Sir?"

Craven looked uncomfortable as if Paget was tempting fate, and only seconds later they heard a whistle blow out nearby. Not with the full lungs of a healthy soldier but one who struggled and finished by coughing violently.

"Look what you did," complained Craven.

"Me, Sir?" Paget protested.

It was the sort of whistle a British officer would use, and so they were compelled to investigate. Craven brought the column to a halt. He drew out his sword in readiness to defend himself against any threat and listened for another short blast to know the location.

"Come on," he declared, knowing his closest friends would follow and the rest would see to the column. Just eight of them rode away from the road and towards a ledge and dip beyond. Coughs and splutters continued with the occasional weak blast of the whistle until finally Craven rode into view of the cause of it all.

"Well, well," he smiled as he sheathed his sword calmly.

Before them was a ragged and bloodied Timmerman. He lay flat on his back against an embankment. His uniform was cut to ribbons, and he was bleeding from many of the cuts that had done the damage. He had no hat nor a sign of a horse or saddle, or any other possessions beyond what he was wearing. His characteristic ivory gripped and gilt sabre lay beside him and was covered in blood. He had two black eyes and a bloody nose and swollen left cheek. He looked as though he had been through hell, and yet he still managed a smile at recognising Craven. Matthys was the first to approach the Major to see to his wounds without hesitation.

"The French finally get the better of you, did they?" Craven asked.

"French?" Timmerman chuckled before breaking into a coarse cough once more and spitting blood.

"Who did this to you?" Paget asked curiously.

"And where are your men?" Craven added.

"They are the bastards who did this," snarled Timmerman.

"What?" Paget was amazed.

But Craven began to chuckle before breaking out into laughter.

"Yes, enjoy it, Craven," smirked Timmerman.

"You recruited a bunch of degenerate cutthroats and were surprised when they turned on you?"

"But why now? Why should they turn upon you now?" Paget was more curious than anything else.

"You have some deep cuts but nothing that should not heal in time, but I will have to sew you up." Matthys ignored the discussion and focused on Timmerman's wounds.

"Do what you must to stop me leaking."

But Paget's curiosity was infectious as Craven now wanted to know.

"Well? Why now?" Craven got down from his horse and stepped up closer.

"The boys I gathered were here to loot and enjoy themselves. They would take anything from anyone."

"And you finally said no to them?" Paget asked.

"Why?" Craven appeared to be confused.

"Don't you see, Sir, he finally has a conscience," beamed Paget as if a great wish had come true.

Timmerman sighed as he finally gave in and explained.

"This is all on you, Craven, and Hawkshaw. Both of you could have killed me or at least have left me to die."

"What are you saying?"

"I demanded that the men under my command be better, that they show some decency."

"And they tried to kill you for it?"

"Mr Paget, they said I had gone soft, and so they left."

"And so you tried to stop them?" Craven said.

Timmerman winced as Matthys got to work with his needle, working with such speed and precision which only a man with great experience could manage.

"No, I let them go, but they didn't do the same for me."

"How so?"

"They tried to take from me everything I have, my horse, my weapons, my pocket watch. They would have my boots off my feet if they could. They took everything except what I was able to defend myself with."

Craven didn't look as sympathetic as Paget would expect.

"He has lost everything, Sir."

"Hardly, how much do you have back in England? Land and money and everything else?"

"Nothing."

Craven did not believe him and looked angered by the statement.

"Why would you lie so severely whilst we work to save your life?"

"Craven, I have not led a good life, and you know that much. I was once a man of means, but it is long gone. Squandered on all of the worthless things which I have nothing to show for."

Craven was stunned, and he could hear the sincerity in his old adversary's voice.

"You did not just come out to this war to pursue me, did you?"

Timmerman shook his head.

"I left my old life in England to pursue a new one here. To find a fortune and perhaps rebuild my name. I thought I could do that with this." He picked up his beloved sabre, "And now it is the only thing of value I have left in this world."

Craven was stunned as he took a deep breath and gasped at the humbled scene of Timmerman looted and heavily battered and beaten.

"What is this all about?" Bunce had approached them.

"It's a long story," replied Paget.

Craven moved out of hearing distance from Timmerman and gestured for Ferreira and Paget to join him, but Bunce joined them, too.

"What do you think?" Craven asked them.

"That is a British officer in need of our assistance," declared Bunce.

"He is that and a whole lot more," replied Ferreira.

"Everyone can change, and I believe he has. He has proven that already," added Paget.

"Why is this even in doubt?" Bunce pressed.

"Captain, these matters are beyond your understanding and so please refrain from interfering," growled Craven.

"I am an officer in this regiment now, aren't I?" he snapped.

"Yes, and if I want your opinion, I will ask for it," scowled

Craven before leaving them to address his old enemy alone.

Bunce looked angry and looked to Paget for help, but he only shrugged in response. Craven had not made his decision, but as he looked down at the humbled Timmerman, he remembered all they had been through together, both the bad and the good.

"When we sailed back from England earlier this year, can you remember what I told you?"

Timmerman shrugged as he was exhausted and near delirious.

"Welcome to the Salford Rifles. I said it, and I meant it. You came here to make something of yourself and to build a fortune. Well so did I. What say we do it together?"

Timmerman gasped with relief as a tear almost came to his eye.

"Let me ride with you, and I will see you all the way to Paris," he replied sincerely.

"We will ride there together."

Timmerman breathed a sigh of relief to know he had some purpose and reason to go on.

"What were you doing out here anyway?" Paget had walked over to them.

"They say King Joseph flees from Madrid, along with every French soldier and Spanish sympathiser. So much loot to be had, but the men under my command would take it from anyone by any means, which is how I got into this mess."

"Wellington will march into the city later this day."

"Yes, and we should be there to see it."

"You are in no state to travel," replied Paget.

"Seal my wounds, a mouthful of rum or anything like it,

and a horse between my legs, and I can go anywhere."

Craven looked to Matthys for his assessment.

"He needs rest, but it is only a few miles to the city where we can find him a comfortable bed."

Craven went back to his horse and took out a small bottle from his saddle and passed it to Timmerman.

"Thank you." He bit off the cork with his teeth and took a whiff of what was inside before recoiling in horror, "God what is that?"

"The worst brandy you ever tasted. You want it or not?"

Craven smiled as he reached for the bottle, but Timmerman pulled it away protectively. He took a mouthful and swallowed as quickly as he could, his eyes widening in horror at the flavour. Yet he soon took another mouthful, and his senses were now dulled enough that he could stomach it without such a violent reaction.

"Why do you even have this?" he asked in amazement and disgust.

"Asks a man with nothing. Would you rather that or nothing?"

"Fair enough."

"I need to get this jacket and shirt off of you," declared Matthys.

Timmerman obliged as he peeled them off him with some help. He had four sword cuts across his torso and was black and blue from blunt blows, but he also had a great many old scars from previous wounds.

"I've never seen such a beaten body," said Bunce.

"I have," replied Matthys who had patched up Craven so many times over the years since his stage gladiator encounters and through years of the war in Portugal and Spain. Matthys took the bottle from Timmerman who reluctantly gave it up and poured it over several of the wounds, causing him to wince further before handing the bottle back as he continued his work. Matthys was quick and efficient, but there was a great deal of work to be done.

"How long will you need?" Craven asked.

"I am working as fast as I can, perhaps twenty or thirty minutes."

"Alright, everyone take a rest, but I want pickets posted and eyes in every direction. Let's not have a repeat of yesterday, shall we!"

Ferreira leapt into action as he barked his orders, though Moxy and Ellis were already on duty well ahead to ensure their safety.

"What happened yesterday?" Timmerman asked curiously.

"About two thousand French troops attacked Wellington's advance guard."

"And you were there? Of course, you were," he smiled.

"What is that supposed to mean?"

"It is who you are, or who you have become. I remember a Craven who would have run from such a responsibility, and now you fight like you were appointed as the King's champion."

"Is that such a bad thing?"

"If I did not know your reasons I would laugh at it, but because I do I cannot."

"What do you mean?"

"Most men who ride out into trouble the way you do, they do it because of some blind loyalty or desire to impress people who never cared for them. You might be a rogue, Craven, but you are the most honest rogue I have ever known."

"Coming from you that means almost nothing, but thank you," smiled Craven.

He left Matthys to do his work as he went back to Paget and Bunce, seeing a good opportunity to get to know the newest recruit to their regiment, one he was still not at all comfortable with.

"You have a great deal of history with that man, Sir?" Bunce asked.

"I do."

"And would you have left him to die if he did not answer your questions in a way you saw fit?"

Craven was stunned.

"Understand this, Captain. I did not recruit or request you, and your rank does not count for much here. That Sergeant over there, Matthys, he is senior to you as far as I am concerned."

"But…"

"But nothing. I make the rules here, and if you cannot accept them, then you can leave anytime. Say the word, and I will have you transferred to anywhere that will have you. Go to the Royal Waggon Train if you want an easy time of it."

"I do not, Sir. I only enquired about…"

"Stop right there!"

Bunce looked quite uncomfortable but did as ordered.

"There is a time and place for discussion and questions, and I often welcome it, but you are new here. Use your ears before you use your mouth until you understand what we are and how we work, is that understood?"

"Yes, Sir," he replied sheepishly.

Craven left them to be with Ferreira, for he could not take any more of the complaints of the new officer.

"Looks like the new boy isn't fitting in to well," whispered Quicks to Nooth.

"And did you?" Nooth smiled.

Quicks shrugged.

"There will always be a clash between proud men, were we any different?"

Quicks shook his head for it was true.

"Give them a little time and all will work out, but more importantly let us look to Madrid."

"It is all I have thought about," smiled Quicks.

"A rich city with soft beds and beautiful women who have resisted French urges all these years, and here we are to sweep them off their feet and save them."

"We will be heroes, do you think?" The idea was such an alien one to Quicks. In all his days as a pickpocket on the streets he had been used to living in the shadows, hated and maligned by the people he interacted with.

"That uniform you wear means something."

Quicks looked down at his tunic with pride.

"If we keep going forward like this, the war will be over in no time, and then what will we do?" he asked as he couldn't imagine his new life coming to an end.

"The militia and the volunteers back in England is fine work. The same job you do now but without the French shooting back at you."

"But was the vast militia and volunteer movement a response to Napoleon?"

"Yes, of course."

"And when that threat is over, will they no longer be needed?"

Nooth was stunned. He had never really thought about it that way. He had lived a life of luxury back in England based entirely on the threat of Napoleon looming over them.

"There will always be a British army if we wanted to stay on."

"I think I will go wherever Craven goes," Quicks said.

"And if that is back to the gladiator contests?"

"Then so be it. He has looked out for us like nobody ever has in my lifetime."

"Not even me?" Nooth jabbed.

Paget watched as his old friend Buncy studied everything around him. He looked on with great suspicion. There was a coldness to him that Paget did not remember, and he imagined it had to be because of the uncomfortable nature of stepping in as a fresh face among friends who had been through so much together.

"You did pretty well with the singlestick," he declared, trying to spark up a friendly conversation as they always used to.

"It was humiliating, to have to be tested like that before everyone, and for what?"

"We have all done it and continue to do so."

"Why? We are here to fight a war not to win duels," snapped Bunce.

Paget smiled at his naivety.

"How long have you been in the Salford Rifles?"

"A matter of days."

"And have you drawn your sword and used it in anger in that time? Against the enemy, I mean."

"Yes, you know I have."

"After being with us for a fleeting moment. Now tell me how many times did you cross swords with the enemy in your previous duties?"

"Well, I unsheathed my sword, and I carried it in battle…" he began but soon tailed off, realising Paget had a point.

"As an infantry officer of the line, your sword is really only a symbol of your rank and a means with which to defend yourself in the worst-case scenario, but this is not a line company. We are not even infantry in the typical sense. The Salford Rifles are not like a regular infantry outfit in the British army, and it took me some time to understand and accept that. We go after the enemy in the most irregular of ways, and sometimes that can mean a desperate clash of steel in some remote Spanish village. It can be a chaotic fight at night. We can oppose French cavalry and yes, we can also stand in line with the infantry, too. The Salford Rifles works precisely because we are not just soldiers, we are a band of fighters. We take the fight to the enemy wherever and whenever we can, and in the chaotic nature of it all, a sword can be a man's most faithful companion. I cannot count the number of times that my sword and my trained hand and body at using it has saved my life and the lives of those around me. That is the life you have now stepped into. I doubt you had any inclination of it, and neither did I, but I do now. Trust me as an old friend. Your sword is the most dependable weapon you have, and you must always work to be as skilled with it as you can be. That is the same for you, me, and even Major Craven."

"The Major still attends sword lessons?"

"Of course, and not just among his friends. He went to

study with a Spaniard!"

Bunce was taken aback as he had assumed it was a cruel and unusual punishment he had been subjected to as the latest arrival. Paget drew out two single sticks from his saddle as he now carried his own. He passed one to Bunce.

"You honestly train with these all of the time?" Bunce asked as he took one.

"Yes."

"Like the common pugil players at village fairs?"

"Yes, but by applying all of the lessons and skills of fencing with live blades. I know you remember some of the skills you used to have, for I saw them. You were most proficient with the foil when we used to cross blades."

Bunce groaned as he was not so sure.

"Do you know the French attach a sword master to every infantry regiment so that they might train their common soldiers to use the sword, even those that do not carry them, and those who carry their little piquet hangers?"

"I did not."

"Would you go into battle knowing that the Frenchman opposing you has trained better and more often in the sword than you?"

Bunce shook his head as his pride would not let him accept such a shameful situation.

"The first time you used these was indeed a test to see if you were worthy of being here, and you passed. But there is much training to be done, for we must never stop learning."

"Will you teach me?"

"I will."

Ferreira watched on as they went back and forth with their

sticks, and Paget gave him pointers and feedback after each exchange. Craven was drawn by the crack of the sticks meeting with one another. He joined his Portuguese friend who still looked melancholic after the humiliation he had felt because of his countrymen the day before.

"Wellington is right, and you know it," said Craven.

"Yes, but it is not easy."

"There are a great many of my countrymen I am ashamed of, but I refuse to be judged because of them and their actions."

"This is an Englishman's army, and you are judged on merit, but when a Portuguese soldier acts badly, we are all condemned and judged for that man's actions."

"They are not important," insisted Amyn as he joined them on a rare occasion. He rarely had much to say, and so they listened as he continued, "You cannot control the actions of your countrymen, but you can show the world a better side with your own actions."

"Yes," agreed Craven.

"They are ready, Sir," declared Joze as he pointed back to Timmerman. He was being helped to his feet by Matthys. He looked sore and quite unstable from a combination of his wounds and the bottle of brandy he had consumed that now lay empty on the ground.

"Can he travel?"

"Onwards to Madrid!" Timmerman slurred.

"He is a stubborn fool, and so yes," replied Matthys.

"Get him a horse and let us be on our way. We have a parade we do not want to miss!"

Paget's face lit up as it was a triumphant parade he had long dreamed of, and what better way to do so by chasing

Napoleon's brother and puppet King out of the capital city that had been his seat of power. There was a great excitement among them all.

CHAPTER 4

Crowds cheered and flags were waved back and forth, mostly Spanish colours, as if they were being liberated by their own people. Paget looked around in ponderous wonder. He could barely believe what he was seeing as thousands of people cried out in relief and jubilation. He had thought he had witnessed such scenes on parades in London, but they had never come close to the ecstasy being experienced before his very eyes. Local men and women swamped all around them to hug and kiss them and give them gifts. Seemingly every local person carried gifts, flowers, bread, wine, grapes, lemonade, sweetmeats, and much more, including laurel boughs which they placed like crowns upon the heads of many of the soldiers who they celebrated as heroes.

Many British soldiers had already mingled with the locals and were seen drinking wine and kissing the local women. The crowd chanted, "Long live Wellington. Long live the English."

Bells rang out all across the city in celebration. It was a joyous and welcome scene after the looting and horrors they had witnessed at Badajoz, where blood-soaked and furious soldiers had run rampant until order could be re-established. But here in Madrid, the British soldiers were treated as returning heroes, and they were in far better spirits, eager to spend their wages on food and wine and celebrate alongside the city's populace.

"I have never seen a people so overwhelmed with joy," said Bunce.

"Nor I, but then I have never seen a city freed from the shackles of the enemy without a bloodthirsty assault. The places we have taken have been starved out, burnt, bombarded, and looted," admitted Paget.

"I was there at Badajoz, you know. I did not make the assault, but I manned the trenches."

Paget nodded in acknowledgement, as he kept treating his old friend as though he had been idle in all the years they had been apart. It was a reminder that neither man truly knew the other at all anymore.

"A frightful thing to have been at Badajoz, no matter what one's duty was."

"Thank heavens this city was not defended so."

"No, but I am sure Badajoz will not be the last."

"Were you there, at the assault?"

"I was."

"Incredible that you are still here to tell the tale."

"Many had it far worse, for we were not the first nor second to make the attack. A great many men went before us."

"I am sorry that I was so quick to judge you and your Major. This appointment was not one I wanted nor expected, and it is quite the change."

"I know how it feels, for I was just the same. Lord Wellington appointed me to Craven on a whim. Quite honestly, I think he did it in jest or to punish me. I imagine he thought Craven nothing more than a selfish wretch who would put me off army life within a week and have me on my way back to England."

"It was hard for you to take this path, too?"

"Very much so, and it still can feel most odd, but I have seen and lived more than I ever could have imagined in these past years, and I would not give them up for any life of luxury back home."

"Truly?"

"I would not lie to you. It has not been an easy life, not in any way, but it has been a fulfilling one, and even if I do not survive this experience, I will have lived more than most men could ever dream of across all of their long lifetime."

"And women, what of women?"

"There is one," smiled Paget.

"How could there not?" Bunce laughed, "Though I see a woman rides with Craven? An armed one, no less," he declared as he looked to Vicenta without a clue about Charlie's identity.

"She is a guerrilla, fighting for her country like so many others," replied Paget defensively.

"Women fighting a war, whatever next?" Bunce sneered.

"I suggest you do not repeat such a sentiment in her presence. For she would beat you to the ground, whether by her sword or her fists."

"Truly?"

"Truly, she is a force to be reckoned with. So many

ordinary people of this country have taken up the fight, it is hard to imagine without one's own country having been overrun by an enemy. Something we as Englishmen have not known for many hundreds of years."

Indeed, it truly was difficult for most of them to comprehend the extent of the relief and jubilation. It was not just that the capital of Spain had been freed, but that the French had now lost half of the territory they had gained in in Spain since 1808 in just eight months. All the hopes of the campaign that had begun with Talavera were finally being realised. After three gruelling years with so many ups and downs, few believed they would ever see such days of triumph as they now experienced today in Madrid. Though as they passed one street the scene of several dead bodies hanging from ropes soured the experience a little.

"They have hanged French soldiers?" Bunce asked in disgust.

"I doubt it. Those are most likely Spanish civilians, men and women who supported the French. Traitors to their people and their country."

"Savages," gasped Bunce.

"They betrayed their country. It is treason, and we would do the same," replied Paget unsympathetically.

"After a fair trial, perhaps, but not by the mob!"

"You have not seen the horrors that have been inflicted upon the people of this country. Looting, murder, torture, rape, and pillage. The oldest crimes conducted on a grand scale, and often encouraged by the French to terrorise and belittle the Spanish. I do not think you can begin to fathom it until you have seen it for yourself."

Bunce was silenced, but he felt no more comfortable with the situation even with Paget's explanation.

"What would you do if people in your home city worked for the enemy and against you?" Vicenta was vexed by the newly arrived officer's opinions and didn't much appreciate his condemnation of her compatriots.

"I would act as a gentleman and see the law and punishment was enacted fairly," he replied boldly.

Vicenta laughed.

"You mock me, Madam!"

Bunce turned back in anger to furiously make eye contact and put her in her place. But Vicenta met his gaze like an infantry square to cavalry, and she would not waver.

"Nothing bad has ever truly happened to you, has it, Captain?"

Bunce fumbled to find his words, but it was clear that it had not.

"You have served in this war and that is admirable, but you have not seen the worst of times."

"Have I not?" he demanded defensively, thinking back to his experiences at Badajoz.

"You have seen men shot and killed in battle, but those men had a fighting chance. And every man in your army volunteered to fight for pay, including yourself. But have you seen your family members tied, beaten, raped, and murdered? Not soldiers, but civilians. Can you imagine that happening to your sister, your mother?"

Bunce had no answers. His stomach turned as he imagined the possibility, and it left him feeling rather more sickened than the sight of the hanged bodies.

"What a horrible war this is," he sniffled.

"Yes, horrible indeed," agreed Vicenta.

Craven took a bottle of wine from a man, and he gladly took a mouthful before looking back to the generous soul who had passed it to him. The man was gaunt, and he looked about to see it was a common theme. The whole populace looked thin and malnourished and not so far from starvation. He tried to pass the bottle back to the man, but he would not take it.

"How can these people be starving?" he asked Matthys.

"Last year's harvest was terrible, and so many armies have stripped the land of food and all other resources."

"We were told the whole of Spain would rise up against the enemy and form an army one hundred thousand strong or more, but how can such hungry and desperate people do that?"

He noticed that many wore tired and worn-out clothing. Madrid might have once been a great city, but the inhabitants who remained looked exhausted and weak.

"The French have taken a great deal from this country and its people. They treat them like a conquered people, like slaves in some cases, but it is their undoing. For they hate them in return with such a passion as it will be the enemy's undoing," suggested Matthys.

"But where will the army come from? Look at the people here, old, tired, sick. They are relieved to be freed, relieved that their struggle is over, and yet we expect them to take up arms and march against the armies of Napoleon?" Craven pondered.

Matthys had no answers. He was sympathetic to their plights, but like Craven and the rest of the army, they expected and needed a great Spanish army to march with them. In spite of some great victories against the French, the enemy still had vast armies across Spain.

"Give them time. They are mere hours from being released from Napoleon's grasp."

Craven groaned in agreement.

"Enjoy what we have today, for you do not know what tomorrow brings. Look at what we have done here. Years of hardship and sacrifice got us here, enjoy it."

They came to a standstill in a large square where the local populace continued to flock to them to celebrate. Yet even more elated cries soon rang out as waggons were driven into the square, bringing provisions, which quickly drew the attention of the crowd and brought Craven some peace. Major Spring approached through the opening in the crowd with a large and suspicious smile.

"What surprise do you have for us this time?" Craven groaned.

"Only good news, Major. Supplies of food and drink flood towards the city. What was a miserable place for the locals only yesterday will be a paradise by comparison."

That was music to Craven's ears.

"No resistance at all, Sir?" Paget asked.

"The last remnants of the French soldiers here have taken refuge in defences on the Eastern edge of the city. We will watch them closely, but let us concern ourselves with that obstacle tomorrow, for today is for celebrations!"

He was seemingly as ecstatic as the locals at the liberation.

"Did anyone ever doubt we would make it this far?" Bunce grumbled.

Craven chuckled.

"What is so funny, Sir?"

"I'll leave you to it, Craven," insisted Spring, leaving Craven to suffer the new young Captain.

"Throughout the winter there were many at the highest positions of this army who doubted we would ever make it out of Portugal."

"Who told you this?" Bunce asked defensively, as if Craven could not possibly know such damning information.

"General Le Marchant, who had heard it with his own ears," he replied coolly.

Bunce was silenced. He dared not question the words of the recently deceased British hero, not for his own pride and also for risk of causing offence to Craven and the others who knew the General personally. And yet he was clearly left pondering whether Craven really did know best, for he had a hard time stomaching the fact he might himself be wrong.

"We should find a bed for him to rest." Matthys gestured towards Timmerman who was still in the saddle but barely conscious.

"Will he survive?" Bunce asked.

"Of course, he will. Nothing can kill that bastard, not even me," replied Craven with a smirk.

Bunce did not understand the dynamic and looked most put out that Craven would talk about one of his fellow officers in such a way. Paget noticed his disapproval as Craven went to see to their wounded comrade.

"You do not like the way the Major speaks about Timmerman?"

"I do not. An officer must respect his fellow gentlemen first and foremost."

Paget chuckled.

"Tell me, how many times have you heard a gentleman speak softly and gently whilst the meaning of his words are scathing and stinging below the surface?"

"Plenty, for sure."

"Then know that Major Craven often speaks in the reverse manner. He speaks brashly of his friends and comrades whilst meaning the best for them. We once spoke in a similar fashion."

"When we were but children, but…"

Paget interrupted the Captain, much to his surprise.

"Wouldn't you like to see a return to such a time? For they were a more honest time for many of us."

Bunce shrugged as he didn't fully comprehend the soldiers he was now serving with, and yet he was aware of their reputation and was trying to understand them in context.

"BP?" he asked in a friendly fashion.

"Yes?"

"Tell me honestly, do you trust Major Craven?"

"I do, with my life, and he mine, and we have both had occasions to test that trust."

"And you believe he is a good man?"

"Mostly," smiled Paget.

But Bunce looked most out of sorts as he felt quite out of place and uncertain.

"What do you really want to know?"

"I suppose I must know if Craven is a good thing. If he is good for the war effort, for the army, and for everybody around him?"

"Then let me assure you of those things. For there is no other officer I would rather serve under."

"Not even Lord Wellington? What if you could be his

aide-de-camp?" Bunce asked curiously, as if trying to trip Paget up and find a hole in his argument.

"I would not give this up."

"Come on, BP," protested Bunce as if his response was absurd.

"Truly, if you had asked me the same three years ago, I would have done anything for such an opportunity, but now I know what I have here, I would not trade it for anything in the world. Not just because I have found a place and a family here, but because I believe together, we can make a difference. Hell, I do not just believe it, I have seen it. The evidence lays in our wake as we have cut our path across these lands."

Bunce smiled as he could see the fiery passion in Paget's face and that spoke volumes.

"Family? I heard what your father did…I am sorry."

"I am not. None of that matters to me now. I am not out here to earn my father's respect. For it means nothing to me. If he cannot see me for all I have achieved, then so be it. He is lesser for it."

Bunce sighed in amazement.

"I cannot imagine the BP I one knew ever saying such words. There was nothing more important to you than the approval of your father."

"We are all young and foolish once."

"You have changed, far more so than I would ever have imagined."

"For the best I believe."

"Then perhaps your father will realise it someday."

Paget shrugged.

"How will you manage otherwise? For a man cannot live

on army pay alone."

"They do," he replied, looking to the soldiers all around them, including many who served in the Salford Rifles.

"Common soldiers, perhaps, but…"

But Paget caught a glimpse of Charlie and cut him off.

"We are not better than them, Buncy. We are just luckier. Lucky to have been born with money and all the fine things one could hope for, but out here those fine things account for nothing. All that really matters is what is in here." He pointed to his heart, "and here," as he pointed to his mind.

"A man advancing merely on merit, that is something Napoleon would say."

"A terrible man can have a good idea," admitted Paget.

"And so, I suppose a good man can have terrible ones?"

"Yes."

"Nothing in this country or this war is what I expected it to be, but now I am even more puzzled than before, having joined you and Major Craven. Wellington says you are the finest of men, and so who am I to question it?"

Paget slapped him on the shoulder in a friendly fashion as if they had done the same so many times before, but Bunce was taken by surprise by the strength in Paget's arm. He stumbled a little before catching his balance and they both laughed.

"Give Craven and the others a chance. They are not what you were expecting, and I know all too well what that experience is like, but I know them, and I know their hearts are true and they are devils in battle."

"I will take your word for it, and what choice do I have? Wellington himself put me here, and so how can I fight it?"

Charlie watched the two old friends chat and make merry.

"Do you worry for him?" Vicenta asked who was always eagle-eyed.

"Worry?"

"An old friend from when he was a different sort of man, do you not worry he might change?"

"No, because I believe in him."

And yet as much as she wanted to believe her own words, there was a little doubt and concern in her tone, and so she quickly changed the subject.

"How does it feel? To walk triumphantly into your nation's capital? And without a fight, no less."

"We all fought a great deal to get here, all of us, but I must admit, it is not all I had hoped for."

"No, but why is that?"

"I had thought the day we marched into Madrid would be the day France was defeated and my country was free, but the enemy is still out there, biding their time and regaining their strength so that they might make an attack against us once more. This is a victory, and I will enjoy it, but the victory is not complete."

"But we will make it so. We will not stop fighting."

"I truly hope and pray for it to be true, but there is no peace until every French soldier is cast out of Spain."

"I will keep on fighting, I can promise you that, and I know Craven has made the same vow, and he will keep it. I will make sure of it."

They watched as Timmerman was helped from his horse. He tried to support himself but was weak and delirious.

"Craven, is that you?" he mumbled.

"I'm here," replied Craven.

"I am going to kill you, Craven, if it is the last thing I ever do," he slurred.

"Of course, you will," smiled Craven as he wrapped one of Timmerman's arms over his shoulder. "Ferreira, see to our horses and find some quarters for all the Salfords before the whole damned army gets here."

Caffy took up Timmerman's other arm and helped him on as most of Craven's closest friends handed the responsibility of their horses over to their comrades, but not Paget. He would see Augustus to some stables or similar by his own hand.

"I will be along shortly."

"I will come with you," replied Charlie.

Bunce followed him.

"This way, Sir."

Joze had already found them some place for Timmerman to rest. His feet dragged along the street, and Craven and Caffy hauled him several hundred yards through the crowds and finally to a public house of some sorts. It looked decadent, and upon entering they were struck with the wafts of sweet perfume, a far cry from the stale beer and urine in many of the watering holes they had travelled through. Birback, Matthys, Moxy, and Amyn followed them inside, at which they were instantly greeting by a frenzy of congratulatory cheers and whistling by a dozen women who were dressed in their finery as if ready for a ball.

"What is this?" Moxy asked.

"It's a whorehouse," smirked Birback. He looked as though he had stepped into heaven as his eyes lit up.

Craven looked to Joze for answers.

"You brought us to a brothel? I said to find somewhere comfortable for Timmerman to rest and heal his wounds."

"Yes, the ladies have been most welcoming. When I told them I was with Major James Craven they were all too happy to help."

"Help?"

"Free bed and board for a dozen of us for one week. We pay only for our drinks and well, nothing more…"

"The girls are on the house?" Birback almost fainted at the prospect.

"We are all eager to show our gratitude to the fine English soldiers who have fought so hard to save us," said one of the women.

"He is Scottish, and I am Welsh," replied Moxy.

"I'll be anything you want," replied Birback with his jaw almost on the floor.

"A little help?" Craven demanded of Joze as they were still propping up the half-dead Timmerman.

Joze and one of the women led them upstairs, struggling to haul Timmerman up the narrow stairway. They continued on down a corridor on the next floor which passed dozens of rooms as if the place as a labyrinth. It was vast compared to what it appeared on the street, and yet even now they could still hear Birback's roaring laugh from downstairs. They finally entered a secluded room far to the back of the building to find it was quite plain but had a comfortable-looking bed. They lowered Timmerman down onto it, and he slumped into a deep sleep within seconds. Craven peered about in confusion, for it was as if they had stepped into a different world to the decadence of the brothel they had travelled through.

"She says this is where women come to labour. It is the most peaceful room in the house," Joze said.

"Until that bastard wakes up," smiled Craven as he knew Timmerman would not stay restful for long.

"Does he need anything?"

"Leave him water. I'll ensure Matthys sees to him."

"I can care for him," the woman said in a thick Spanish accent.

"Yes, please, much obliged," replied Craven.

He and Joze left her to it as they went back to the bar, hoping to find some replenishment, but ahead they could see Birback giggling like a schoolboy as he followed a woman into a room. They vanished inside, but Birback's cackling could still be heard as they went on by. They went back to the bar downstairs to find drinks and food had been laid out for them. They quickly sat down and got stuck in. It was nothing more than bread and oil with some cured meat and wine, but it was like the nectar of the gods after the many weeks and months of chasing the French back and forth across the countryside, which had been largely laid barren by the French armies.

A most beautiful woman who was a few years older than the rest, and held herself with the grace that Lady Sarmento did, gazed upon Craven. She held herself with such authority that she could only be the Madam who ran the establishment.

"Thank you for…well everything," declared Craven.

"What is your thanks worth?" she replied seductively. She paced up beside him and ran a hand gently down his arm.

"Is it not the women who give their services here?"

"Yes, but I am not for sale, but you…you have lots to trade," she smiled.

Craven was stunned at the realisation that his services were being requested in payment in a whorehouse of all places.

He smiled and lifted his glass. It was an enticing thought, as she had done so much for them and was also quite beautiful.

"Excuse me, but it has been a long road and I must see to my men."

"Then be quick, for my girls will see to them quite well."

Craven sat down amongst some of his closest friends and gasped in relief at resting his feet and relaxing in a place with walls and chairs. He wanted to go on making merry, and yet they all came to a stop, looking to one another and marvelling at the situation they now found themselves in, as though it were a dream. Craven took up his glass with which to toast as it felt appropriate.

"We have come a long way, far further than many believed possible, both individually and the whole bloody army, but on this instance, and I never thought I would say this, to Timmerman, may that bastard live forever," he smiled.

"To Timmerman!" They held up their glasses to toast just as Paget and Bunce stepped inside. They stopped at the bizarre scene before them.

"What on Earth is this?" Paget gasped.

CHAPTER 5

Craven awoke in a delirious state with a pounding headache. Yet he could hear Birback roaring with laughter as he continued on with one of the women of the house. Craven shook his head. He couldn't understand how the Scotsman was even still standing. The bed beneath him was soft and welcoming, but he was both hungry and thirsty in equal measure. He looked beside his bed to see his boots, which were the only things he had managed to remove the night before. He had slept in his unbuttoned tunic. He pulled on his boots and gathered up his sword belt but did not even bother buttoning his tunic as he staggered out of his room. He found the corridor reeked of stale sweat, but it was half masked by sweet perfume, which was a small relief, but the combination made Craven's stomach churn. He stomped heavily down the stairs and made it back to the bar where they had spent the night before. The establishment looked just as good in the light of a new day as it had the day before. Decadent colour fabrics and murals hung from most of the walls, and candles and delicate lanterns lit up the room.

To Craven's surprise he found Timmerman awake and sitting at the table where they had toasted the wounded officer the previous day. He looked to be in remarkably good spirits with the life having returned to his cheeks and eyes. As he tossed food into his mouth, a beautiful young woman brought him another plateful.

"Ah, Craven!" he roared excitedly as he continued to consume food like a starving wild animal.

"What are you doing up and about?"

"I had the most amazing sleep and awoke in this magical place where I have been treated liked a king and fed like one, too."

"It's a whorehouse."

"Yes, and a damned fine one!" Timmerman roared again with a great smile as if he had found his new home.

Craven took a seat beside him as the Madam herself brought food and wine for him. He knew that was no ordinary occurrence.

"Thank you, truly."

"And thank you," she replied with a cheeky smile.

Craven looked a little surprised as he did not remember anything between them the night before, but in truth he did not remember much at all as she strutted away mysteriously. Timmerman was much amused and took up his glass of wine to salute Craven.

"Bringing a dying man to a brothel, you are a great man, Craven."

"Are you dying?" Craven pressed.

"Not anymore!" He then howled like a wolf to celebrate being alive before breaking into laughter, but he soon winced from the pain of his wounds, "Damn," he snarled.

His mind was fully recovered, but his body needed many days or even weeks to catch up.

"You are lucky you do not have a fever. Do you remember how we found you?"

"In my own blood, and leaking far too much of it, I believe."

"If it were anyone else, I don't imagine they would have survived, but you are too stubborn to die."

"Damned right!"

"You are lucky we found you, though. You could have bled out there, or been set upon by the enemy, guerrillas, or wolves even. Many a sick or drunken fool has lost his life to the wolves in this country."

"The only wolves are the ones who did this to me."

"Will you go after them?"

Timmerman shrugged.

"Truly, you are the angriest man I have ever known. Yet your men do this to you, and you do not even care to seek revenge upon them?"

Timmerman shrugged once more as he continued to eat and drink quite at peace.

"No, you can't leave it at that. Why will you not go after them?"

"It's not what I want anymore. They only did what I would have done not so long ago. It was not personal, not like your Bouchard."

Craven sighed in amazement.

"I knew you would always find ways to surprise me, but not like this."

"Being angry at the world is exhausting. I am getting too old for it."

"Don't leave it all behind, for we need a little of that fire in your belly when we face the French."

Timmerman laughed.

"I do not need to be fuelled by anger to face them, for that is pure pleasure."

"Major Craven!" a voice cried out.

He slumped and sighed, as the call was reminiscent of his time at Salamanca and the arduous and brutal struggle against the forts that had held out there. Forts which all reports and intelligence had informed Wellington would be of little consequence. A young officer raced into the establishment. He stopped to stare at several of the women in the room who were in their evening finery despite it being early morning.

"What is it?"

"Sir, Lord Wellington requests your presence."

"Of course, he does," replied Craven sarcastically.

"I will take you to his Lordship, Sir," replied the young man who was still awestruck as if he had walked into heaven.

"Come on, then." Timmerman groaned as he struggled to get up. He took hold of a single crutch that he used to support the weight of his ruined body.

"You are not needed here," insisted Craven.

"A walk will do me well, and I do not need nursing by you!"

It was clear he would not be stopped, and he moved to the door with remarkable speed as if to display the strength he had recovered. It was hard for Craven to argue with him, as he buttoned up his tunic and hooked his sword belt on so that he was prepared and ready for whatever the world was about to throw at him. Nobody else was awake, not even Paget and Matthys who were the early risers Craven might have expected. And so he went out to meet with Wellington with the most unlikely of comrades by his side.

They went on with great attention from the locals who smiled and clapped as they went by. None of them could know who Craven was, and so it could only be general jubilation at seeing British soldiers instead of French ones in their streets.

"They are rather animated, aren't they?" Timmerman smiled.

"They applaud a wounded veteran, Sir," replied the young man leading them as he looked to the state of Timmerman whose numerous wounds were clear to see and behold. He still wore many bandages, and his uniform was patched and ragged as if he had led the Forlorn Hope at Badajoz and survived the ordeal. The way the locals treated him made Craven chuckle.

"If only they knew," he whispered to Timmerman.

"I have spilled enough of my blood in the face of the enemy," he replied defensively.

It was hard to argue with him, as despite his motivations not being the most honest in the past, there was no doubt he got results and was quite the thorn in the enemy's side.

"What was it they called you? The Fantasma? The Ghost?"

"That was you, Sir? What an honour!" The young officer had overheard him and stopped them to offer his hand.

"I will shake the hand of the Fantasma, Sir!"

Timmerman did not know how to respond and looked to

Craven for help.

"Well, it's true, isn't it?"

"Yes, but…" began Timmerman.

"Give the man a hand. You are a hero in this country."

Timmerman reached out to find his hand violently shaken by the enthusiastic young officer who was positively beaming at the experience.

"Major Craven and the Fantasma, gosh what a delight!"

Craven laughed. "And what is your name?"

"Lieutenant Sayer, Sir."

"It is a pleasure to meet you, Lieutenant."

Sayer was taken aback.

"Well thank you, Sir," he replied with a huge smile as he continued to lead them on.

"The Fantasma? I was little more than a brigand, a Bandido really," whispered Timmerman.

"Yes, and it is those cutthroats who are winning this war for us. Even the very worst of them are heroes in this country now. For they fight an enemy far worse than themselves."

Timmerman found that most curious.

"Yes, this is not a gentleman's war as much as so many would want it to be, and fighters like you and I have finally found a place that is just right for us."

"Is that what you believe?"

Craven nodded sincerely.

"I spent years fighting upon a stage, when in truth this is what I was born to do. I have found my calling here, and I think you have, too. And that is what has brought us together. Bitter enemies now fighting side by side."

"What does that make us?"

Craven had to stop and think for a moment. They'd had a mountain of strife in their past, and yet none of it seemed to matter anymore.

"A man who fights by my side and has my back is my brother," he replied sincerely.

"As simple as that? After all we have been through?"

"You think I would still have Birback around if not?"

"What has he done to you?"

"What hasn't he?" Craven smiled back at him.

"Have my back and I will have yours, that much I can promise."

"Then we understand one another."

Timmerman smiled at the prospect without saying another word. They were led on to the Eastern edge of the city where Wellington and many staff and advisors were looking out at a French defensive position on the heights beyond. A great number of British soldiers were in place to surround the enemy advances but made no attempt on them.

"It is the Salamanca forts all over again," gasped Craven, realising his fears were coming true as he looked at the formidable defences.

"Perhaps a taste of those days, but hardly as great an obstacle," replied Major Spring.

But Craven was not so sure as he studied them with his own eyes. On the heights to the East the Retiro Palace and museum had been fortified. A star fort with loopholed walls, ten bastions, and deep trenches and palisades.

"It will be no walk over," admitted Craven.

Though in truth the defences had not had half as much time and effort put into them as the forts of Salamanca that had been converted into a formidable fortress.

"I want it stormed this night," Wellington stated.

Craven looked most uncomfortable with the idea. The memory of the initial assault on the Salamanca forts was still fresh in his mind, as he had witnessed the slaughter with his own eyes.

"Without a bombardment, Sir?"

"The enemy might think they can march to relieve these defences and therefore this entire city, and I will not have it. We must destroy their hope."

"What do you say, Craven?" Major Spring asked him.

"Me, Sir? I am no engineer nor expert in these matters."

"And yet you always have something to say. Say it," ordered Wellington.

Craven carefully studied the defences for himself once more.

"The outer defences do not look all that much. If they can be taken this evening, we might well force a surrender without an assault on the stronger parts."

"A show of strength without risking too much?"

"Not just strength, we can take those walls." He pointed to the walls around the park and botanical gardens of the old palace that formed the outer lines of the defences.

"It would certainly drive whatever defenders are there back into a small space, which might make them hesitate to keep up the contest," added Spring in support.

"Will you see it done?" Wellington asked him.

Timmerman laughed as he realised Craven had just put his foot in it and volunteered himself to make the assault. But Craven did not even hesitate. He was quite willing to try and save them all from another brutal outing as he'd witnessed at the Salamanca forts.

"I will, Sir."

Timmerman was silenced and amazed, but also impressed. He liked this bold and assertive version of his old enemy, a rogue who once ran from many hardships, but now he held firm.

"I want three hundred men to breach into the park area there, and another three hundred against the walls of the botanical gardens there."

"You are giving me command, Sir?" Craven asked in surprise.

"Heavens, no. I am ordering you to join the assault and to make certain it is a success."

"I will see it done."

"I know that you will."

Wellington led his staff away without another word.

"You've really stuck your neck out this time, Craven. Be sure the French do not cut it off, for they are rather fond of doing so!" Timmerman chuckled.

"I never volunteered for this, but I will see it done."

"I know you will, because you have too much pride to fail. Perhaps that is what makes you such the different man you once were. You never cared for pride, and now it might just be the death of you," Timmerman smiled back at him.

"And you never cared for any man, only women, and look at you now!"

Timmerman laughed as he was most certainly right in his assessment of him.

"Who knew that all we needed to become better men, was the greatest war this world has ever seen?"

Craven looked back at the French defences. Wellington was right about them not being anything like as strong as those they encountered at Salamanca, and yet they were still an intimidating sight.

"You aren't coming with us." Craven was looking at the crutch Timmerman was resting on.

"You're damn right, I'm not," agreed Timmerman who was in no fit state for a fight, or even the climb to the heights themselves.

The day passed quickly as they could hear celebrations continuing across the city, and soon enough the sun was setting. The time had come. He led his way forward. Caffy, Birback, Moxy and Ellis followed on after him hauling two great wooden beams, the sort that might be used structurally. They tossed them down, hitting the ground with a hefty and solid impact and no bounce at all.

"What are those for, Sir?" Paget asked.

Craven gestured towards the hundreds of soldiers who had gathered ready for the advance. Plenty of them were carrying pickaxes, and Craven pointed up to the walls they had to overcome.

"Those walls must come down, and I do not intend to chip at them with picks."

"So, you will batter them down?"

"Yes," grunted Birback with glee at the destructive thought.

But Paget shook his head in disbelief as if it were the most ridiculous of ideas doomed to fail the moment it was conceived, and yet he was loathed to condemn them to bad luck by knocking their enthusiasm. The last rays of sunlight on the horizon were the countdown to their attack, and tensions were heightened as Timmerman hopped over to see them off.

"All okay?" Craven asked Paget.

"I fear these moments are getting too familiar, the assault of a most heavily guarded fortress and all the risks it entails."

"Get used to it. For Spain is full of castles and walled cities. Either we assault them, or we withdraw and defend in the same fashion as the enemy, which foot would you rather be on?" Timmerman asked.

Paget shrugged as it was not much of a decision to make. Nobody had it easy in these sorts of battles, though he remembered what it was like being on the back foot, and it felt far worse, for at least momentum was in their favour and morale was dragged up with it.

They waited for darkness to finally settle on the heights and then they knew the time had come. The two forces advanced towards the Retiro heights, and Craven signalled for his party to go on in support. He commanded just thirty of the Salford Rifles, a small party to support the assault that numbered three hundred British soldiers at each of the two points that would be the targets of the assault. On they crept, hunkered down low and hoping to not be seen until the last moment. For the enemy must surely expect an assault this night, as Wellington's cautious reputation was now rapidly giving way to a more aggressive one. They were within one hundred yards of the walls when the first musket shots rang out, and the chaos of alarm calls and sporadic volleys filled the night sky.

"Charge!" one of the officers cried.

Both storming parties hurried towards the walls as musket fire ignited before them, but not with any serious ferocity that would slow them. Only a few men were struck before they reached the walls and began at them with picks as they tried to rip them down and clear a way for a larger assault force. But Paget watched in amazement as Birback led one of the beams forward being used as a batter ram. He and Caffy positively sprung with the hulking lump of hardwood with such momentum that something had to give, either the wall or them. To everyone's surprise they struck the wall and crashed right on through it. A ten-foot-wide section of the wall gave way, and Birback went barrelling in through the debris as the beam followed him.

"My God, it worked!" Paget cried.

Craven looked just as surprised, revealing how he had no more faith in the plan than Paget did, and yet the next one carried by Moxy and Ellis thumped into the wall. Though it struck with less of a dramatic effect, it caused the already weakened wall to collapse along a length from the first breach. A cry of elation rang out from the troops who could barely believe their early luck as they rushed for the breach. Cries of panic echoed out from the French inside, and it was clear they were already fleeing from the outer defences. Craven rushed on through to see a scene of chaos as the French troops fled, including from the palace as they abandoned the outer line of defences completely. A few shots rang out from either side, but the battle was won, and soon enough those who had taken the walls cheered for all on the Eastern edge of Madrid to see. Their cheers of celebration were so loud they drowned out the jubilant cries of those upon the walls.

They watched as the enemy fled to their inner defences, abandoning so much of the defensive works, as well as a great many cannons and an aqueduct which brought fresh water to the place. Paget could hardly believe how easily it had been achieved, and it was a great relief to them all.

"They won't hold out for long, Sir, will they?" He was looking to the enemy taking up the defence of the star fort.

"Not a chance," smiled Craven.

But they heard coughing at their feet and looked down. Birback was pushing stones from himself as he tried to dig himself out of the rubble that had collapsed on him as he went through the wall. Craven sheathed his sword and helped to haul him out and get him to his feet. He was covered in cuts and bruises from the impact and the collapse which followed it, but he had a huge smile on his face at the success of his bullish battering ram charge.

They watched as hundreds of British troops poured into the French position, surrounding the inner defences completely as they settled in for the night knowing the enemy had nowhere to go. Craven soon found a bench inside the palace that would provide more than enough comfort that night. It was placed beside open glass doors that looked inward to the last French bastion. Paget sat down beside him and sighed with relief.

"Only a handful of casualties and our mission is complete. Quite remarkable, isn't it, Sir?"

"Yes, but our task here is not done until all remaining French soldiers are gone. They must have two thousand soldiers in there." He gestured towards the fort. They were in shooting distance of the French troops atop it, but nobody fired for fear of recourse from the other side as they settled in for a peaceful night.

CHAPTER 6

The first light that struck the palace awoke most inside, and they were relieved to wake to a peaceful morning, as a battle had not erupted in the night and the morning seemed to bring no change. Paget was at the open doors which looked out to the enemy position, and a French officer was peering back at him, both waiting for their orders to know whether they would fight one another or not. At their backs they could hear a lot of activity towards the city, and they moved to windows on the far side of the room to get a good look for themselves. Cannons were being drawn up in readiness to bombard the enemy position.

"Craven!" Moxy cried. He had not taken an eye off of the enemy positions. He rushed back to the Welshman's side to see a flag of truce being carried out from the star fort. The enemy came to negotiate in some way.

"Do they come to surrender, Sir?" Paget asked hopefully.

"We can only hope, for there does not need to be any more blood spilled here. We will have complete victory no matter how hard they resist, and so why fight it?"

"Would you give up?" Timmerman asked.

It was a hard thing to answer, but Craven nodded in agreement.

"If it was between complete destruction of the soldiers under my command, my friends, or surrender, I would surrender."

"Truly, Sir?"

"Of course, and then I would promptly ensure a successful escape attempt at the first opportunity."

"We had to do it at Almeida," added Ferreira as he remembered the disaster of that place and how they were almost caught by Bouchard amid the greatest explosion of the powder magazine there.

"Does an officer not have a duty to his captors if he has given his word to surrender as a gentleman, Sir?"

"Yes, and what is more important to you, a promise to the enemy or the promise you made to your country? If you are ever captured, it is your duty to escape so that you might go on fighting against them, is that clear?"

"Yes, Sir," replied Paget in amazement as he thought capture would mean the end of the war for him and the end of everything he knew.

"Major!" Nooth called.

Craven rushed back to the window where they had viewed the guns being dragged into position, and his eyes opened wide in surprise as Wellington approached with a small party of officers.

"Paget, with me!"

He did as asked, but Bunce followed on as well. He could not resist the opportunity to be seen by Lord Wellington as part of the triumphant party that had taken the defences the night before. Craven was not even in charge of those who had made the assault, but Wellington clapped eyes upon him instantly as he entered the palace.

"Sir, the enemy send out a flag of truce."

"And you will go to meet with them."

"Me, Sir?"

"You will bring the party to me, and I will speak with them personally."

"Yes, Sir."

Craven was relieved he did not have to conduct the negotiation. He rushed on outside with Paget and Bunce following. They carried no weapons in their hands, only their swords and pistols about their bodies. They passed by many of their own troops, closing the distance with the five Frenchmen who advanced under the flag of truce. The most senior of them quickly spoke, as if fearful he might be shot despite the flag if he did not explain himself quickly.

"Monsieur, I bring the compliments of Governor Lafon-Blaniac and terms with which I would discuss with your commander."

"Follow me."

Craven led them on. The Frenchman was surprised as if he had expected a more abrasive response. They were led into the palace and stopped in disbelief as they realised they were meeting Wellington himself, who they treated with much respect.

"My Lord," declared the French officer.

"Your Grace," Paget snapped.

But Wellington signalled for silence.

"You ask for terms?"

"Sir, Governor Lafon-Blaniac asks me to inform you that if you make any attempt to press further on our position, he will fire upon the city of Madrid with many cannons which we possess."

Paget was stunned as he had expected a demand for preferable terms of surrender. Yet Wellington made no reaction at all as he thought about the man's words and studied the faces of the other Frenchmen. There was an uncomfortable silence for some time until finally Wellington replied.

"Mr Bunce, please see these men to the next room and provide them with refreshment whilst we continue this discussion."

Bunce looked disappointed as he wanted to see and hear how it went on, but he did as he was ordered to do. Craven smiled and Paget could not understand why.

"What is it, Sir?" Paget whispered.

"Just watch."

The doors were soon shut behind Bunce and the rest of the Frenchmen, leaving the French messenger alone with them all. There was a tense standoff for a few moments as Wellington seemed to consider his words, but Craven knew he was just letting the Frenchman sweat a little.

"What do you say?" The Frenchman could not take the pressure any longer, and Wellington finally gave his response.

"You will not fire upon the city. For to do so will lead to your complete and total destruction, which will occur unless you accept my terms."

Craven smirked as it was a masterful negotiation, and Paget was starting to understand what was going on. Wellington had sent the other Frenchmen away so that there was no need for the man to hide behind any bravado in front of his comrades. Wellington went on.

"You will surrender the fort and march out with your honour and lives intact. Officers may keep their swords, horses, and baggage. Your men may keep their knapsacks and they will not be searched. All arms and stores are to be given over intact. These are my terms, and they may not be negotiated. Your defences will fall quickly, but you may decide at what cost."

The Frenchman was stunned but also relieved, as he clearly did not want to die there.

"What do you say?"

"I must take your terms to the Governor."

"You have until 4 o'clock, after which no terms will be offered. Is that understood?"

"It is."

They watched as Bunce led the party out of the palace so that they be returned to the fort.

"Craven, have your men ready," ordered Wellington.

"Yes, Sir. Are you not certain they will accept the terms, Sir?"

"I am most certain of it, but I would be a fool to not prepare for any other possibilities. If the enemy make any attempt to fire their guns, you will have your sharpshooters silence them at every opportunity."

"Yes, Sir."

He went back to the position he had held overnight and

knew he did not need to give any warning. Everyone was on high alert, ready to shoot down upon the enemy at a moment's notice. They had covered them since first light and especially since Craven himself went out to meet them across open ground.

"What now?" Ferreira asked.

"We wait."

"For what?"

"Either the French lay down arms and march out by 4 o'clock, or they make some attack on us before."

"And will they make an attack?"

"They would be fools to do so, but we know many fools."

They could hear the crash of a crutch striking the stairs nearby, and they knew it was Timmerman. No other would be foolish enough to come so close to the enemy whilst having to use a crutch to do so.

"Here comes one now," smiled Craven.

Timmerman hobbled into view to a cheer from the Salford Rifles around him. It was a bit of a surprise, as they had often treated him with indifference if not a bitter hatred which was most deserved at the time.

"Alright, I'm not dead yet," he smiled as he played to the crowd.

Craven was impressed. It must have taken a lot of energy and determination to climb up to the heights and join them, and there was nothing to gain for it except to be with his comrades.

"Wellington has given terms. Lay down arms by 4 o'clock or we go in," said Craven.

"Do you think they will give up?" Paget asked.

"They have every reason to do so, but only time will tell."

"Imagine the riches inside. I hear much of the wealth the French acquired in Portugal and nearby was placed there," replied Timmerman.

Craven smiled as now he understood why Timmerman had come.

"Everything inside is the property of the army until Lord Wellington decides otherwise," growled Paget.

"Of course," smirked Timmerman.

It was a long wait. Every soldier there knew the alternative to the enemy surrendering would be an assault, and most of them were painfully accustomed to the terrible nature of an attack on a robust fortification. Even those who had not witnessed it had heard of the horrors from those who had.

"Should we get some sword practice in?" Bunce asked after only a few minutes of waiting.

"No, we should save our strength in case it is needed," replied Craven.

The hours passed by slowly, but finally the time was drawing close, and there was a great anticipation as well as tension. They waited for the enemy's response, all the while they could hear cannons being readied and prepared to fire upon the enemy should they not submit to Wellington's terms.

"Only a few minutes now." Craven checked his pocket watch.

"Something is happening, Sir!"

Paget had been watching carefully for any sign of movement from the same window as before. Craven rushed to his side and could see the first French troops march out empty-handed. A cheer rang out from the British and Portuguese troops as it was not just a triumph, but a relief that they would not have to fight a most awful ordeal that day.

Yet the French soldiers did not go entirely peacefully. Many hobbled and swayed in a drunken state, venting their rage against their governor for having surrendered without any serious contest. The prisoners were promptly led onwards back towards Lisbon so that they could be placed far from the front and any risk of escape or troublemaking. Craven rushed on out of the palace with the Salfords behind him. Even Timmerman raced on with them, using his crutch to catapult himself forward. They soared inside the remaining defences. The star fort had been built around the old royal porcelain manufactory where the celebrated Buen Retiro china was made. It would have been the final refuge if the star fort itself had been compromised, but it was also a vast storage space of which they were most curious to see what they might find. They stopped as they entered to see it was rammed full of supplies.

There were vast quantities of uniforms, shoes, muskets, and all manner of accoutrements, enough to equip an army of tens of thousands. They went on through the stores to find a truly astonishing amount of equipment.

"Well, it's hardly gold," muttered Timmerman.

"But that is." Paget took a corner to find masses of stacked paintings, silverware, chests of jewellery, and all manner of wealth.

"And it will all go straight back into the war effort!" Major Spring strode in to ensure the loot was not being seized by the first soldiers to find it.

Provosts poured in behind him to see that all was conducted correctly, but Spring was not interested in the riches. He merely marvelled at the mounds of thousands of shoes and tunics and all that a soldier needed in the field. He picked up a simple and modest pair of French soldier's shoes of which there were many thousands in piles.

"This is the treasure this army needs."

"Treasure?" Paget asked.

"With this we can shoe the whole damned army, and those tunics." He pointed to the blue French uniforms, "They can go to the men of the Royal Artillery and our light dragoons. Those others there can go to the Spanish. Nothing shall be wasted. This is a gold mine for this army," he smiled.

"Sir, look, Sir!" Moxy cried.

He was out of view but soon came charging in, drawing gasps from many, for he carried an Imperial Eagle in each hand. Few could believe the sight as Craven snatched one from him to see if it was the genuine article and not some kind of cheap trick.

"Is it so, Sir? Is it the real thing?"

"It is, Mr Paget. It is," marvelled Craven.

"I'll be taking that, thank you." Major Spring took the other from Moxy, but Craven looked reluctant to part with his.

"Follow me, and let the army see." Spring strode on out, leaving the provosts to protect all that was inside.

Paget led the others after them as they were eager to see the gilt golden eagles glimmer in the afternoon light from the sun still high in the sky. They did not disappoint. The eagles shone like beacons as they were carried out with pride, for there was nothing more valuable to take from the enemy than their Eagles. It was the most important symbol of Napoleon's power, and the soldiers who carried and marched with them were to protect them with their lives. Cries rang out as they stepped into the light and all eyes were soon upon them, as the troops all around erupted into a frenzy of celebrations. They could hardly believe the day could reach even greater heights, and so they could not contain themselves when the Eagles were paraded before their eyes as they marched on. They were presented to Wellington in an impromptu ceremony as the troops continue to roar such loud celebrations, they could barely hear one another. They finally quietened a little as locals from the city arrived with food and wine to hand out freely.

"What to do with them?" Major Spring asked as they marvelled at the two Imperial Eagles. It was a strange thing. They had not been won in open battle, but their capture was an honest one.

"They will go back to England, to the Prince Regent. May he display them as a symbol of all we have achieved here," replied Wellington.

"And what of us, Sir? What of the army?" Craven asked.

Their leader looked about at the weary but jubilant faces of the soldiers all around them. It had been a hard campaign, and they were all sweating profusely from soldiering through the hottest weeks of the Spanish summer.

"Let them rest, and if the people of Madrid will treat them as heroes, let them."

He then marched on with Spring and the Imperial Eagles to more cheers from the army surrounding him.

"We rest here in Madrid, Sir?" Paget asked with glee.

"Not for the sake of the men, I imagine," replied Craven.

"Then why, Sir?"

"The seat of power here in Spain must be properly re-established. There is much work to be done, and once again we do not know the intentions of the French armies to both the North and South."

"How can you know this, Sir?"

"It is the nature of war," replied Matthys as he joined them.

"Do not question it. We have time here and a populace willing to pour food and wine into our mouths. Appreciate it, I know my body will," added Timmerman.

But Paget looked anxious.

"What is it?" Craven asked.

"I do not know if I can relax and celebrate when I know there is so much more to be done, Sir."

Timmerman laughed.

"A soldier should always take every opportunity to eat, drink, and sleep."

"He is right. We have earned this, and there is so much more to be done, we must recover our strength." Craven looked back to the city which was still the heart of the party as people danced in the streets and food and wine flowed freely.

"Then what do we do here, Sir?"

"Live a life of leisure, as the gentlemen we are, Mr Paget."

Craven led them back to the city limits as their work was done. Madrid had been taken with barely any fight at all, but it had all come off the back of the magnificent and decisive victory at Salamanca. A victory so complete that many felt the French army would not stop running until they reached France. That was the prevailing feeling amongst the army, and it did wonders to boost morale. It finally felt that Wellington's army was the dominant force in the Peninsula, for all fell to them or fled in a great reversal of when Napoleon had led his army through Spain in 1808. But unlike Napoleon's army, who were despised, Wellington's soldiers were now treated as liberators and heroes. They were the talk of the city as they were given every gift and attention that they had to give.

Craven led them to the nearest tavern they could find and stormed into a cry of elation from the family who owned the establishment. They had no idea who Craven and the others were, but they wore the uniforms of British soldiers and that was enough.

"Thank you, thank you, please all have a drink at our expense," declared the barkeep.

Craven took out his purse and poured many coins across the bar top.

"Keep them coming," he replied.

The drinks flowed, and all were drunk before the sun had even gone down. For there was much to celebrate, and they continued in the same fashion for day after day as the populace continued to lavish praise and gratitude upon the army. The parties continued on with no sign of coming to a close. But on the third day of excess, Matthys had seen enough as he looked across the bar room of the brothel they had made their home for a little while.

"My Paget, will you join me at church?"

Paget did not have the heart to say no, as Matthys rounded up many more, including Moxy, Ellis, Caffy, and Bunce.

"You must join us," Paget insisted to Charlie.

She groaned. She did not have much care for the church or any faith left after her hardships, but just as Paget could not say no to Matthys, she could not deny him.

"I will join you," added Vicenta.

"Where is Craven?" Matthys asked.

Nobody had any idea, though many of their party were missing, likely still spread out across the city enjoying the celebrations. Matthys shrugged as if it did not matter. He led the group like a shepherd as they were marched up a hill towards a peaceful-looking place of worship, and Nooth dragged Quicks to join them.

"They are Catholic," insisted Vicenta.

"It will do just fine," replied Matthys.

The party was in good spirits, despite being dragged away to a seemingly dower service, but the fresh air was a welcome relief after the stuffy bars and brothels. They entered to find it was almost full, but they were welcomed just as they were all about the city. The service was about to begin, but most of them could not keep their eyes off of a line of beautiful young women sitting on the far side of the pews.

"Will you look at that," exclaimed Nooth.

"Shh," insisted Matthys angrily.

It then struck Paget how this was a place for the wealthy. It was filled with Spanish officers, officials, and wealthy locals. There was not another common soldier in sight, except those the Salfords had brought with them. He imagined they might not have been allowed in if it was not for the presence of Captain Bunce and himself, and they had arrived just at the moment the service was about to begin so there was no time to eject them. Several of the local men scowled at the common soldiers they had brought into their place of worship.

The sermon soon began, and none had much understanding of the language except for Vicenta, and Matthys who knew the text well enough that he could recognise which verses were being read. Both whispered explanations as to what was being said. Paget clung to Vicenta's words as she translated bits or paraphrased for them, and it was not long before the topic turned to one that was most sensitive to him.

"Listen to your father. The father of a righteous child has great joy. A man who fathers a wise son rejoices in him."

It was hard for him to hear, and he moved to step out.

"Are you okay?" Charlie asked.

"Yes, I just need a little air."

Though she knew precisely why it bothered him so, and so let him go where he might find some peace to be alone with his thoughts. Paget stepped out from the church and closed the doors behind him. He took a deep breath, for such talk of fathers was more terrifying to him than facing a French column. He moved about the church and down a small side street where he might be left in peace and not gazed upon by all passersby. He could hear the sermon go on, but it meant nothing to him now that he had no one to translate it. He leaned back against the stone church and took a deep breath, trying to calm his nerves as so many emotions swirled about his mind.

"A good service?"

Paget almost jumped out of his skin in surprise as he thought he was alone. He looked up to see a stranger leaning against a small doorway on the opposite side of the street. He was unarmed and dressed as a wealthy and decadent local gentleman. He wore a dark scarlet red jacket that was well cut to him and tailored black trousers. He had a broad felt hat decorated with a feather. Everything was in its place. A man who took much pride in his appearance and had the money with which to do so. Paget was impressed. He had a slightly swarthy complexion and well-kept short black hair.

"I am not much one for the Church, though I believe and trust in God as much as the next man," insisted Paget.

"Then you believe God sends you signs?"

Paget could not put a finger on the mysterious stranger's accent. He spoke English extremely well but sounded not quite Spanish nor French. He was evidently well educated which disguised his origins.

"I suppose I do, yes."

"Then let me give you a sign, Lieutenant Paget."

He could find no words, and yet he soon smiled, knowing his name and rank was no surprise after the days of celebrations he had enjoyed in the city.

"A sign?"

"You want the head of Major Bouchard."

This was far more a concern for Paget who now became suspicious and defensive. His hand reached for his sword as if he perceived the man was a threat and he was in imminent danger.

"What of Bouchard? Who are you?"

"Who I am is not important. Not yet."

"If you…" began Paget angrily.

"I can give you Bouchard."

"What?" snapped Paget in amazement.

"When the time is right, I will tell you where you can find Major Bouchard, and you may do with him as you please."

"Who are you?"

But the man said nothing. Paget looked up and down the street as if expecting trouble. He drew out his sword as he looked for any sign of attack, but he then looked back to the doorway where the stranger had casually rested, and he was gone, confounding Paget even further. He kept spinning around with his sword out in front of him, trying to find the man. He was anxious and confused as he rubbed his eyes as if to wonder if he was seeing things which did not exist.

"Paget?"

He spun about, causing Charlie to have to duck under his blade as he lashed it about wildly.

"Sorry, sorry." He lowered his sword but continued to look about in all directions with a terrified expression.

"What is it?"

"It's…It's…" But he realised how crazy he sounded to her as if he were fighting ghosts, "It's nothing. I just thought I saw something." He then slowly sheathed his sword.

"Are you alright?"

"I think so." He rubbed his hands down his face as he tried to snap back to reality, or what he thought was reality. He dared not explain what he thought he saw, for he wondered if he was going insane.

"Come on, I've heard quite enough of this nonsense."

"You do not believe in the words of that priest and the teachings of Jesus Christ?"

"I believe we are on our own in this world, for no God has ever saved my life or the lives of those I love."

Paget groaned as he did not know what to believe.

CHAPTER 7

"Have you heard the news?"

Vicenta rushed into the room in the most excitable state any of them had ever seen her, for she was typically stoic and calm. Paget was the first one she encountered, and yet he appeared lost in his own mind.

"Did you hear, Paget? Cadiz is free!"

And yet he did not even notice she was talking to him.

"Truly?" Ferreira asked in amazement.

"Paget?" Charlie asked. She was concerned for him as he looked stunned.

"Yes?" he finally replied.

"Cadiz, the siege of Cadiz has been abandoned."

His face lit up as the realised what that meant. Their brief time at the besieged city felt like a lifetime ago. It indeed had been well over two years since the French surrounded the Spanish Naval base that had been strengthened by the British

Army and Royal Navy, and become the seat of power for the reformed government in Spain. Its ongoing survival was a humiliation to Napoleon and all of France, that they could not take such a small patch of ground from the British and Spanish, and this news that the siege had been broken was the final nail in the coffin.

"The enemy abandon the siege for fear of being cut off after our success at Salamanca. This was because of us. We freed the city all these hundreds of miles away," Vicenta beamed.

"Do you know the significance of this?" Matthys asked Craven where they leaned together at the bar.

"I know that Napoleon has not failed in any siege across all of Europe, until now," smiled Craven.

Matthys looked impressed as the others cheered in celebration. Even if they did not know the full implications for it, they knew that Cadiz has been surrounded by the enemy for years, and so this was just one more victory.

"Yes, the first ever to stand against the armies of Napoleon. This news will spread all across Europe and the world. It is a great blow to the Emperor."

"So much depended on the outcome of Salamanca, didn't it?" Craven was reflecting on the previous months, "All of that posturing back and forth, it was not in vain, for we could not afford a victory like that of Talavera, could we?"

"No, a decisive blow had to be achieved or it was over. Le Marchant knew it, too, and so did so many others."

"He was just one of the few who believed it possible," sighed Craven.

"And he achieved it, and he will be remembered for that forever."

"Is that what we want for ourselves? To be remembered for dying achieving our goals?"

"That is for each man to decide for himself, but the time and manner of our end is rarely our decision to make."

"And if a man doesn't wish to die at all?"

"Perhaps he should not lead charges against the enemy," smiled Matthys.

But Craven looked about the room the comrades who had become his closest friends and family.

"I could not order them to do that which I would not do myself."

"And that is why they love you."

Craven was stunned as Matthys went on to explain further.

"Think back to the number of occasions where you have shirked your responsibility? Avoided the worst of jobs and left it to others, you remember?"

"Yes, a long time ago."

"Precisely, that is the man you used to be. They would not follow that man, but this one, they would do anything for. Even Timmerman has come around." Matthys pointed to Craven's old adversary casually sitting in the same room and making friendly conversation with Nooth and Quicks.

"Will we winter here, do you think?" Craven asked. He was quite enjoying the comforts of the city and the most amazing welcome the populace had given them.

"It is too early to say, for there are months left in the campaigning season and so much can happen in that time."

"And yet we have not moved. We have been here for several days with no sign of moving on," replied Craven hopefully. He would gladly remain in the city to enjoy all it offered until the next year of campaigning. But Matthys was already shaking his head.

"I do not think we wait here to replenish our strength, although it is needed."

"No?"

"No. Wellington has extended his reach a long way from our safe havens in Rodrigo and Badajoz. I think he waits to see what the enemy does. We are strong enough to march out and oppose one of the French armies, but not both."

"And if we wait for them to come to us, they will combine into a force too large for us to overcome?"

"Yes, just like at Salamanca, it is a fine balancing act, and the timing must be just perfect for the moment that we strike."

"You do not think the French armies will withdraw from Spain now? Accept their defeat?" Craven pondered. He had clearly thought the capture of the Spanish capital might end the war in the country and take it to French soil.

"A French army before Napoleon might have done just that, but those who follow the Emperor are far more stubborn and steady. They will not accept defeat here in Spain, not yet, and why should they, for they still have far greater armies than us."

"Larger perhaps, but not greater," smiled Craven.

Ferreira suddenly crashed into them and partly fell into their table, as he giggled with Quental and Gamboa. Craven looked angry as he pushed the Portuguese Captain away, but Ferreira looked almost disappointed.

"My dear James, we are in Madrid! Madrid! We have succeeded in doing what nobody believed we could, and you sit here in solitude. Get out and see the city and all of the beautiful people who are only too eager to show their gratitude."

Craven was stunned at the revelation, and who he had to hear it from.

"Right!" He slammed his fist down on the table and shot to his feet, "This is our party and we earned it. Now let us live it!"

Cheers rang out as the room emptied, and they hit the streets of the city to enjoy themselves. They filled the street with their laughter and general noise. It only served to add to the chaos of the illuminated city which was still as alive as it was on the first day they had arrived. Although the drunken rowdiness was getting worse as they could hear arguments echo out and glass be smashed upon the ground. There was utter chaos, and Craven spotted Major Spring observing and judging it with several other officers, and so he went to him as the party went on.

"Will you join us?"

"I am afraid I must set an example for the army, not that it will be noticed."

"If it will not be noticed, then it serves no purpose. Come, drink with us!"

The Major looked a little uncomfortable and conflicted.

"Major, if you cannot celebrate at a time like this, when can you?"

Spring groaned, but Craven knew he had him as he came forward.

"I'll see you gentlemen in the morning," he said to his companions as he left them to join Craven.

"Don't make me regret this," he insisted.

"No promises, but you would regret not making the most

of your time here. The people want to lavish you with praise, and you have earned it. Enjoy it."

Spring shrugged as he no doubt agreed. It had been a long and arduous campaign, and it felt good to relax and forget about all the work that was ahead.

"The enemy have abandoned Cadiz, did you hear?"

But Spring smirked at the prospect he might not have.

"Oh, yes, of course you did," smiled Craven.

"It is damned fine news no doubt," agreed Spring.

"And so where is next? Where will Wellington lead us?"

"Even if I knew I could not tell you."

"Of course, then let us not worry about the future and celebrate the present!"

They went on from bar to bar, drinking and making merry as the sun went down, but Paget remained anxious and unsettled as he stepped outside from one bar to get some air. He could not help but think of the mysterious stranger who had appeared before him and disappeared seemingly as quickly. It was as if he had merely vanished as if he was some kind of premonition, and yet he looked and seemed as real as day. Paget could not help but wonder if he was going a little mad. Perhaps he had been on campaign too long, or maybe he had taken too many hits to his head? It had been a tough and gruelling few years, and they were taking their toll, for he was not the fresh faced and eager young man he once was. Was he falling into the horrid state Craven once had? It was deeply concerning.

He looked out to the soldiers passing by and was drawn to one officer who he recognised. He thought it was Ellis, and yet he hesitated to say a word, wondering if it was another vision. Ellis had not worn the uniform of an officer since the hospital at Elvas where he had impersonated one to get the best quarters. Paget rubbed his eyes, shook his head, and looked again. He knew he must be mistaken, and yet the officer had already passed, and now he could see the back of his head.

"It can't have been," he whispered to himself.

It was yet more reason to worry. He could hear the cheers and good times going on inside and decided to shrug off his woes as best he could and go back in to join them.

A week went by of continuous celebrations in the city of Madrid when one morning Craven awoke on a bench in the bar of the brothel that was their quarters. He had not managed to get to his bed, for he had passed out not even from liquor but from exhaustion, and so he had slept well. But he awoke to the curt voice of Matthys.

"What is the meaning of this?" demanded the Sergeant with an authoritarian tone.

Craven got up to see Matthys confronting Ellis who was trying to quietly sneak back inside without being noticed, and what's more he was wearing the uniform of an officer.

"What the devil do you think you are doing?" Bunce entered the room and looked upon the common soldier in the uniform of an officer with disgust and contempt.

"I was an officer once."

"Do not lie to me," snapped Bunce.

"That much is true," replied Craven.

Bunce was stunned as he could not imagine an officer relinquishing his position to join the ranks.

"What is going on here?" Matthys asked.

Ellis said nothing.

"By God you will answer," demanded Bunce angrily.

"He is right, you must explain yourself," added Craven.

Still he remained tight-lipped.

"This is about a woman, isn't it?" asked Matthys.

Ellis said nothing, but the glow in his eyes and slight smirk confirmed it.

"What have you done?" Craven shouted at him.

Ellis sighed as he did not want to reveal anything more.

"Out with it now, for you would be flogged or worse for this," Matthys said.

"And so you should be," agreed Bunce.

"You have a chance to explain yourself here and now, but if you will not, then you will be punished accordingly," roared Craven.

"I meant no harm. I do not wear this to assume any power nor authority," protested Ellis.

"We do not want to hear excuses. Tell us what this is about, now," growled Matthys.

"It began when you took us to church. You remember those beautiful young women we all gazed upon," sobbed Ellis.

"I took you to a house of God, and all you could think about was women?"

But Craven was far more sympathetic, as he did not hold the church in such high regard as his old friend.

"What happened?"

"I got talking to one of those ladies, Julianna," he smiled.

"Oh, God," jeered Bunce.

"We are in love, but I could not continue to see her at service, not as a common soldier."

"This must stop, now," growled Craven.

"I cannot."

"You are a disgrace and should be whipped for this," snarled Bunce.

"Enough!" Craven was sick of Bunce's interruptions.

"Sir, he must pay for his crimes."

"Let me remind you who commands the Salford Rifles, Captain. The punishment for a soldier's crimes is at my discretion."

"Yes, Sir."

Ellis looked down at the floor in shame, but he would not apologise. Paget barged into the room looking weary, but he stopped in amazement as he gazed upon Ellis in the officer's uniform.

"What...can you see him, too?"

"Yes, it seems Ellis here has been sneaking out in the dress of an officer," replied Craven.

"Has he?" smiled Paget as he chirped up at the scandal and also the realisation that he was not going mad. It confirmed that he had seen what he thought he had. It was one of two mysteries solved, "Well, what on Earth is this all about?"

Craven did not scold him as he had Bunce, and that irked the Captain, but he said nothing. Craven was happy for Paget to go on with his questions as Ellis already looked more willing to open up, for Paget was far more forgiving and kinder than the rest of them.

"There is a lady who I have been corresponding and meeting, Julianna."

"How wonderful," declared Paget. But he looked to the others to see the scowls upon their faces, and he could not understand why. "It is not wonderful?"

"He has impersonated an officer to carry out his affair,"

replied Bunce.

"A serious crime indeed, though one of passion, for there was no attempt of a crime against the army here was there?" Paget replied defensively.

"Is this uniform not a crime enough?"

Paget shrugged. A few years earlier he might have agreed, but now he had come to realise that life was not so simple. He used to think rules were absolute, but now he knew they were more frameworks in which to work. Guides which could be moulded and twisted to one's needs to long as one did not overstep. Craven had taught him that.

"You cannot keep doing this." Craven was happy to let Ellis off so long as he desisted.

"I cannot, for we are in love, and I wish to marry her."

"Congratulations," replied Paget.

"There is just a small problem."

"That you are not an officer?" replied Bunce.

"No, that her father is a general, a Portuguese general."

Bunce burst into laughter at the absurdity of the situation whilst the others were stunned into silence. Craven had dealt with all kinds of ridiculous situations as the leader of a bunch of rogues, but he never would have expected it from Ellis, who had always been the quiet one.

"A general's daughter? Are you insane?" Matthys asked.

"You really are full of surprises these days, Ellis, but I am not sure you realise the severity of the situation you now find yourself in," added Craven.

"Please, Sir. I love her, and she loves me. I have a plan for her to elope so that we might be married."

"No, I cannot allow it. You would have us steal the

daughter away from an ally and all the while impersonating an officer in Wellington's army? I am sorry, but this has to stop."

"But, Sir?" Ellis begged.

"But nothing. I am sorry but I cannot allow this to go on. You will surrender that uniform and return to your own. And you will make no further contact with this woman, do you understand?"

"That is all the punishment he will receive?" Bunce demanded.

"It is plenty punishment enough," added Craven as he looked at the distraught expression on Ellis' face as he stripped off his officer's tunic.

"I do not want to hear nor see any more of this, is that clear?"

"Yes, Sir," replied Ellis.

"Matthys, you are to keep a keen eye on him, for I will not be so kind in the case of any more offences."

"Major Craven, Sir?"

It was the same young officer who had been sent to summon him last time. Lieutenant Sayer.

"Yes?" Craven groaned.

"Lord Wellington requests your presence, Sir."

"Of course, he does." Craven groaned again as he buttoned up his tunic and picked up his sword belt. He stopped for a few final words as there was still a great deal of tension in the room.

"This is the end of the matter, for all of us. There will be no more offences nor punishments, do I make myself clear?"

"Yes, Sir," the response came from them all.

Craven followed the messenger out and sighed in

frustration as he got outside. It was a difficult situation to have to deal with, especially considering the stubborn parties involved. He had called for an end to the matter, and yet somehow, he had a feeling in his gut that it was wishful thinking.

"Ellis, you dog," he smirked.

CHAPTER 8

Wellington was living quite the comfortable life much like the rest of them. His table was full of food and drink, and yet he looked as buried in his work as ever, for he did not pause to celebrate with the rest of the army.

"Major Craven," he sighed.

"Yes, Sir?" he replied as if expecting to be in trouble.

"Major, the victory we won here is one which has had massive implications across the world, both politically and militarily. Of course, the victory was at Salamanca, but it won us Madrid."

"Yes, Sir."

"Now I quite understand that there is much to celebrate, but when will it end?"

"The men are in good spirits, Sir."

"Too good, for the British soldier can be the most disciplined warrior upon the battlefield, but he can also be the scum of the Earth when he is not held back by the restraints of his officers."

"Yes, Sir," smirked Craven.

"And yet it has come to my attention that many officers in this army are truly no better. The men run amok, drinking heavily, fighting, gambling, and getting up to all manner of mischief. This city has treated them too kindly, for I fear Madrid might be the death of this army."

"There has been a lot to celebrate."

"Yes, but there is also a war to go on fighting."

"And yet we remain here stagnant."

Wellington groaned with frustration. He clearly felt the same way as he looked to the map propped up behind him and pointed towards it with a cane.

"The enemy were beaten at Salamanca, but they were not finished. Reports suggest Clauzel has reformed and rebuilt the army which we defeated at a remarkable speed in the North. Joseph and Soult to the East and South remain strong, too. In fact, some say Clauzel and his second Foy are now running amok, attacking all of the positions which we had secured."

"And you will let them do so, Sir?"

"No, I bloody well will not!" Wellington angrily slammed his fist down on his desk.

"Very well, Sir, when will we depart?"

"That is the dilemma His Grace explains," added Spring from the sidelines, "The enemy press and present danger in three directions, and so we may not abandon Madrid, for it must be held."

"Indeed, I will set out after Clauzel, but not you, Craven. We must hold Madrid."

"I am not a layabout to stay in the rear," protested Craven.

"Major, enjoy your time here, for you will be in battle soon enough."

"Yes, Sir," replied Craven as he remembered how good they had it now.

"But perhaps do not enjoy yourself too much," added Spring.

"Yes, it seems as though it is not just the men who have excited themselves a little too much here in Madrid. Curfews and patrols will be enacted, and any soldier of the King found in a drunken order will be punished accordingly," Wellington ordered.

"Yes, Sir. Will that be all?"

"We will have work for you soon enough, Craven, and so be ready for it. We must do everything in our power to stop the French armies attacking Madrid as one. Hill marches North to take up the defence here, and all but a few men in Cadiz and elsewhere now march to this city and the whole of Castile."

"You have seen us this far, Sir, and I know the army has faith in you. We all do."

Wellington was touched, for it was a beautiful gesture from a man who was far better with his sword than his tongue. Wellington sat back and suddenly opened up with a frank and honest concern.

"Though I still hope to be able to maintain our position in Castile, and even to improve our advantages. I shudder when I reflect upon the enormity of the task I have undertaken, with inadequate powers myself to do anything, and without assistance of any kind from the Spaniards."

"They will not fight, Sir?"

"I have spent near two weeks here trying to convince our Spanish allies to get their affairs in order and raise up a great army to fight beside us, but they resist me at every turn."

"But why, Sir? Will they not fight for their country?"

"I had hoped so. I had hoped all of Spain might rise up if Madrid were to be freed, and that is what we were promised here and by those at home, but there is a dreadful exhaustion here in the central provinces. The famine of the past year and the toll the enemy have taken on the land. The absurd ineffectiveness and inefficiencies of most Spanish officials hinder things at every turn. Just as we have seen time and time again, the people of Spain want to fight, and they frequently do so passionately, but those whose job it is to lead and organise them fall short in near every instance, and so much now falls to us and the Portuguese. I am apprehensive that all this may turn out ill for the Spanish cause. If by any cause I should be overwhelmed, or should be obliged to retire, what will the world say? What will the people of England say? What will those in Spain say?"

Craven was astonished by the glimpse into Wellington's mind he was experiencing, and yet it was heart-warming to know he shared the fears of any other man.

"As a swordsman I do not concern myself with what people think of me, only that I win my battles. For that silences even your worst critics."

"If only war was as simple as a duel, for if we must withdraw there will be no progress made here in Spain until spring."

"That did not stop you this winter, Sir. For I remember marching through the snowstorms."

Wellington welcomed the sentiment.

"Sir, whatever lows we face in the coming months, nobody can take these successes away from us, not without defeating this army in battle."

"I pray that the people of England and Spain see it the same way."

"Good luck in your pursuit of Clauzel, Sir, and know that the Salford Rifles are always ready should we be needed."

"I have no doubt that you will be."

Craven saluted and left, but his enthusiastic demeanour soon fell away once he was out of sight of their leader, revealing it was all an act. He had heard Wellington speak with such bleak honesty only a few times, and he knew how severe a situation must be to see such a thing.

"Are we to march, Sir?" Paget saw Craven approach, and yet he could see the low spirits he was in.

"We do not, though others do."

"Then we lie here idle as the war goes on without us?"

"Wellington has a plan, and we must trust in it."

"I should hope so, Sir, for I feel as though we need a plan ourselves."

"What?"

"It is Ellis, Sir. He is positively mutinous."

Craven growled angrily.

"There is something else you should know, Sir."

"Yes? What is it?"

"You have a visitor," replied Paget mysteriously.

Craven stormed back into the brothel that was their billets and found a most familiar and welcome face waiting for him. It was Amalia. She jumped to her feet and rushed into his arms. It had felt as though they had been apart for many years, and yet they had indeed seen little of each other in the past year. He wondered if she had moved on, for many soldiers' affairs were merely fleeting by the nature of how they were forever on the move. Yet she kissed him passionately to confirm nothing had changed between them. Many of the Salfords cheered at the sight, and even the prostitutes joined in by clapping at the reunion.

"It is wonderful to see you," she beamed.

"And to you, too, but I am sorry you must excuse me. For there is a matter I must attend to."

"Yes, I am aware, and I should ask for a few moments to speak with you first."

She led him to a table and sat down. They were brought wine which was given so freely in Madrid since they arrived.

Charlie pulled Paget aside as the rest of them gave Craven and Amalia some space, but it felt like he was being led into a trap.

"What is this?"

"I came here to see you as I was passing through, but then I heard about Ellis."

Craven sighed as he knew he now had a fight on his hands.

"Ellis is a fool."

"They are in love, he and his Julianna."

"What of it?"

"The Craven I knew would fight for his friend to be with his love."

"Would he?" Craven fell silent and thought it over, but Amalia was not done applying pressure.

"You have become quite the leader, but do not forget your bonds to those who are closest to you. The army might not approve of this pairing, but when have the rules ever been an obstacle to you?"

Craven shrugged as he had always done things his own way and they both knew it. He looked over to Ellis at the loss and heartache on his face, and then around the room to see he was being judged by all but Bunce, who nodded as if to confirm he should stand firm in his position. It had the very opposite effect. He would never side with the stubborn officer over his closest friends, and so he began to wonder if he was on the right side of things.

"What would you have me do?"

"Let him do what you would do. Follow his heart and his gut."

Craven smiled. She had twisted him about her little finger by using all of his own beliefs against him. She saw her opportunity as if looking upon a wounded opponent and made her final strike.

"Listen to what Ellis has to say, please, because I know he would do the same for you."

"He already has, more times than I can count," he admitted as he finally gave in.

"You cannot be considering this? You cannot let this madness go on?"

"Shut up, Buncy!" Paget scolded.

Bunce did so, for despite being Paget's senior, he remembered what Craven had told him. He was not in a position of authority in the Salford Rifles as his rank would suggest, and an angry expression from Craven only confirmed it. Amalia got up from her seat and ushered Ellis into her place where he sat down opposite Craven.

"Tell me you have a plan?"

"I do. I have bribed two of the manservants at Julianna's household. Tomorrow night I will go to her, and with the aid of a ladder I will carry her from her room. The two men who have been paid will have a horse loaded with her things out the back of the house. These men will keep a good look out so that we might elope into the night without any trouble."

"What do you think?" Amalia asked.

Craven thought on it for a few moments, but he could not contain the cheeky smirk on his face. The idea was so absurd that he loved it.

"You were going to do this with or without me, weren't you?"

"I have to, I love her."

Craven shook his head in astonishment. Ellis had always been the quiet and mysterious one, and the very last person he would expect to fall in love in the most difficult and dangerous of situations.

"Then let us see this done together."

The room erupted into celebration, all except Bunce.

"How can we go along with this?" he whispered to Paget.

"Because we fight for one another, and you will not tell a soul, not unless you want to bring down the wrath of the Major upon you."

"Tell me more. How are we going to achieve all of this?" Craven asked Ellis.

But Matthys stepped in before he could reply.

"You will not be anywhere near this, for you are too recognisable a face."

"Secrecy is key. The General must have no idea where his

daughter has gone," added Amalia.

Craven sighed as he could see the others agreed.

"Have you not considered asking the General for his daughter's hand?" Bunce asked.

"He would not give it, not in a hundred years."

"Is it not his right?"

"You do not believe his daughter should be able to choose who she marries?" Amalia asked.

"Yes, with the consent of her father," he snapped.

Craven laughed. The Captain once again reminded him of Paget when they had first met.

"This is funny to you, Sir?"

Craven had heard enough as he got to his feet and loomed over the upstart.

"Leave us, and speak not a word of this to anyone, or I will have your tongue. Do you understand me?"

Bunce looked sheepish and soon backed down as he left the room.

"You must forgive him, Sir, for he still believes that all things are as he has been told they should be, and that is not always a bad thing," declared Paget in his defence.

"And if he does tell others about this?" Amalia asked.

"We must give him a chance to be trusted," pleaded Paget.

Craven nodded in agreement.

"You all fought this hard for me to do this, but you would not have me there?"

"You cannot be, but you can assist us in all of this," said Matthys.

"Then I will go," declared Paget.

"You are almost as familiar a face as Craven."

Paget groaned, realising he was being sidelined the same as Craven was. He hated the feeling. Not only did he want to help, but he hated being left behind. Craven went over to the bar and reached behind to pull out a folded tunic and handed it to Ellis.

"You will be needing this."

Ellis unfolded it to find it was the officer's tunic he had worn as a disguise to let him pass among the wealthy gentry and officers who roamed the city.

"I will need two to help me, but no more, for it will attract too much attention," declared Ellis as he took charge as the officer he once was.

"I will go," declared Charlie boldly, as she could not think of anything more noble than fighting for love. For she had finally realised that was what she fought for now, having cast off the poison that was her insatiable lust for revenge.

"I will go, too," declared Vicenta, who had come to enjoy Charlie's company.

It was a good team. They were both capable fighters, and Vicenta's language skills could be most useful.

"Not dressed like that," replied Craven.

For Vicenta's clothing drew a lot of attention. She dressed like a guerrilla and also made no attempt to hide the fact that she was a woman.

"What would you have me do? Dress as a lady?"

"Yes, and on Charlie's arm."

"A lady on a common soldier's arm?" Matthys asked.

"And at night during the curfews, no, you will need to be an officer for a night," declared Craven.

"Here, have this." Paget took of his tunic and helped

Charlie into it. It was a remarkably good fit as they were of a similar build.

"Now we must find you a dress." Craven looked to Amalia for help.

"I have no need of such finery in these days but look where you are. Ask her." She gestured towards the Madam who had shown much interest in Craven.

"What do you say? Will you help us?" Craven asked.

"Yes, but what do you offer in return?"

"Not him." Amalia looked to Craven defensively.

The Madam peered about the room until she locked eyes on Ferreira and looked him up and down like a slab of meat as she licked her lips.

"He will do."

Ferreira looked a little put out but then shrugged as if he was not opposed to the idea, which caused Quental and Gamboa to chuckle.

"I will go with them," added Amalia.

"What? Why?" Craven protested.

She looked to Vicenta who sat casually straddling a chair and her head slumped.

"Because I can pass as a lady."

Vicenta shrugged and agreed. She might be able to look the part from afar, but she was a rough and tough soldier at heart. Craven did not look content. He did not much like having to sit this one out, and yet it was clear that Amalia would not back down and so he accepted it.

"Do you think this can be done?" Craven asked Ellis directly and sternly, for so much was now being risked in the endeavour.

"Yes, I believe it can."

"Then see it done."

"And if they are caught?" Paget asked.

"Then the Major will do everything he can to speak on your behalf, but he cannot admit to having known about this plot." Matthys looked to Craven to ensure they were on the same page. Craven didn't much like being on the outside of things, but accepted Matthys was looking out for them all and allowing him to go as far as he possibly could.

"Don't get caught," he insisted as he couldn't imagine it would end well.

"No drinking tonight. Get a good night's rest and be as firm and fresh as you can be," Matthys said.

"Is she really worth it?" Craven asked.

"Worth dying for," Ellis replied earnestly and without hesitation.

"Then you will need that tunic to be more than just a costume."

"What are you saying?"

"You will need an officer's pay if you are to keep a woman like that. What do you say, Lieutenant?"

Ellis could not believe the offer, and had it come at any other time he would have refused without hesitation, but he thought of Julianna and the future they might have together. Yet he still struggled to accept.

"You were an officer once, and you might have hidden that part of your life away for all this time, but it is still a part of you. I am not asking you to be any common officer, I am asking you to be an officer in the Salford Rifles, what do you say?"

Craven offered his hand out with which they could shake

on it. But Ellis still looked uncomfortable. He looked to his closest friend for an opinion, the Welshman he had spent so much time beside. He feared it would be a betrayal to elevate himself above the man he had fought beside for years as an equal.

"What do you think?"

"When a beautiful woman falls into your lap, do not hesitate."

"I meant the promotion."

"We all must do what we must. You just struck out with all the luck, you lucky devil," he smiled.

It was all Ellis needed to hear as he took Craven's hand.

"Mr Ellis," smiled Craven.

Cheers erupted as they celebrated the promotion of one of their own, for the only man who would not celebrate the promotion had left, the angry Captain Bunce.

"Wine!" Craven ordered.

Matthys gave a scathing glance. He had demanded those conducting the mission tomorrow be sober this evening, and yet even he could not ruin the moment by enforcing those conditions. The women brought wine and also their company, and yet Amalia did not at all seem bothered by what she was seeing. For as a surgeon she had seen enough that nothing really shocked her anymore.

The wine flowed and the conversation and laughter went on for many hours, as Craven and Amalia caught up whilst the party went on all around them. She seemed to have as many exciting stories as he did as she continued to support the militia and guerrilla forces and anyone else who needed medical attention. Finally, a lull came when they sat back and realised how much had gone on since last they had seen one another.

"It's really happening, isn't it? Spain is finally being liberated?"

"I hope so, but the work is not yet complete," admitted Craven.

"Does Wellington not march to destroy the remaining French armies? The newspapers say he is on an unstoppable path."

Craven looked awkward and said nothing. That spoke volumes.

"Oh," she replied with concern.

"I cannot tell you too much, but this war in Spain is far from over."

She looked disappointed, and he understood why. The fighting had gone on for several years, and the success throughout this year might well suggest it was coming to a close. He wished it was.

"We beat the French here in Spain, but I do not think it will be this year."

"Thank you, for being honest."

"Sorry, I did not want to be so blunt."

"I deal in medicine and surgery. Wishful thinking is useless to me. I want the facts or nothing at all," she retorted.

Craven looked relieved.

"It is great to see you."

"Yes, but I suppose there have been many women in the life of James Craven," she smiled.

"Not of late."

"No?"

"I have had no time for it, but I have thought of you a

great deal."

"James Craven, have you gotten sentimental?"

"What if I have?" He knew there was some truth to it. He was not the same man who had arrived in the Iberian Peninsula. In fact, he was barely recognisable beside his ability with a sword.

"Take me to bed," she insisted with a smile.

"Here?" he asked in astonishment.

"I do not care where. It is not important. Do you always choose where you do battle?"

"If I can, yes."

"And if battle is upon you and you can only fight or retreat?"

"Then I will stand and give it my all," he jested as he got up and took her hand to lead her away.

CRAVEN'S WAR – RUNNING THE GAUNTLET

CHAPTER 9

"Are you ready?" Ellis called out.

They heard a grown. Vicenta was not happy at all as she muttered under her breath in the next room, but soon enough she stepped out to join them. Birback's jaw dropped as he gazed at her in amazement, as if only just realising she was a woman. The sight of a woman dressed for battle might be a most peculiar sight to most British soldiers, but not to any in the Salford Rifles, but none of them could have imagined she could look so graceful. Paget smiled and was equally enthralled, which only made Charlie smile. For she far preferred Paget's tunic that she felt most at home in, especially as it smelled of him.

"Here, you will need these."

Paget handed Charlie his sword and hat. She took them graciously but with bewilderment, for Paget would never give away his sword so easily.

"I will protect it with my life."

"And it will protect yours should the need arise," he promised.

"There should be no need of any fighting." Craven looked to Amalia with concern.

"But if there is, we shall be ready." Vicenta hoisted up her dress to reveal a dagger tied to each of her thighs. Birback groaned with delight at the sight.

"Never forget that her beauty is suppressed by her ferocity," Matthys whispered to him as he tried to avoid any strife.

"I know," smirked Birback as if he was gazing upon his perfect woman.

Matthys smiled to himself, knowing Vicenta would beat him black and blue. Now they only waited on Ellis who came down the stairs to join them. He was dressed as an officer should be and held himself a little taller and prouder for it. Though his rifle was slung on his shoulder out of habit.

"You won't be needing that." Craven held out his hand to take it from him.

"But what if I do?"

"No officer would walk about town with a rifle on his shoulder. You will only draw attention to yourself. Attention is the last thing you want, for this must be a quick and quiet thing."

"It will be. Everything is in order. We will merely go for a walk and spirit my love away."

It was bizarre for most of them to hear him talk this way. The quiet and reclusive man they once knew seemed to fall away, revealing the romantic officer now standing before them.

"Are you ready?"

Ellis took a deep breath as he knew he was risking everything if he went through with it.

"I am," he replied confidently.

"Then I wish you luck, Lieutenant."

"Thank you, Sir."

They watched the party of four step out into the evening light as they began their mission.

"What will happen, Sir, if they are caught?" Paget asked Craven.

"Honestly, I am not sure."

"It would be a grave offence against the General, our ally," explained Matthys.

"But what punishment might Ellis suffer?" Paget pressed.

Both men shrugged as it was a strange situation which they had never encountered.

"Pray they escape with his lady and his identity a secret," added Craven.

"And if he does not?"

"Then we cannot claim to have known anything about this plot," insisted Matthys.

"Sir?" Paget couldn't imagine they would not support their comrade.

"If Wellington discovered Craven had any involvement in this, he could lose his command."

It finally dawned on Paget how serious the implications might be.

"And yet you still helped him?"

"It's the right thing to do."

Matthys nodded along in agreement and that confirmed it to Paget.

"How can the right thing be against all the rules?" he pondered.

But nobody had any answers for him as he put on another coat. The one he had loaned Charlie was not his only one, like it was for most of them, and he had another hat, too.

"You would go with them, wouldn't you?"

"I would, Sir."

Craven picked up his sword belt from the chair where it hung and thrust it into Paget's hands.

"Then go."

"Thank you, Sir!"

Paget ran on after them. Ellis strode on at a determined pace like a man on a mission, with Vicenta being forced to keep pace with him just as Paget caught up with them. Nobody questioned it, for the help was most welcome.

"Slow down," insisted Charlie.

"Yes, we are merely out for an evening stroll, not marching on Moscow," joked Paget.

Ellis slowed down but he was positively boiling over with excitement. None of them had ever seen him so animated. He seemed to spring to life at the very thought of Julianna. Up ahead was a party not unlike their own with two British officers with women clinging onto their arms.

"Let me do the talking," whispered Paget.

"I was an officer long before you ever put on the uniform," reminded Ellis.

Paget kept forgetting that fact, and it was still hard to imagine. He noticed Ellis tip his hat and exchange pleasantries with the passing officers as if he were quite comfortable in the position.

"You really are a gentleman," smiled Vicenta.

But her words grated on Paget.

"You will not pass as a lady," he declared.

Amalia squeezed him violently to tell him off.

"I meant no offence," he added.

"But he is right. Speak only in Spanish and nobody will be the wiser," added Amalia, who was well versed in the language, also being a native of Spain.

That suited Vicenta just fine, as she didn't much care for conversing with English gentlemen. They only saw her as some sort of savage or a novelty because of the trousers and weapons she customarily wore. They continued on as they saw an officer decrying several men for being out at night whilst provosts saw to another rowdy group of drunken soldiers. But nobody said a word to Ellis' rescue party besides simple pleasantries. For as far as anyone knew, they were sober gentlemen with their upstanding ladies.

"How has Craven been?" Amalia asked Paget as they finally had a quiet moment in which she could enquire after him.

"Very well I should say."

"You would never say any different, would you?" She smiled at him.

"To most people that is true, for it is my duty to protect the Major's name and reputation as well as his body, but I speak the truth to you."

She could tell he really meant it.

"And you? It is so good to have you back with us."

She looked a little awkward.

"I am sorry, did I misspeak?"

"I did not want to give the impression that I was returning, for my visit is merely fleeting."

"What a shame, and I am sure Craven will be saddened to hear it."

"I am sure he will be just fine."

"He will survive, but he will be less happy for your departure. He speaks of you often."

She seemed pleasantly surprised by the notion.

"How do you ever move in these things?" Vicenta awkwardly walked on, hating every moment of the restrictive nature of her new attire.

"I manage just fine," replied Amalia.

"But you do not fight."

"I've seen her barrel a Frenchman over," replied Paget in her defence.

Vicenta looked impressed.

"I fight for my country in my way, and I think you do, too, don't you?"

"I do what I can as a nurse. Never has there been such a need for such skills, I am sorry to say."

"This is the place." Ellis looked up to a grandiose old residence that was fit for royalty. Two servants waited at one of the doors with a loaded horse at the side of the grand house. They nodded towards Ellis in recognition.

"Those are the men you paid?" Paget asked.

"Yes," he replied, but his eyes soon wandered to a woman on a balcony on the floor above. Her long black hair and billowing dress fluttered in the light wind as she leaned out gazing upon them, waiting for her rescuer.

"My Juliet," he smiled as he thought of Shakespeare and the famous balcony. He could not help but think of the most famous of romantic scenes.

"Let us hope we are more successful than her," muttered Paget.

But nobody heard him. They were fixated on the beautiful woman and the fairy tale-like scene before them.

"Through here." Paget took them to a side street, "This should be it," he added, spotting the ladder that had been placed in readiness for their daring escapade.

"Wait." Ellis stopped him for a moment.

"What is it?" demanded Paget angrily, as he wanted to see the job done promptly.

"Thank you, all of you. None of you had to be here, and it means the world to me that you are," gushed Ellis as he looked sincerely from one to another.

"You can thank us when we are free and clear."

Paget hauled the ladder up and shoved the other end into Ellis' hands. Charlie and Vicenta peered out from the alleyway to check for any signs of passersby. The scene of two officers fumbling with a ladder at night would surely draw suspicion, as they could be up to no good. They both nodded towards the pair with the ladder to signal that they were ready.

"Just as we planned it," smiled Ellis, realising his dream was about to come true.

They rushed out from the alley and stormed on towards the house as if they were assaulting a great fortress. They expected to be fired upon in any moment as that had always been the experience of a night assault, but this was no fortification. They soon reached the foot of the balcony without any commotion or surprises at all. They raised the ladder slowly and carefully, laying it gently against the wall beside the balcony.

Paget looked back for any signs of trouble as Ellis shot up it, and he held the base firm. He watched Ellis reach out for Julianna's hand in the most touching gesture before signalling to Vicenta and Charlie to go and collect the horse from the servants. It was heavily loaded with bags and cases and all the possessions and clothing Ellis' wife-to-be could cart away with her. Paget watched Ellis guide Julianna down the ladder as Charlie handed over a bag of coins to the servants, the rest of their payment. She led the horse away. He could hardly believe their luck.

"It's working," he muttered to himself with a smile.

For the plan was working precisely as intended. Julianna reached the ground and leapt into her lover's arms. They embraced and kissed, but out of the corner of his eye Paget noticed a glimmer of fast movement. He looked to the doors where the servants had kept watch just in time to see them vanish inside with some urgency. Panicked cries echoed out just moments later as the two awful characters raised the alarm to all inside.

"We have to go, now!"

The time for secrecy was over, and urgency was needed. Ellis took Julianna's hand. They rushed on after Charlie and Vicenta, only to find that they could manage little more than a fast walk for the horse was so heavily laden.

"We have to go faster!" Paget cried desperately.

"We can't!" Charlie was trying to hurry the animal on. They turned into a fairly narrow street only five yards wide as Paget kept looking back in the hope that no one was giving chase, but soon enough a mob of eight Portuguese men stormed into view. They were gaining on the party for they were not heavily encumbered, carrying only sticks and large knives. Though Paget knew an angry mob was quite capable of doing awful things with such simple tools.

"They are upon us!"

Charlie brought the horse to a halt as there was no choice but to stand and fight. She ripped Paget's sword from her side. Paget did likewise, taking Craven's sword in hand, the beloved Andrea Ferrara blade he had carried when they first became acquainted. He could feel a sense of power flowing through the sword into his hand as if it made him invincible. The two of them went forward as Ellis drew his sword and backed away with his precious Julianna held close to his side. Vicenta took out the two daggers from under her dress and took up position in front of the couple and behind Paget and Charlie.

"Do not kill them. These are not enemy soldiers. We must not add murder onto the list of our crimes," insisted Paget.

But the mob was an intimidating sight, and it would be hard to break them without doing serious harm. Their pursuers stopped for a moment, surprised to find such resistance. Some of them were servants of the household whilst others appeared to be rather wealthier. Family members, perhaps.

"Give her back to us," declared one of the men, knowing they were speaking to Englishmen.

"No!" Ellis roared.

"Julianna, you must return home!"

"I will not!"

"Very well, then we shall take you!"

The man rushed forward and lashed out at Paget with his stout and heavy long stick. Paget parried it away, but the blow forced him back, and the mob surged in through the opening as the peaceful street descended into a chaotic brawl. Paget braced his sword with his left hand as he was shoved backward by an aggressive barge. He could only watch as another of the men lunged at Charlie with a large knife. She beat it aside and rotated into a cut against the man's head, which was far forward where he had overreached. She had riposted out of instinct but pulled the blow just in time, stopping short of what would be a fatal blow to the head, and merely slicing the man's forehead. Blood poured down his face, and it was enough to make him pause for a moment, but the shock soon subsided. Rage took its place as he rushed forward with another by his side. Charlie punched one in the face with her ward iron and sent him staggering back, but the other rushed in against her, the man she had cut open. He tried to thrust in at her stomach, but she grabbed hold of the knife hand and managed to hold it in place. Although she had to give ground as more of them broke through. Vicenta looked ready to kill as she was the next line of defence.

"Do not kill them!" Paget cried.

He tussled with one of them and felt a stick crash into his head, sending his hat flying away. He stumbled back and was forced to turn his attention to his own safety. Vicenta did as she was asked, but she did not look happy about it. She slammed the pommel of one dagger into a man's stomach and the other into another's jaw, but she was struck across the face with a large stick and staggered back. The path to Ellis and Julianna was now clear as three of the men surged through. One grabbed the horse and the others kept wailing on the other three of Ellis' companions who were severely hindered by not being able to inflict any serious blows. Amalia took up a broom resting against a wall nearby and swung wildly as she tried to keep their attacks away.

"Let her go!" growled one of the men who closed on Ellis.

"She wants to be with me. You cannot have her!"

"It is not her choice to make!"

The man rushed in against Ellis, but the newly appointed Lieutenant lashed out in defence and caught the man's hand, cutting off two fingers with his razor-sharp sabre. The agonising cry in horror of his victim brought them all to a halt as they realised how serious the situation had gotten. None of the Portuguese men wanted to fight with soldiers if they were willing to inflict serious harm with their long blades. The two sides separated as the Portuguese made away with the horse and all of Julianna's possessions, but she remained firmly at Ellis' side.

"Back away." Paget held his sword out in a threatening fashion as the two sides parted, "Keep going, go on," he insisted as much to the enemy as to his comrades. Soon enough both sides had backed away far enough that they vanished into the night.

"Come on. Let us be on our way with haste." Paget sheathed his sword and led them on. "Put that away," he said to Ellis as a naked blade would attract a great deal of attention to them.

They ran on at much speed and were soon coursing down one of the main streets, passing many other officers who must have assumed they were merely rushing on to their beds, and so they said nothing. As they approached the brothel, they could see Craven and Matthys waiting outside for them. They clapped at their triumph as they approached and got them inside where cheers rang out as celebratory drinks were thrust into their hands. Craven stepped up onto a table with glass in hand to toast to the happy couple and all eyes turned to him.

"Joseph Ellis, rifleman, officer, common soldier, officer for a second time," he joked, drawing much laughter, "I have known this man for many years, and yet I must admit I am only recently discovering truly who he is and who he was, but I can tell you what I have always known. Ellis is a man you can depend upon in the best and worst of times. Julianna, you have chosen well!"

The crowd roared once again as Craven got down and helped Ellis up to take his place.

"Thank you, thank you all. I am sorry I have not always

been able to share with you all that much, but all of this changes tomorrow. For tomorrow morning we will go to a neighbouring chapel to be married, and I beg you all join us in celebrating the best day of our lives!"

Cheers rang out once again.

"Let's drink!" He leapt down from the table to down a glass and look for another as Craven approached his wife-to-be.

"James Craven, your future husband's commanding officer, Ma'am," he said politely.

"I have heard much about you, Major, but you need not put on an act with me. I am not the lady my father would want me to be, or I would not be running away with an English soldier," she replied honestly.

Craven appeared stunned as he looked to Amalia in amazement.

"You will fit in just fine," added Amalia.

"I am afraid none of my belongings have made it with me, for they were wrestled from us by members of my father's household."

"Craven will see that you get everything you need."

"Yes, I will," replied Craven suspiciously as he wondered what had gone on that they were not telling him. He soon pinpointed Paget, knowing he would be the first to cave and explain it to him.

"Excuse me, ladies," he said as he made his excuses.

He stormed across the busy bar and butted into a conversation between Paget and Charlie.

"It went as planned, then?" he asked as he poked and prodded to try and get a confession.

"Why yes, Sir, the ladder was in place and the lady was as

she was supposed to be."

"And you had no trouble making your escape?"

"No...no...no, Sir," stuttered Paget.

"They came after us," admitted Charlie.

Paget sighed in frustration, but he did not fight it any longer.

"Who?"

"The two servants that were bribed and many more of the household."

"And you saw them off?"

"We did, Sir."

"And they gave you that?" Craven was looking at Paget's swollen forehead where he had been struck by a stick.

"Yes, Sir," he groaned.

"And what did you give them?"

"Paget insisted that we not kill them," replied Charlie defensively.

"What damage did you do?"

Craven knew there was more to the story.

"Mr Ellis, Sir, he cut off two of the fingers of one man," whispered Paget.

Craven's eyes rolled into the back of his head as he threw back a large glass of wine, knowing that was going to come back to haunt them.

"He really had no choice, Sir. A mob of men was beating on us with sticks and knives."

"It's true," added Charlie as Craven looked back at the happy couple dancing among the tables.

"I hope she was worth it. I really do."

Craven reached for a bottle and threw it back without even

pouring.

CHAPTER 10

Craven and the rest of Ellis's closest friends watched as he and his new wife kissed in the chapel. It elicited a roar of celebration seemingly as loud as the crowds upon their arrival in the city. The Priest did not much appreciate the vulgar British soldiers as they roared like they were cheering on a game of sports, but he was powerless to hold them back. He was glad to see them be on their way as they poured out of the tiny chapel to leave him in peace.

They soared on through the streets triumphantly with the happy couple as they marched on back to the brothel where food and drinks had been laid out for them so that the celebrations might continue.

"A lady of much standing, and she celebrates in a place such as this?" Paget wondered as he watched the couple laugh and kiss and make the most of it. Craven was leaning against the wall beside him and smiled at the notion, wondering when Paget would realise the parallels to his own life.

"You should have seen it, the palace from which we took her from," Paget went on.

"Did it remind you of home?" Craven smiled.

Paget finally cottoned on to what he was doing.

"You think our situations are alike? Surely not!"

"She wilfully left a comfortable and wealthy life for this and stayed down here in the muck for love."

"I…" began Paget but he stuttered, realising he did not have a leg to stand on.

"I do not just stay for Charlie, Sir," he replied defensively.

"I know, but it is love, nonetheless."

"I suppose it is," he sighed.

"You have seen all the highs and the many lows this life we share here. Would you give it up if you could go back to all you had?"

"There is not a chance of it, Sir. I did not want to merely exist, I wanted to live."

"I know what you mean."

"You do, Sir?"

"Yes. I was not born into the sort of wealth you were, but nor was I poor."

"No?"

"My father is a merchant. A rather successful one, and I could just as easily have followed in his footsteps in the family business. It would have been a good life, or an easy one I should say. For what makes a good life depends on who you ask, but that was not it for me. I could not imagine being on my death bed and thinking it was all I had ever done."

"Is that why you became a gladiator?"

"That, and so many more things. I wanted to truly live the good and the bad, all of it. I said I came here to Portugal and Spain to make myself a rich man. If I find those riches, then it will be another accomplishment, but if I do not, it does not matter. I think you understand that now, too. You might have come here out of a sense of duty and loyalty to your family and to your country, but I think you realised a long time ago that there are things in this world just as important, perhaps more so."

"Yes, Sir, I believe there are." They both looked to the newlyweds and could see one of those reasons before their eyes, "Of all of us, I never would have picked Ellis to be married first," smiled Paget.

"Indeed, he is full of surprises."

Ellis caught a glimpse of the two of them watching him and his new wife. He tipped his head and held up his glass to thank them once again.

"It feels good, to do a good thing, doesn't it, Sir?"

"It certainly can," he agreed.

The party went on all day and well into the night, but Craven was awoken the next morning by somebody banging violently on his door. His eyes shot open to find Amalia resting against him, but another crashing on the door awoke her also.

"What is it?"

"Nothing good."

He leapt from his bed and hurried to get his clothes on. She threw off the sheet and went to do the same.

"What are you doing?"

"Whatever this is I will face it with you," she declared.

Craven did not try to stop her.

"Major Craven, Sir!" Paget cried out from beyond the door. He sounded flustered.

"Yes?"

"Sir, you must get out here!"

Craven sighed as this only confirmed the severity. He tore the door open before he had even buttoned up his jacket, and Amalia was only just covered as she hurried on after him without a care.

"Sir, Major Spring is calling for you, I think he knows what we did, Sir," wept Paget.

They hurried on downstairs to see Major Spring enjoying a morning coffee and looking most content and relaxed.

"Is there not some emergency?" Craven demanded.

"That is certainly the attitude presented to Lord Wellington by a certain Portuguese General," replied Spring with a wry smile.

"I do not know what you refer to." Craven tried to play innocent.

"Wellington will see you immediately, and you, too," he replied as he turned to Paget.

"Me, Sir?"

"Yes, you."

He downed his coffee and got to his feet. His manner was confused, perhaps intentionally, as he seemed both angry and calm in equal measure, as if he were putting on an act before an almighty outburst. Paget lowered his head as he submitted entirely like a naughty schoolboy who had been caught in the act. Craven fixed his uniform as best he could as they followed on after the Major.

"Do not admit to anything," Craven whispered to the

worried Paget.

"You would have me lie to Wellington?" Paget asked in horror.

"Yes, if you know what is good for you."

Paget looked most uncomfortable as they were led on and soon enough, they were before Wellington. He seemed remarkably calm, although also very tired as he went explained why they had been summoned.

"Gentlemen, I prepare to march and pursue the enemy, and all the while I have been in this city, I have endeavoured to build support with our allies, that is both from the Spanish and the Portuguese. Any small thing can sour relations enough to ruin negotiations and see support whittle away, and so when a Portuguese General comes to me to protest that a British officer has made off with his precious daughter in the middle of the night, you can imagine how this might strain relations somewhat?"

"Yes, Sir, how awful," replied Craven.

"And what do you think the punishment should be for such an offence to one of our allies?" Wellington pressed.

"It is hard to say, Sir," replied Paget.

"But you understand an officer who conducted this action must be punished, yes?"

They both agreed, for there was no way to defend the actions without admitting to their involvement.

"Then explain this to me."

He revealed an officer's cocked hat and threw it down on the desk before him. Paget recognised it instantly. For it was the one which had been knocked from his head as they fought off the Portuguese mob in defence of Ellis and Julianna.

"What of it, Sir?" Craven asked.

"Have a look inside," smiled Wellington.

Craven took it up only to find it was embroidered inside the headband.

"What does it say, Major?"

"LT B Paget, Sir," he groaned, looking to the young man with disbelief, that he would be so foolish.

"Sir…I can…" began Paget.

But Craven put a hand on his shoulder and stopped him.

"Enough." He would not let Paget take the blame for a scheme that they were all in on.

"Let us have the truth of this, every bit of it!"

"Sir, one of our own is in love with the General's daughter, and she him. They were spirited away to be married in the morning of this past day."

"And you did not think to ask the General's permission for his daughter's hand in marriage?"

"No, because he never would have given it, just as I don't ask the French to give up Spain, I take it back from them," replied Craven defensively.

"Except the French are our enemy, and the Portuguese are not!"

Wellington lay back in his chair and sighed.

"I am sorry, Sir, but I only did what I thought was right, and I supported my fellow officers and friends," declared Paget.

"Who is this officer who is so madly in love he would risk it all?"

"Lieutenant Joseph Ellis, Sir," replied Craven.

"Ellis? I do not know him. Is he a good man?"

"A very fine one. For he has served beside me since before

our first acquaintance, Sir. He has been instrumental in our successes."

"Damn it, your minds should all be on more important things than marriage at this time!"

"Would you have your men give up on hope, Sir?"

Craven was as stunned by Paget's confrontational response as Wellington was, but Paget did not give them any time to respond as he went on the offensive.

"This army does not just fight for pay or fear of the lash, they fight for hope. Hope in their future. Mr Ellis found a little of what we are all looking for, and nobody has the right to take that away from him, or they should not, for it would be for shame. I have seen how that couple gaze upon one another, and I say that is worth fighting for."

Wellington was not even angry. He was impressed by the nerve of the man he once knew as merely a feeble child.

"All that being the case, the General wishes to pursue proceedings against your man. I can absolve the two of you of your part in this, but Mr Ellis must be held accountable," replied Wellington with compassion as they had won him over.

"Yes, Sir," replied Craven.

"You will inform Mr Ellis to consider himself a prisoner, and he shall submit to any proceedings which are brought against him."

"Yes, Sir."

"And Ellis' wife, the lady Julianna?" Paget pressed.

"They were married in a proper service?"

"Yes, Sir, and witnessed by many."

"Then they are bound in the eyes of the Lord, and none shall part them unless it be decided by any proceedings which determine it so."

Paget could not have been happier at the result, but Wellington looked both amused and exhausted by their misadventure. He picked up Paget's hat and tossed it into his arms.

"Let us get on with this war, shall we?"

"Yes, Sir!" Paget roared triumphantly.

"Now get out of my sight, and do not bring any more trouble to my table!"

They rushed on out, relieved to have gotten away so lightly.

"What will happen to Ellis, Sir?"

"I do not know, for I have never known a thing like it."

"I am sorry for the hat. This is all because of me," snivelled Paget.

"No, Ellis was always going to get caught, for who could honestly believe we could get away with it?"

"Then why did we do it, Sir?"

"Because it was the right thing to do, and it was the only chance they ever had of being together. No, the blame is not yours. You stepped up to help one of our own, and you even took a stand against Wellington to fight for what you believe in. I only wish I could have been as good a man as you when I was your age."

"You didn't have the friends that we share now," smiled Paget.

They marched on back to their billets in good spirits, for they could not have hoped for a better outcome in the face of them being discovered. They arrived to find everyone awake and waiting impatiently for news, but none more so than the newlywed couple. All were silent.

"Ellis, consider yourself a prisoner," declared Craven.

"And Julianna?" he asked with little concern for his own life.

"As your lawful wife, she may remain with you for now."

Gasps of relief followed before the room erupted into chatter.

"You fought for them?" Amalia approached Craven.

"Paget certainly did."

"Thank you, Sir, but in truth I do not think Lord Wellington truly wanted to punish us," he replied as he left Craven to Amalia.

"What will you do now?" she asked Craven.

"For now, we have some time here in the city, but soon we will march once more, for there is much to do. You could come with us?"

She blushed a little as she seemed to consider it for a few moments.

"You are a great man for seeing this through, a hero to your men and this army, and to me also. But I want to be my own hero. I have helped a lot of people through this war, and I will continue to do so. I can no longer stay with you than you could have stayed with me."

"And when this war is over?"

"What will our lives be then? For each year looks so different to the last. All we can do is make the most of the days we have and fight to make the ones ahead better."

Craven did not try and resist as he could see the determination in her eyes. She might not be a soldier, but she was a fighter in her own right. He could appreciate that, and so he did not fight her, not having the heart to try and stop her.

"Where will you go?"

"To a village to the South, they have been caring for wounded guerrillas and they need my help."

"How far is it?"

"A week's ride maybe."

"And you will go alone?" he gasped.

"With two other women who travel for the same purpose."

"It can be dangerous out there. Let me go with you."

"Do you not have duties here?"

"For now, we do not. Wellington has insisted we take some rest here in the city, and many more troops will be remaining in place also."

"He marches on, then?"

"Yes, in pursuit of the army we defeated at Salamanca."

"Should you not rest as you have been ordered?"

"A week on the road by your side sounds most restful after the year we have had."

"Then I would very much appreciate your company in escorting us."

"Very well, when will we depart?"

"Today, for I have already stayed too long."

"I shall gather up a few of the men and we will be on our way by noon."

"Not Paget. Let him rest, for he deserves it."

"He certainly does. You know he took a stand against Wellington. He really set at him in Ellis' defence."

"That does not surprise me at all."

"No?" Her response took him quite by surprise.

"That young man would fight God himself to protect his own," she explained.

Craven laughed, but he also knew it was true.

"Are you sure about this? Serving as my escort?"

"You did not hesitate to go with Ellis. It is only fair we return the favour, and I should much like to see you safely to your destination."

"It is not the first dangerous journey I have taken in this war."

"No, but it is one I can make all the safer, and so I will."

"Thank you, truly. I will gather my things." She kissed him and then went on her way to gather her things.

Craven turned back to see Paget waiting for him as if he knew something was up.

"You are leaving with her, aren't you, Sir?"

"I will escort Amalia to where she is needed, but I will not be gone for long, perhaps two weeks at the most."

"What about Ellis, Sir? Who will fight for him?"

"You will, and Ferreira, too. Ferreira is one of the General's countrymen, and you are the best man for the job."

"But, Sir, I am merely a junior officer."

"No, you are more of a gentleman than any of us, and you have Wellington's ear. You will be more than capable of seeing to this, more capable than I."

"But what if I cannot?" he fretted.

"Know that you can, and remember, never let an adversary see weakness, not unless you want them to."

"Yes, Sir."

"You believe Ellis and Julianna are worth fighting for, don't you?"

"Of course, Sir."

"Then you will see it done."

The others could see some wheels were turning and so they waited for the news.

"I am escorting Amalia on the next part of her journey. The roads are dangerous as you all know. I need three fighters to help me see Amalia and the other women to safety. Who will come with me?"

Birback shrugged as he was surrounded with beautiful women in the brothel and so saw little of value in leaving.

"I will go," declared Caffy.

"Yes," replied Matthys.

"I will help you," added Vicenta.

"Thank you, let us ready our horses. We will need a week's supply, two if it can be done."

"I will see to it." Matthys rushed on to see to everything as he always did.

"You would go just to spend some more days with her?" Vicenta asked him.

"Yes, but why do you?"

"I am not one for the city. It is loud and ugly."

"And you?" he asked Caffy.

"I go where you go, Sir," he replied calmly.

"You don't have to, you know that?" asked Craven as he thought of the man's life as a prisoner and as a slave.

"It's a better place than most," he replied honestly.

Craven was curious by his response.

"And when it is all over, the war, what then?"

"What will you do, Sir?"

"Honestly, I am not entirely sure."

"Well tell me when you do, for I should like to know."
"Why?"
"It could be where I go, too."

CHAPTER 11

After managing such a large force and marching with a vast army, it was quite the relief to be in such small a company. Craven and Amalia rode on through the countryside, though Craven kept a keen eye on their surroundings and all of his weapons were ready and within easy reach. He knew bandits might make an attempt on such a small party, which they would never risk against the force he typically rode with.

"My country is not as dangerous as you think," Amalia smiled as she gazed upon his suspicious face.

"Yes, for the most part that is true, until it is not. I imagine bandits have always lived among these hills and far more so since this war began."

"I cannot blame them, for what else can men do in the face of such oppression?"

"I don't have a problem with the ones who fight the French. It's those others who will rob and kill anyone who crosses their path which concern me."

"Well then, I am lucky to have a good strong man to protect me, aren't I?"

They went on for several days in peace before reaching a small river late in the day.

"Wait here."

Craven went forward to test the depth. He drove his horse on, but it was becoming increasingly deeper, and he could feel the animal was about to start swimming. So he quickly pulled the reins about and led them both out.

"We will camp here for the night." He didn't much want to risk them being soaked through just as the sun was going down.

"Keep your weapons handy," he added to the others, as he was suspicious of every place they went. They soon got a fire started and had some supper.

"It is quite the beautiful country, isn't it?" Matthys asked as they sat comfortably around the flames, "I think I should like to return here one day when war does not grip the land."

"You would travel here, to what end?" Craven asked.

"To see the majestic sights and to walk it in peace in my own time and not on the orders of another."

"Nobody ordered you to make this journey."

"You know what I mean. To wander these lands in a time of peace would be a most joyous experience."

"The only people who make such a journey are pilgrims and those wealthy enough to not have to work for their money."

"Could that be you one day?" Amalia asked Craven.

"I wish it could be."

"And why not? After all you have achieved here, why not

that?"

"Yes, a Major with your reputation might find himself with great favour on your return to England," explained Matthys.

"But I am not of noble birth," he sighed.

"That does not matter anymore. Do you think the men who run the factories across England are of noble descent? No, they made their wealth and now reside in great palaces as if they were."

"But I do not own nor operate a factory. I use a sword, and what money is there in that?"

"But you are also a hero," added Amalia.

"Yes, you are, and if you live long enough to return home, you will be much celebrated. There is power in that. You might even get the ear of the King or the Prince Regent, just like General Le Marchant. Le Marchant had a hand in shaping this army and with the swords and methods of their use. Perhaps you could one day fill that gaping hole he left behind when he fell at Salamanca?"

Craven looked rather curious at the prospect, but then became doubtful once more.

"You think the army would care what I had to say?"

"Le Marchant didn't care what the army thought. He went straight to the King and Prince Regent with the power and influence to implement change."

"Then you would have me befriend royalty?" Craven smiled as if it were a ridiculous dream.

"If the James Craven I knew four years ago could see you now, what would he think? Would he think anything was impossible?"

Craven shrugged as his old friend made a good point.

"And you? Would you follow me into the King's court?"

"I would," he replied bluntly, as it was not a joke to him.

They soon settled down to get some sleep, but Craven stayed on guard for the first watch. It was close to midnight when he heard the tramp of a horses' hooves among the stones on the far bank of the river. He looked over to see a lone rider gazing upon their fire. Craven's hand reached to his sword, but he did not draw it, for he did not want to instigate a battle if it was not necessary. The rider clearly knew the place well, for he did not hesitate to jump into the flood and crossed with ease. He was upon them within seconds as the rest of Craven's party awoke to the noise. The stranger looked to be a local, but Craven was forever suspicious as Bouchard and the likes were not beyond disguising themselves as foreign soldiers and civilians. He had even done so himself when there was no other choice. He leapt from his horse quite casually as if they were old friends and not complete strangers.

"May I have a light?" he asked as he pulled out a cigar from his pocket.

"Be my guest."

Craven watched the man's movements carefully. He pulled a burning stick from the fire and began to smoke quite casually, but he was surveying Craven and the others and their weapons. A whistle echoed out from the far side of the bank, and another cloaked rider leapt in and cantered up to the party.

The two men exchanged words for a moment in Spanish. Vicenta gave no indication of understanding, and beneath her cloak her Spanish attire was concealed. She smiled as she nodded towards Craven's sword, and so he knew that is what the men were discussing.

"Where are you going?" the new man asked in a curt tone.

"None of your business," replied Craven.

"You are very late," added Matthys who did not much appreciate aggressive strangers coming upon them in the night.

The two men spotted three rifles stacked against the tree nearby, their barrels and locks glistening in the fire light.

"This is our place, and I would know who travels here."

"An officer of King George's Army, that is all you need know," replied Craven.

But the man smiled as if he did not believe him, and Craven's cloak concealed his uniform as well as Vicenta's. He wore a simple forage cap with no regimental markings, for it was most warm and comfortable in the cool night. The two strangers seem to eye them up and down as if they measured their strength to wonder if they might overpower them. At which point Craven cast the left side of his cloak over his shoulder to reveal his sabre, and the pistol that was stuffed into his officer's sash. He carried them as though he were in battle, as the fears of a night attack were quite similar. The Spaniards looked surprised but were convinced.

"You should travel with more companions. This can be a dangerous place at night," declared one of the men.

"We have met the French in battle from Porto to Salamanca. I think we will be quite fine," insisted Matthys.

The two men leapt back onto their horses and rode off into the night without another word, and Craven felt vindicated in insisting he accompany the women, who were unarmed.

"You see, a dangerous place."

"Those men meant us no harm," replied Amalia.

"Perhaps, and we may never know, but if they did, there would not have been anything you could have done to stop them."

"We wouldn't have to, for we would have stopped at villages along our way. We would not have slept under the stars."

Craven was stunned as it had not occurred to him. For he marched like a soldier as far as he could and then made do with wherever they stopped for the night.

"We would have been just fine, but the company is most welcome," whispered Amalia.

* * *

Paget strolled on through the streets with Ferreira, Bunce, and Quental as they returned from some peaceful drinks away from the rowdy brothel, where the men were contained due to the night curfew. Not that most of them had any complaints.

"Do you really think you can win the General over, Sir?" Paget asked Ferreira as his thoughts turned to Ellis and his wife's father who was now pursuing him relentlessly.

"Wellington cannot afford to lose good fighting officers in this war," replied Quental hopefully.

"But he isn't really an officer, is he?" Bunce asked.

"As much as you or I, and he was an officer in the service long before either of us," replied Paget defensively.

"Maybe that was once the case, but the way Craven raised him up from the ranks?"

"Like a great many officers in these times," replied Ferreira.

"That is the Major's decision, and we must respect it," added Paget.

"How can a common soldier ever truly be one of us?"

"Lord Wellington believes they can, for he has overseen more officers raised from the ranks than any other."

"Even Napoleon? For does he not give generals' batons to common soldiers?" Bunce moaned.

"Perhaps they earned and deserved those batons?"

Bunce was stunned. Paget was not at all the boy he once knew, but he had no time to protest as Paget went on.

"I have seen generals who were not deserved of wearing the uniform of a common soldier, and I have seen common soldiers who I'd gladly follow as an officer of my rank or above should he have earned it. The buying of commissions is a great unfairness that I would see abolished one day. A man's wealth bears little resemblance to his ability as a soldier or as an officer."

Bunce was shocked.

"And so you do not think Wellington deserves to be where he is now?" he retorted with a smirk as if he had gotten one over Paget.

"Now he has, but there was a time where I might not have agreed. The fact that such a capable man as Wellington now leads us is luck for all of us in much part. For many useless men have risen through the ranks to the very top based on wealth alone."

"Has a rich man not already proved himself more capable than those with less?"

"No."

Bunce shrugged. He could not understand Paget at all, but they were arriving back at their quarters. Yet in the distance

Paget noticed a shadowy figure leaning against a doorway, seemingly the same mysterious figure who had appeared beside the church many days before.

"Go on, I should do well with a little more of this evening air," he insisted as the others went on into the brothel.

Paget stopped and gazed upon the stranger from afar. At their last meeting he was unsure if he was a real man or a ghost or some other thing that only he could see. But after the confirmation that it was indeed Ellis in the officer's uniform he had seen, he no longer doubted his own mind so much and so approached with no fear. That fear was now replaced with curiosity as he wondered what he could glean from the man who had promised to deliver Bouchard to him.

"Lieutenant Paget," welcomed the man as he approached.

"I am afraid I do not know your name, nor your rank or even which army do you serve? But I imagine it is the French, for you would not be so secretive if it were not."

"And if that were true?" he replied dryly.

"You wear no uniform and do not appear to have come here to do harm. And so, it should not matter unless you are a spy, making plans against us?"

"Sometimes the aims of men on either side of a conflict can be aligned."

"You have reason to see Bouchard dead?"

"My reasons are my own."

"And why should I trust you?"

"You have no reason to. I will tell you where Bouchard is, and I can assure you there is time enough that you could ride to his position before he moves on."

"Or I could ride into a trap of your making?"

The man shrugged as if he did not even care to defend against the possibility.

"Why do you not bring this to Major Craven?"

"I bring it to you."

He gave no further explanation. Paget sighed in frustration as the man was deliberately obtuse and difficult, and yet what he offered was also very enticing.

"We will be enemies someday, won't we?"

"Almost certainly," admitted the stranger, "You may call me Joachim for the present."

"But it is not your true name?"

The stranger merely smiled as he reached into his pocket. Paget's hand moved towards his sword in readiness for the stranger taking out some weapon, but it was only a piece of paper that he held out for him.

"The location of Bouchard."

"For how long?"

Joachim smirked as he could see Paget had taken the bait, but Paget was still not certain of the stranger's motivations.

"Two days at the most."

"You could just as easily be an agent of Bouchard?" Paget tried to push the man's buttons to elicit a response so that he might reveal more.

"Nothing I say will convince you either way."

There was both an arrogance and confidence in his voice. Paget snatched the folded paper from him.

"If I go through with this, and I have not yet decided whether to trust in this, but if I do and it is any way a trap, I can assure you that I will find you. Others have tried to lead me to my death. But I am the one still breathing," growled Paget.

"I can see why Craven likes you," he replied before leaving without any further explanation. This time he did not seemingly vanish into thin air but walked calmly off into the night, leaving Paget deep in thought.

"What game are you playing?"

He opened the folded piece of paper to find the name Fuensauco, which must surely be a town or village that he was not familiar with. He folded it back up and took out his map as he stepped closer to the lamps hanging from the front of the brothel. It did not take long for him to find the place and track back to their location in Madrid to realise it was not far at all.

"A single day's ride at a good pace," he muttered to himself, and he shook his head, knowing nobody on foot could make the journey in time. He didn't like the pressure the stranger was putting him under, but the chance of a shot at Bouchard was greatly appealing. He stuffed the map back into his jacket and stepped inside. His comrades were in high spirits as they had been since their arrival in the city. Charlie thrust a glass of wine into his hands, but she quickly noticed the troubled look in his eyes.

"What is it?"

"I have to make a decision, and it is not an easy one."

"About what?"

Paget looked quite uncomfortable with sharing, but as he looked into her eyes, he knew there was nobody more he could trust with the question in his mind.

"If you had a chance at Bouchard, but you knew it would be dangerous, would you take it?"

"Yes, I would."

"Without any doubts or fears?"

"None. Bouchard has been a great menace to us all, and any chance at him would be worth taking."

Paget nodded in agreement as it had clearly tipped the scales in his own mind. He strode towards Ferreira with such a serious expression that Ferreira knew it must be of importance.

"What can I do for you?"

"Sir, you have command here, and you are responsible for Ellis' future."

"Yes, that is correct."

"In which case, I request permission to take a party on a matter of great importance."

"What matter?"

But Paget looked weary as so many others were listening in.

"Secrecy is of the utmost importance, but I assure you it is of great importance."

Ferreira shrugged as he trusted Paget enough to not ask further.

"How many do you need?"

"Just nine good men."

"Then they are yours."

Paget grabbed a fork and began to tap it against his wine glass. He called for silence and drew all eyes upon him.

"I need nine volunteers who can be mounted and ready to ride at first light!"

"I'm in," declared Charlie without hesitation.

"Do we have to be sober?" Birback asked.

"Yes."

Birback groaned as he took another gulp of wine and ruled himself out, but Charlie gave him a brisk punch on his shoulder that caused him to spill his drink and choke a little. He knew exactly why, for she was furious that he had not stepped up to help.

"I'm in," he muttered as he reached for a wine bottle to refill his glass. Charlie went to snatch it away, but he lurched out and scooped it up with remarkable speed as he held onto it defensively.

"I said I'll do it, not that I'd become a saint," he declared defensively, drawing laughter from many.

"I will ride with you of course," added Bunce.

"We will come with you, Sir!" Nooth called out enthusiastically as he leapt to his feet to volunteer and dragged Quicks up beside him.

Several more volunteers soon completed Paget's small party.

"Thank you all!" He held up a glass in toast to them all, "The Salford Rifles!"

Cheers rang out and wine was spilled as they thrust their glasses into the air. The celebrations which had begun upon their arrival went on. Paget realised what a risky venture he had set in motion. He retired to the quietest corner of the room where Charlie came to join him.

"We are really going after Bouchard?" she whispered with excitement.

"Yes, we are."

"With only ten soldiers? He is the most dangerous enemy we have ever known, and you think it will be enough?"

"Dangerous with a sword in hand or when he lurks in the shadows to strike, but I know where he is in this very moment. We will approach with the same secrecy he has used upon us, and then we will shoot him dead before he even knows he has been discovered."

Charlie was taken aback by the plan.

"What?"

"I should have expected you to want to make a challenge and win honourably."

Paget shook his head.

"That would have been me some years ago, but this isn't a matter of honour. Craven wants that bastard dead by any means, and he has good reason to order it. I will see it done."

Charlie looked impressed as he was remarkably level-headed and pragmatic regarding Craven's nemesis.

"Unless you think Craven would want to do this himself?" Paget asked with concern.

"Is there time to wait for Craven's return to do this?"

Paget shook his head.

"Then it falls to us. You heard Craven in regard to Bouchard. He is to be stopped for the good of us all, for the Salford Rifles, for Spain, and for the whole war effort."

Paget took a deep breath and exhaled in relief, taking comfort in the knowledge he had the backing of those closest to him. Though as Ferreira approached, he remembered how much he was hiding from them all.

"Are you sure you will not take more of the men with you?"

Paget shook his head.

"We need speed above all else. Any more soldiers would only slow us down or draw more attention to us."

"Is it safe, this venture?"

Paget chuckled.

"We ride the roads of Spain where armies battle back and forth and troops and guerrillas are constantly on the move, how could we be safe?"

"Fair enough, but do not take chances that you do not need to. Ten men cannot change the course of the war, and the deaths of ten certainly will not," insisted Ferreira with compassion.

"Begging your pardon, Captain, but I think you forget who you are and who we are. One man can and has changed much."

Ferreira shrugged.

"What of Ellis and Julianna?" Paget quickly shifted the subject for fear of revealing too much and having his mission aborted before it had even begun.

"The General is a stubborn man, but I will grind him down into fine powder," smiled Ferreira.

"Captain Ferreira, Sir?" asked one of the men, and he left to deal with some business.

"You should tell him. Tell him who we are going after," insisted Charlie.

"I cannot, for he would never agree to it. Ferreira has become a good man, but he will not let us take a chance like this, and in this instance he would be wrong. We must do what the Major has asked of us. We must end Bouchard.

CHAPTER 12

The cries of local people rang out as Craven's party rode into the small village that was their destination. Many knew one of the women they were escorting by name as the happy reunion followed. The village looked untouched by war as if it were a hidden valley that the enemy had never discovered. But it was also evidently a refuge for the sick and wounded, as he could see men bandaged from sword cuts and others were missing limbs.

"Thank you," insisted Amalia.

"It was my pleasure."

"Will you stay the night?"

"I am afraid I cannot. For we must return to the Salfords with all haste."

As it had only just gone noon, they could cover many miles if they turned back then and shave a day from their return journey.

"Have you received some news?" she asked with concern.

"No, but our work is not done. It never is, and if they have not found trouble in my absence, then Wellington will have."

He turned his horse about to leave just as soon as he had arrived.

"James?"

He wheeled back around as the others went on.

"Come back to me, whether it takes a year or ten years."

"You have my word," he promised as he tipped his hat before going on his way. He then rushed on to join the others as they began their journey back to Madrid.

"We could have stayed a night," declared Vicenta.

"I could have stayed for good, and perhaps I would have," smiled Craven.

"We are right to return to Madrid with all haste, for a lot can happen in two weeks. Wellington leaves a sizeable force at the city for he fears the French armies which may march upon it. We should be there and ready to fight," insisted Matthys.

Craven looked back to see Amalia watching him leave, and he sighed. It was not an easy decision to make, and the Craven who had first come to Portugal and Spain would not have hesitated to stay and think of himself first and foremost.

"Let's get back to this war, shall we?" he asked them.

* * *

Paget drew Augustus to a halt at a road sign and took out his map to check against it. "We are close now, come on!"

He raced on down the road towards Fuensauco, quickly veering off onto a farm track so they could approach in secrecy.

Soon enough he slowed his beloved horse down to a walking pace so as to not give away their advance. As they came towards a crest ahead, he dismounted and passed the reins to Quicks.

"Wait here," he ordered to the small party.

He pulled out his spyglass and took a deep breath as he went forward cautiously and quietly. The anticipation was building now, as was the fear. For there was both a great risk and great responsibility weighing on his small shoulders. He could hear some activity ahead and ducked down low. He crept ever so quietly until he peered out over the dusty ridge.

In the valley below was a small village with only a few houses, but soldiers' horses were tied up behind one house and a few men went back and forth. And though they were armed, they wore no uniforms. He spotted one man sat atop a well in the middle of the village as he spoke with another. He lifted his spyglass but hesitated for a moment as he looked up to the sky, wary of any sunshine that might reflect from his glass and give a warning to any potential enemies.

He watched as a large cloud moved across the sky and blotted out any direct sunlight and finally brought up the spyglass. He tracked back and forth, studying each man. He could see they carried French cavalry sabres and other French equipment, and whilst the guerrillas were known to do the same, this was too regimented. These were French soldiers in disguise, and he knew it. He panned across each soldier. There were eight in view with enough horses for at least seven more. Finally, he got to the well, and his eyes opened wide in amazement.

"It's him," he gasped.

He was looking at Bouchard himself sitting upon the well. He could barely believe his luck. The villain was just where the mysterious Joachim had said he would be. He would never have believed the stranger until he had seen Bouchard with his own eyes. He peered back and forth at the surrounding hills as if expecting to see some sign of a trap, but there was no indicator of one no matter how carefully he looked. He had to take another breath to calm himself, his heart racing at the prospect of achieving what they had tried to do many times. He looked again to the man he believed to be Bouchard to be certain, and there was no doubt in his mind. He reached for a patch of grass on the dry and semi-barren landscape and tore it from the ground, tossing it into the air to watch how the wind took it, but there was only a small movement from the light breeze. He looked back at his target with the naked eye and assessed he was just under two hundred yards from the centre of the small village. The conditions were as perfect as one could hope for, and he was confident he could make the shot. He shook his head back and forth in disbelief as if all the stars had aligned. He scurried back to the party with a great smile on his face.

"Is it him?" Charlie asked.

"It is." Paget took out his long rifle from Augustus' saddle.

"Do you want me to take the shot?" Moxy asked.

"No, I have this."

Bunce and Charlie followed him to the edge where Paget checked with his spyglass once more to be absolutely certain it was Bouchard. There was no doubt in his mind as he passed it to Bunce so that he could ready his rifle.

"You are really going to do this? You are actually going to assassinate an officer?"

"That man is our enemy, and he has done more damage than you can imagine."

Paget brought his rifle to full cock, resting it on the ridge as he lifted it to his shoulder.

"Are these the actions of an honourable Englishman?"

Paget took aim. Bouchard was in his sights, and he was confident of making the shot as his finger rested gently over the trigger.

"Breath gentle and hold as you squeeze," whispered Moxy.

But Paget was dialled in as he knew what he had to do and how to do it.

"Surely there is a better way? Are we not gentlemen?" Bunce protested as he lifted the spyglass to see the target for himself, "This is not right. This is not how gentlemen conduct war."

"Shut up, Buncy."

"I don't know how you could ever live with yourself for this," he muttered.

Paget attempted to ignore him, but the waiting had caused his trigger finger to become sweaty. He rubbed it off on his tunic before taking aim once again as sweat trickled down his face from both the summer heat and the thick tension of their situation.

"You have him," insisted Moxy in support.

Bunce continued to watch through the glass in disgust, as to him it was not a fair nor honourable fight. Paget slowed his breathing and gently braced his finger on the trigger of the rifle. He finally held his breath ready to shoot, but as he did so, a parting of the clouds above let the sunlight through, and it glimmered brightly against the glass in Bunce's hands. Paget had not noticed and squeezed the trigger, but the Frenchman shot up from where he was seated at the exact same moment to investigate the reflection.

Paget's long rifle roared to life, but where the shot would have found Bouchard's chest it now glanced his forearm, alerting all of the enemy to their presence and intentions. Moxy quickly lifted his rifle to take a second shot, but Bouchard was already in rapid motion as he ran for his horse, and the Welshman's shot whizzed past him and struck a house behind. Bouchard cried out to rally his comrades as they rushed for their horses.

"What do we do?" Bunce asked in a panic.

"Run!" Paget dragged him away from the edge and hurried back to the others. He could already hear the gallop of the French horses approaching as he leapt into his own saddle.

"Did you get him?" Charlie asked excitedly, but she could see the answer in the disappointment and concern in Paget's face.

"Come on!" he roared as he led them in a rapid retreat.

"Why do we not stay and fight?" Bunce cried out.

"Because that man is a killer! There can be no victory here!" Paget barked.

Bunce looked stunned as the severity of the risk Bouchard posed finally dawned upon him, seeing the fear in the faces of such capable and accomplished soldiers around him. They rode on as quickly as they could, regularly looking back for any sign of their pursuers, and yet they did not emerge.

"Have they fled? Did they think we were far more away than we are?" Bunce asked with a smile.

Paget shook his head as he didn't believe it for a moment. He knew Bouchard would not take an attempt on his life lightly, and there was no reason to assume they were a sizeable force or threat. The main road was ahead and provided some hope of escape, but as they rode on to it, they converged with Bouchard's force who had galloped hard along the route to cut them off. Bouchard swung a hard cut towards Paget's head which he ducked under. It was not delivered with the same finesse Paget might expect, but he noticed a wince on the Frenchman's face as the wound from the shot on his forearm had weakened him slightly. Paget ripped his sword from his scabbard and parried a second blow. The two parties went at it with cold steel as they rode on in parallel.

Charlie hacked one across the shoulder blades and then against the face of the same man, causing him to pull back on his reins and give up the chase. Birback hammered away with thunderous blows, which his adversary parried easily, but it was enough to keep the man occupied, having no window of opportunity to strike back for fear of being cleaved in twain. Bunce lashed back and forth with his sword with a great passion but little effect. The adrenaline pumping through his body had got the better of him, and he thrashed about as if he were using a stick. He could not even get his edge aligned in most of his attacks, but the flurry was at least keeping him from being struck, as it was with Birback's thunderous blows.

Quicks took out a small dagger and threw it with a quick throw, burying the weapon into the chest of one of the enemy. He drew his sword out to join the melee, but a sword was thrust through his shoulder before he could land a blow. He cried out in pain as Nooth veered in between him and his attacker to take up the fight.

Moxy looked most uncomfortable parrying away the

strokes of a sabre, for he did not much like being so close to the enemy. Back and forth the two sides clashed as they rode on. Paget battled it out with Bouchard, the most terrifying opponent he could ever imagine having to face. On they went, hoping the French horses were more tired than their own. He had no doubt Augustus could outrun them all, but he would not leave his comrades at the mercy of the murderous Frenchman.

"You would dare try and shoot me dead!" Bouchard lashed out against Paget using more strength and finesse in his fury.

But Paget firmly parried each of the blows, and in between the Frenchman's wild blows, he flicked a quick cut against Bouchard's face. The blow struck home and opened a deep cut on his forehead and cheek. Blood poured into his eye, and he struggled to see as he swung a hard back handed blow in return, which Paget braced for and only just managed to hold off.

Back and forth the blades went with a furious clatter of steel on steel as light blows were landed on both sides. Blood flowed freely, but not a single wound severe enough to stop any of them as they furiously went on.

"Look!" Charlie cried.

Paget and Bouchard both stopped to follow her gaze. Dozens of guerrillas were appearing from the cover of rocks on the hills ahead of them as they entered a shallow valley. Paget smirked as he knew they were saved. Bouchard glanced over at him in furious anger before pulling back on his reins to bring his riders to a halt.

"Yes!" Paget roared in triumph.

But as Bouchard came to a stop, he took out a pistol from his saddle and quickly fired. The ball struck Nooth in the back, and he slumped over his saddle. Quicks braced his own horse against his and rode on. He held Nooth in the saddle as they galloped on to safety. Paget led them for another two hundred yards so that they were well beyond Bouchard's reach and within the safety of their saviours before coming to an abrupt halt.

He leapt from the saddle and let Augustus wander as he rushed to Nooth. He and Moxy helped the wounded man from the saddle, and they laid him down on the ground. He looked weak as blood poured from his mouth. Moxy ripped open Nooth's jacket to find his shirt below was soaked in blood. Quicks rushed to his side, instantly realising that there was no saving him. He took Nooth's hand as tears began to stream from his own face, but the wounded man could find no words and managed only a small smile before drawing his last breath.

"No!" Paget furiously shot to his feet and looked back at Bouchard with rabid anger in his eyes, the Frenchman relishing his anguish.

"No, no, no!" Paget rushed back to Augustus and leapt into the saddle as he wheeled about to launch back towards Bouchard. But Charlie rushed to his side and held onto his reins and held Augustus back. He seemed as reluctant to let Paget go on as Charlie was and so did not go on, despite Paget digging in his heels.

"No, do not die for nothing!"

"He must die!"

"And he will, but not at the cost of your life," Charlie wept emotionally.

"I can beat him!"

"No, no you can't, and no amount of anger nor determination can change that."

Paget huffed angrily as he looked back to Bouchard who held up his hands as if to goad him further into doing battle.

"Please, do not do this!"

"You would have me let him live?"

"No, I would have you live."

Paget looked back to Quicks who now cradled the dead Nooth in his arms. The two men had become the best of friends despite once holding one another in contempt. It was a bond only death could break, and so it had been broken.

"This was because of me," wept Paget, his anger towards Bouchard transformed into a bitter disappointment in himself.

"No, never," replied Charlie as she tried to console him.

Bunce was stunned by the whole affair.

"He…he shot him…he shot him in the back," he muttered in horror.

"That is the kind of man we are facing, a man who must die!" Charlie screamed at him.

He dared not speak out even though he would never normally allow a common soldier to speak to him in such a way. Paget kicked his heels in once more as he tried to spur Augustus on, but his beloved friend would not move, as if he understood the danger he was being asked to take his master into and refusing.

"Please don't go. This is over."

"How can it be over, Charlie, whilst that bastard still draws breath?"

"We will get him. I promise you we will end him, but not today. It cannot be today. Do not let us lose any more lives for nothing."

Paget stopped resisting and slumped his head into his

hands, knowing they were defeated. Bouchard wheeled his sword about his head in triumph before turning and riding away. Paget had lost his shot at the French Major who had plagued them for years, but the cost of the attempt was unbearable. He climbed out of the saddle and into Charlie's arms as he cried and did not even try to hide it. Though nobody thought any less of him for it. In fact, it was the very opposite. Few officers would ever shed a tear for the loss of one of the rank and file, and in that moment, Bunce finally understood the connection Paget had to the Salford Rifles, and not just the man who commanded them.

He could never imagine that the French officer could have done such evil as to warrant being shot down in cold blood, but as he looked down at the body of Nooth and Quicks still clinging to his lifeless body, and then back to the distraught Paget, he was beginning to understand. Paget suddenly turned to face him and glared with such an angry intensity.

"Why did you interfere?" he demanded furiously, "Why could you not let me take the shot when we had the chance?"

Moxy was the only other among them who had seen the events unfold, and his shrugs confirmed to Charlie that Paget was justified in his fury as he stormed towards his old school friend and shoved him violently.

"Why? Why!" he kept yelling.

Bunce offered no resistance but would say nothing either until Paget's emotions got the better of him, and he lashed out with a punch which caught Bunce square on the jaw. It snapped his head back, but he still would not fight back nor even attempt to defend himself.

"Why!"

Quicks rushed in between them and held Paget back.

"Stop, it won't bring him back!"

Paget staggered back as tears continued to stream down his face.

"You did not kill Nooth. That bastard did!" Quicks insisted.

The guerrillas descended from their positions and surrounded the small group. Paget wiped his tears away with his sleeve as he stepped up to face this new challenge. They were well armed and had not yet shown their intentions. The man in charge faced off against Paget for a few moments. He was only a few years older than the Lieutenant but had lived a hard life. His face was like dry saddle leather from a life spent under the unrelenting Spanish sun. He was dirty and his clothes ragged. He could just as easily be a Bandido as a guerrilla fighter, and some men could be both as the situation most suited. They glared at one another in a tense face off for a short while.

"Come," the Spaniard finally said as he turned to lead them away.

"Where do you take us?" Paget demanded without taking a step after him.

The Spaniard turned back and smiled as he respected Paget's strong spirit.

"To dig a grave," he replied calmly.

Paget gasped in relief as he relaxed a little and nodded for the others to see it done. Quicks unravelled Nooth's blanket, and he and Moxy lifted him onto it for the last time. The two of them and Charlie and Moxy each took a corner and hoisted their fallen comrade. Paget and Bunce led the horses on after them. The guerrilla led them only a few hundred yards to a patch of softer ground, and soon enough the Spaniards returned with several shovels and went to begin to dig. Quicks took one from them and then Charlie took another. They went to work as the guerrilla sat down beside Paget.

"Thank you, we were in grave danger. You saved many lives," declared Paget in gratitude.

"We have a common enemy," replied the man pragmatically.

"Yes, we do," agreed Paget.

They watched silently as the grave was made, and Nooth was lowered into it. Birback crafted a cross with a knife and a tree branch and some twine. Moxy paced over to tower over him and marvel at the care he was putting into the job.

"I didn't think you cared," whispered Moxy.

"But he does," shrugged Birback as he gestured towards Paget and did what he could for the Lieutenant's sake. They formed up as Nooth's body was covered over and Birback handed the cross to Quicks.

"None knew him better than you." Paget let Quicks say a few words. They watched as he thrust the cross into the soft ground and stepped back as he thought of his fallen friend.

"Nooth was the last man I should ever have thought to call a friend. He was an arse, but so am I. We were both Manchester boys, and he will never see the city streets again, but we will remember him."

CHAPTER 13

Cheers rang out from soldiers and civilians alike as Craven rode into Madrid, the festivities still going on. A few weeks of jubilation hardly seemed excessive after the years under French rule. It was a great feeling to celebrate among a liberated city, and Craven's mood could not be better. A few weeks with Amalia had been a wonderful break from the war and general soldiering. They rode on to the stables where the horses of the Salford Rifles were looked after, but he was surprised to find Ferreira there. He looked as though he had been waiting for their arrival, but he could not have known when that would be to within more than a day or two's accuracy, and so he became suspicious and concerned.

"No luck with the General?"

"Not yet, but there is another matter."

Craven would normally not be particularly concerned, but he could see a grave expression and dread in Ferreira's eyes. He knew something awful had occurred.

"What is it?"

"Paget discovered Bouchard's location and went after him."

"And you let him!" Craven roared angrily as he imagined the worst had happened. He furiously stormed on, and Ferreira hurried to keep up.

"I did not know."

"How could you not know?"

"Paget said he needed a few men for something important but that he could not tell me what it was regarding, and so I trusted him. Would you not have done so?"

Craven hissed and shook his head, knowing he would have, but he soon stopped and placed an accusing finger on Ferreira's chest.

"Tell me it did not cost him his life?" he demanded angrily.

"No, not him," admitted Ferreira.

* * *

Paget watched the soldiers of the Salford Rifles arguing angrily amongst themselves as to the rights and wrongs of his efforts that had led to the death of Nooth. He looked pale and gaunt and at a complete loss. Charlie yelled back at several of the men who had served with Nooth in Manchester and were even more angry than the rest, for she would not let them get near Paget. The door burst open, and Craven stormed in. For a moment the room fell silent, but it did not last as the angry cries burst out once more. They ignored Craven entirely.

"Enough!" Craven boomed.

The room fell silent almost instantly as Craven looked to the battered few Paget had taken with him. They were still bandaged and bruised from the affair, but Bunce got a word in before he could say anything.

"Sir, Paget put us at risk in a disgusting mission which no officer or gentleman would ever conduct, but worse than that, he botched it."

Craven was stunned by the public stab in the back by someone who was an old friend to Paget who looked too distraught to even answer. Craven wondered if he had even been listening.

"Major, you cannot…" began Bunce.

"How dare you tell me what I cannot do!"

Craven furiously stormed up to the young Captain and grabbed him violently by his tunic.

"How dare you turn on your fellow officer and friend! For you are no gentleman, you disgust me," snarled Craven before shoving him back.

Bunce looked mortified as he peered around as if looking for some support or outcry over his treatment, but he found no sympathy, and so he hung his head in shame as he rushed for the door to flee from the mob looking ready to beat on him.

"Listen to me carefully. Whatever the rights and wrongs of Mr Paget's actions, he followed the orders I gave. I put a warrant on Bouchard's head, me! Nooth's passing is an awful thing, but this is what I asked of you all. Any chance to end Bouchard was a worthy attempt. That is what I asked of you all. If you want to blame anybody, you blame me, for I put this course in action, and I will not hear any different!"

Everyone was silent, but it was Birback who slapped his thighs and groaned as he got to his feet, for he was one of the few not in discussion or argument upon Craven's arrival.

"What?" Craven asked abruptly as if he was about to have a fight on his hands.

"Nobody in this room is to blame for the death of Nooth. He was a damn fine soldier and he died doing his duty," declared Birback boldly.

Grumbles of agreement echoed out from many in the room, and for a few seconds Craven was stunned. He never could have imagined such sweet sentiment from the Scottish ruffian who he thought he had the measure of. Remarkably, the whole room was in agreement with him. Craven nodded in appreciation, though he seemed the least likely of allies in that situation. Charlie rested a hand on Paget's shoulder in support as he started to return to life.

"Find a drink so that we might toast our fallen friend!" Craven roared.

Cups and glasses were quickly shared around and enthusiastically filled. Craven waited for the room to settle down once more, and he began to address them.

"Nooth was an awkward bastard. He worked harder than any of us to be the best he could be, and in doing so he made fools of many of us, myself included. I'd never admit that he beat me on that Manchester stage, but the truth is he did. He was a fine man and a good swordsman. To Nooth!"

"To Nooth!" They all drank to their fallen comrade before Craven went on.

"Nooth left his mark on this world, but on none more than a friend he once despised, a man he came to call a brother.

Quicks, get up here!"

Cheers rang out as Nooth's best friend stepped forward anxiously, not knowing what was expected of him.

"Matthys." Craven held out his hand towards the Sergeant, who in turn placed something into the Major's hands.

"Corporal Nooth leaves a gaping hole in this fine body of fighters, and who better to fill it than his brother," he declared, holding out a corporal's chevrons.

"Congratulations, Corporal."

Quicks took the chevrons, the same type Nooth had proudly worn. Cheers echoed out all about the room as they all felt some of the grief be lifted from their shoulders. The promotion felt a fitting celebration of Nooth's life.

"Wear them in his honour, and yours," whispered Craven.

"Thank you, Sir," he muttered in shock.

Many others flocked to Quicks' side in celebration as Craven stepped away to let them have their moment.

"You let Paget off lightly," whispered Matthys in surprise.

"He has suffered enough, more than enough," replied Craven with compassion.

"Yes, he has."

Craven took a deep breath as he reflected on all that had happened. Matthys wanted to tell him how proud and impressed he was, but he knew it did not need to be said.

"Who would have thought Birback had such words," he smiled.

"Or that he could time them so perfectly. I think Paget must be rubbing off on him," laughed Craven.

There was a loud banging on the door, which brought them all to silence once again. Craven's hand instinctively reached towards his sword as if he sensed danger. The door opened wide, and a senior Portuguese officer stepped inside. Craven had never met the man, but he could tell from Ferreira and Ellis' face that this was the General who had gone to Wellington to protest the theft of his daughter. He was a slightly portly fifty-year-old with a calm but imposing composure. His daughter was there among them and looked most anxious that she might be taken away.

"Major Craven, I presume?"

"Yes?" Craven responded wearily, his hand slowly dropping away from his sword hilt.

"My condolences on the loss of your man."

"Thank you, but I will not let you take another," growled Craven defensively.

The General smiled and nodded in agreement.

"May I speak to my daughter and son-in-law?"

"You can say whatever you have to before us all," insisted Craven as he was not willing to let them out of his sight where some trick might be pulled to carry her away.

"Thank you," he replied pleasantly, turning his attention to the couple. Everyone watched on to see what the man who held their fate in his hands had to say.

"Julianna, and Lieutenant Ellis. I have to say I was shocked by the news of your marriage, and I must admit that at first, I was most angry, but let me salute you, for it was a brave thing. The man who is to marry my daughter must be willing to fight for her, to die for her, and now I know she has found such a man. Congratulations! I will ensure your possessions are returned to you immediately, and I will make no further proceedings against you, Lieutenant."

Cheers erupted all about the room. It was the perfect news after the morbid and tragic affair they had gathered for.

"A pint of wine for every man on me!" Ellis roared.

The room erupted into a frenzy once more, for as much as wine was freely had in these days of celebration, the soldiers were always eager for more. Julianna's father went to her and to shake Ellis' hand with a smile and goodwill.

"Sir?" Quicks looked rather sheepishly at him as he held the corporal's chevrons in his hands.

"Yes?" Craven replied.

"Sir, I do not know how to feel, taking this. Filling Nooth's shoes?"

Craven smiled, for the former pickpocket reminded him of himself, for he too was hesitant in promotion, unlike most men.

"It is about more than just you, Quicks. It is for all of them," he replied as he remembered how he was convinced to take his last promotion for the benefit of the whole regiment.

"And you think I am up to the task, Sir?"

"I know you are, and Nooth knew it, too."

"Then, thank you, Sir, and I will try to not let you down."

"And I in turn make the same promise to you, for I should have been here for when you set out after that bastard Bouchard."

"I think it was fate that you were not, Sir."

It made Craven think more deeply as he become increasingly curious about the events that led to the tragic affair. Quicks retired to a quiet corner of the room and took out a needle and thread to get to work on upgrading his uniform. It was as if it could not wait and recognised the symbolic nature of it, for it was his last remaining connection to the friend he had lost. Craven was lost deep in thought as he tried to imagine how they could have gotten to this point.

"You want to know what led Paget to Bouchard, don't you?" Matthys knew that expression well, and he too wanted the same answers.

"You think they were led into a trap?"

"That would have been my first thought. But having spoken with Moxy, no, they had a real chance at shooting the Major dead, and I think they might have lost many more lives if Bouchard had been behind this."

Craven groaned. It was a strange situation indeed as he led Matthys to Paget, knowing he was the only one who could answer their questions.

"How did you know where to find Bouchard?" demanded Craven bluntly.

"Can it not wait?" Charlie gasped.

"A present threat looms over us, and so, no, it cannot."

"We must know," Matthys added.

Paget looked reluctant.

"You have to tell us. We must know what dangers surround us."

Paget sighed as he knew he could not keep it a secret any longer.

"Sir, a man came to me with information."

"A stranger?"

"Yes, Sir," admitted Paget as he knew how foolish it sounded.

"A stranger told you where you could find Bouchard and you believed him?" Matthys never would have imagined Paget would fall for such a potentially dangerous ruse.

"Sir," he replied, as he appealed to Craven directly before he was disciplined, "I only did what I thought you would do. I know I took a risk, but I believed it was a risk worth taking."

"But you believed a total stranger and led yourself and others into danger without any inclination of whether it was safe?" Matthys was shocked.

"The stranger was correct. Bouchard was just where I was told he would be, and I had my chance. I could have shot him dead, but I faltered."

Craven sighed in despair at Paget's pain as he put a hand on his shoulder.

"It was a valiant effort, and you are quite right, I would have taken the risk, too," he assured Paget.

"But I failed, Sir?"

"We will never achieve much if we are too afraid to fail."

"Tell us about this stranger," insisted Matthys.

"He called himself Joachim."

"Where is he from?"

"I could not place his accent, but he was no Englishman, and not a Spaniard either."

"You believe he is in the service of the French?" Craven could see Paget was hiding a major fact.

"I believe so, yes."

"And still you took him at his word?" Matthys demanded.

"The French squabble amongst themselves, the Marshals fight one another at every turn. Yes, I believed he was an enemy, but I also believed him when he said we had a mutual enemy in Bouchard," replied Paget defensively.

He looked sheepish as they all knew he had taken a

massive risk.

"I would have done the same," replied Craven.

"You really would, Sir?"

"Of course. Nothing in this war is achieved without risks, and Bouchard is a slippery one. Tell me, why did you not take the shot when you had the chance?"

"I...I tried, Sir, but Captain Bunce made me doubt my actions, and then the thought of cold-blooded murder sent shivers down my spine. It was a moment of doubt which I believe I could have overcome, but the opportunity was lost, and before we knew it the enemy was advancing upon us. All we could do was run for our lives, for I nearly cost us all of our lives. Bouchard nearly took my head clean off."

"You crossed swords with him?"

"Yes, Sir."

Craven looked proudly upon him with a smile.

"You are a strong one, for it is no small thing to escape a battle with that man. You did well."

"Thank you, Sir."

Craven and Matthys retired to the far side of the room and slumped down side-by-side onto a bench, their minds full of thoughts and questions.

"He did not do well," declared Matthys.

"No, but he needed to hear it. Was it foolish to do what he did? Yes, it was. But it is that sort of bold and brazen initiative that has gotten us to where we are today."

"He could have gotten himself killed. He could have gotten them all killed. As Moxy tells it, the only thing that saved them was the lucky intervention of some local guerrillas."

"We all need a little luck in this war, for we cannot parry

cannonballs," smiled Craven.

Matthys backed down. There was nothing to be achieved by flogging a dead horse. "This Joachim, he is a concern," he replied.

"Did he use Paget to try and kill Bouchard, or was it merely another trap, do you think?"

"It was no trap of Bouchard's making, for he would not be so reckless as to be in the sights of one of our sharpshooters for a single second."

Craven nodded in agreement.

"Then whoever this man is, he genuinely wanted Bouchard dead?"

"Or he is indifferent to Bouchard and merely used him as an enticing bait," pondered Matthys.

Craven rested back and thought it over. "This will not be the last we hear of this Joachim."

"Nor of Bouchard."

"Do you believe I should have ended him? Bouchard, I mean. When I found him sickly and weak, should I have ended him then and there?"

"It would have been the best thing for us all, but I am relieved that you did not, for a great many atrocities are committed by men in war and justified by the ends which they seek. I am not sure you would be the man you are today if you had."

Craven sighed in relief as it was regret that he had often fretted over.

"What do we do now?" he asked Matthys.

"Wellington marches on Burgos for yet another siege, but we do not know the location or intentions of the French armies."

"And if Soult comes up from the South?"

"Hill protects the boundaries of the city, but it will not be enough if Soult marches on Madrid, and he might have the support of Joseph's men, too."

"A dangerous position we find ourselves in. I think many believed the capture of Madrid might send the French fleeing to their own border as the whole country rose up against them, but I fear there is not the stomach for it, and the French are far more stubborn than we imagined."

Matthys looked stunned by Craven's astute outlook.

"What?"

"Nothing, only that you have a grasp on these events which I never would have imagined possible."

"You pushed me to be where I am today, and so do not act so surprised."

"We hope and pray for many things in life, but we rarely get all that we desire," smirked Matthys.

"What will we do now? We cannot remain here idle, for I fear it will drive us all crazy."

"Some of us are quite content with it." Matthys gestured towards Birback who laughed along merrily with one of the prostitutes sitting across his knees.

"Wellington ordered us to rest here for a while and we have done just that."

"Some of us have."

"I feel rested, do you not?"

Matthys shrugged.

"Wellington also informed us that diversionary attacks are needed, and he has ordered Spanish forces up and down the country to obstruct French movements at every turn. Few are as effective at this work as we are. Tomorrow we will head out into the body of this country, and we will discover what we might do to assist in these efforts."

"You mean we will go looking for trouble?"

"Precisely."

Charlie came to join them.

"How is he doing?" Craven asked after Paget.

"As good as can be expected. Thank you, for I imagined you to be far harder on him."

"What would it achieve? It was a brave thing he did. How could I scold him for that?"

"Bouchard must die," she insisted.

"Yes, and we will see it done. Do you think Paget could have gone through with it?"

"I have no doubt. You should have seen him fight, stirrup to stirrup with Bouchard at the gallop. He was like a lion."

"Good, because tomorrow we set out to find the enemy."

CHAPTER 14

The makeshift stable once a food storehouse was alive with activity as the Salford Rifles made their preparations to depart. And though they had all enjoyed their time in Madrid and had been treated very kindly, there was an excitement shared by all to get back out on the road and in the fight. Especially as they were eager to put the tragic loss of Nooth behind them and perhaps even seek a little revenge. Yet as Craven secured his horse's saddle, he heard a rider approach at some speed and with great urgency. The horse stopped outside but its rider rushed inside. It was Major Spring.

"Craven, your presence is requested at Burgos urgently!"

Craven pulled out his map from inside his jacket. The Spanish city was one hundred and fifty miles North of Madrid, and a similar distance again on to the border with France. Driving the enemy back into their home country felt almost within his grasp now as he could see how far they had reached across Spain.

"Is it finally happening? Do we march for France?" His face lit up with excitement.

"I am afraid not. Wellington is in desperate need of powder and ammunition. With our siege guns sent back to Rodrigo we are not having an easy time of it."

"What is it that we can do?"

"Hill remains to protect Madrid, and with a great many soldiers tied up here, too, as many as forty thousand as best I can count. I need reliable men to see powder and shot to Burgos. I know it is not glamorous work…"

"We'll see it done," insisted Craven without hesitation.

"Do not let anything happen to these supplies, for I fear if the troops at Burgos do not receive it there can be no victory," whispered Spring.

"When do we depart?"

"A caravan is assembling as we speak north of the city, and they should depart within an hour or two if all is well."

"And the diversionary attacks Wellington put in motion? Are we not needed there?"

"Ballasteros' Spanish army works to impede Soult. Anglo-Sicilian operations are underway on the Catalan coast, and guerrilla raids, including some supported by Navy men-of-war all battle to confuse and constrain French movements. In this time and moment there is nothing Wellington needs from you more than this."

"Understood."

Spring looked a little relieved as he was clearly under a great deal of stress.

"Are we still making progress here?" Craven showed his

concern.

"We are."

"Then why so fearful?"

"I fear the unknown. I fear Wellington underestimates the enemy's strength and their capability to bring it to action."

"You think all the French armies in Spain might unite against us?"

"Wellington does everything to prevent it, but yes, it is my greatest fear. Good luck," he replied sincerely as he hurried away to see to more urgent business.

Craven was rocked by the news, and yet there were so many unanswered questions.

"A change of plan, Sir?" Paget had noticed his puzzled expression.

"We march North."

"North, Sir?"

But his face lit up, as he realised they were going to Wellington's aid. Though Craven didn't much think he would be so enthusiastic if he had heard Spring's news and seen the worry in his face. Craven looked to Ellis and Julianna as they made the most of one final embrace. She was to stay in Madrid, for the march onwards was no place for a lady as they had few luxuries to enjoy. He smiled at their heartfelt embrace as he could feel in his gut that challenging times lay ahead.

He soon led them out to rendezvous with the wagon train they were to escort, but within minutes of stepping out into the open air a rain shower began to hammer down upon them. There was no refuge to be had, as they had a job to do and a place to be. The rain instantly dampened their spirits. Not only was it a miserable experience in the moment, but it would make the journey an arduous one, and they could imagine what it would be like for the poor devils working on the siege works at Burgos.

They were quickly on the road with a great long line of heavy wagons moving at no greater a speed than the infantry could manage. The mounted elements of the Salford Rifles led the way. It was a slow-moving column. In the saddle they could have reached Burgos in three hard days of riding, but it would take them double that time as the slow-moving column snaked its way North.

"Do we expect to meet any trouble on this road?" Bunce asked as he rode behind Craven and Paget and alongside Ferreira. The Portuguese Captain shook his head with disdain. He didn't have much respect left for the newcomer after he had not stood up for his old friend and comrade when it mattered.

"Perhaps, perhaps not," replied Craven dismissively.

"Who would threaten a force such as this as it marched from one army to another?" Bunce attempted to answer his own question, and that only angered Craven further, but Paget answered for him.

"All manner of misadventure might find us. The enemy continue to harass us at every turn, and we do not know all of their strength or movements. The people of this land are desperate and might steal from us, and these supplies would be like gold to the guerrillas and bandidos."

"But not now, for only a fool would attack this force," replied Bunce, dismissing Paget's concerns.

"A man can feel awfully strong right up until the point that he meets a giant," declared Craven.

"And so you think there are giants living among these

lands?" Bunce smiled.

"A marauding French force of several hundred cavalry would feel like giants if they were to attack us as we are. Spread out in column over a great area. Or a great force concealed in the woods. Many a great and powerful Roman legion was destroyed by a force that was unknown or underestimated by them."

Bunce was silenced but did not look happy about it. On they rode without any threat of danger for two days, but the rain continued to lash them on and off continually as the roads became increasingly softer and more arduous. They struck up fires as they settled in for the night and set plenty of pickets. Ellis warmed himself by a fire. He looked lost and deep in thought.

"A shame your wife could not join us," declared Paget.

"No, it isn't. I would not have her suffer through this."

"And yet what would you have done if you had eloped without her father's support and assistance?"

Ellis stopped to think about it for a moment before shrugging as he had no clue.

"I suppose we did not think it through, but she might well have found lodgings with the women of the officers from other regiments."

"With what money?"

Ellis smiled and shook his head.

"We did not think so far ahead."

"And was it worth it?"

"Yes, no matter what our life would become, it would have been worth it, and if that meant Julianna would have to march with us here and now, she would not protest."

Paget shook his head.

"You do not believe me?"

"I think she might have agreed to it, yes, but I do not think she could go on out here."

"Why? How were you any different?"

Paget had led a similar life of privilege and comfort before joining the service.

"Because I am a…" he hesitated as he looked to Charlie and realised how foolish his statement would be, and so he rephrased it, "War is not for ladies."

"Like Lady Sarmento?" He reminded Paget of the fiery Portuguese lady who had supported them throughout, despite enduring great hardships, "None of us were this strong before all of this, but we rose to the occasion, and I know Julianna would have done the same."

Paget smiled and nodded in agreement. It was hard to argue with that. On they rode the next day, but it was not long before they saw movement in the hills either side of them. Guerrilla forces were tracking their movement.

"What do we do?" Bunce asked.

"For now, we do nothing," insisted Craven.

"We could see them off?"

"We stay with the column," growled Craven.

"A warning shot, then?" Bunce sounded anxious.

"Do you even know if they are our enemy?" Paget asked scathingly.

"They certainly do not look friendly."

"Wouldn't you look on with suspicion at foreign soldiers marching through your country?" Matthys joined in the conversation.

But Bunce was not convinced at all as he reached for a pistol from his saddle holsters.

"Do not touch those pistols," Craven said firmly.

"They wouldn't do you any good anyway," added Paget, as they were at musket and rifle range.

On they went calmly and at the steady speed they had maintained over several days. The Spaniards watching soon vanished back into the hills, either content they were not the enemy, or that they were too strong to make an attack against. Craven didn't care which, so long as their progress North was uninhibited.

"Seems they didn't have the stomach for a fight," smiled Bunce.

"Neither do we," added Craven.

"You, Sir, do not have the stomach to do battle?"

"We cannot afford to. We are not a raiding party. The column we protect is more important than we are now," explained Paget.

"And if we destroyed them, we would be all the safer, would we not?"

"And when we ride off to chase them and return to find the wagons raided and empty, what then?" Craven asked.

Bunce shrugged. It was clear to them all that in spite of some time in army service, he had lived a comfortable life marching only with large forces and without the danger posed to the column he now rode with.

On they went, and despite the regular and miserable rainfall they soon reached Burgos within a week's ride. It was a miserable sight. The ground all around had turned to a quagmire with British, Portuguese, and Spanish troops dug into great lines of fortifications and trenches. A cheer went up at the sight of new powder and supplies arriving, but it was half-hearted at best. Everyone knew it would signal a continuation of the siege and eventually a bloody assault, as had been required upon every French-held fortress, and a great fortress it was. A vast old medieval fortification reaching high up into the sky like the great old castles did, made all the more impressive by the fact it was built two hundred feet above the city.

The castle was once the favourite palace of the great Castilian Kings and the seat of power from which the land all around was recaptured from the Moors. It was a grandiose residence and defensive structure steeped in history and rebuilt many times over. And yet its tall old towers were built long before the invention of modern cannons and therefore a great big target for the guns of a modern army. But Wellington had so few, and none of the heavy siege guns that would be required. And the French had significantly improved the defences also.

The old castle was defended by three lines of fortification. The first was an old medieval wall, itself strengthened with an earth parapet. A palisaded fieldwork made up the second line, and the third a revetted palisade protected by a ditch. It was a formidable set of works that was most intimidating. On the top of the castle hill was a church and the ancient keep, now converted into a retrenchment with a newly built casemated work and made into a gun battery.

There was also a fortification North-East of the castle which rose one hundred and fifty feet above the castle itself. It was a horn-work fortification intended to protect the castle further, though it was now occupied by Wellington's troops.

"We have made some headway at least," declared Paget.

But Craven was carefully studying the defences. Two breaches had been blown in the outer wall, but it had evidently not been able to be exploited as the enemy had filled it with anything and everything they could find.

"They call that the Napoleon Battery!" Wellington rode forward to join them.

"Lord Wellington, Sir," saluted Craven.

"You see it, up there behind thick stone and well supplied." He pointed to the French cannons atop the casemated roof up high in the castle.

"We bring supplies courtesy of Major Spring, Sir."

"And they will be much needed," sighed Wellington who was not in good spirits at all as the great long line of wagons trundled on past.

"What can we do, Sir?"

"For now, there is nothing you can do, but what you have done here to bring us these wagons is worth its weight in gold. It is not glamourous work, Major, but it is most valuable indeed. The army camps several miles to the North. You may join them there."

"I'd rather keep the enemy in sight, Sir, if we may."

Wellington laughed.

"Then you are the only men who would!"

Craven looked surprised. "Is the army not eager to win a victory here?"

"Truthfully, I am not sure, for whole companies shirk their duties here. Some nights I can rely solely on the Guards, who are the only men with enough pride and sense of duty to do the work."

Craven watched as the tiny handful of Wellington's guns

fired upon the mighty fortress, but it felt like a futile attempt. They seemed so few in the face of such a thickly walled and multi-tiered defensive position. The cannon balls launched towards the so-called Napoleon Battery were shimmering and smoking for they were red hot shot, just as had been used on the forts of Salamanca. It meant they were not trying to batter down the French positions but cause them to set ablaze.

"You make an attempt on their powder magazine, Sir?"

"We do," he sighed.

It was a desperate measure, and they all knew it, but Craven's memories of the fateful magazine explosion at Almeida would never be forgotten. And so he had faith, but even he knew that the French victory there was as more attributed to luck than skill, and so he could only pray that they too could be so lucky. Craven watched as soldiers toiled in the slushy mud among zig zag trenches running up to the enemy walls in several places. Yet even as they worked, the French cannons raked their positions. The enemy not only had more guns but also enough powder to fire as frequently as they desired. It was a bleak affair.

"Have the enemy sallied out against you, Sir?"

"Yes, in the night two days prior, and they carried away with them a great deal of equipment. We saw them off, but at quite a cost, including Colonel Cocks, a brave officer indeed. Two hundred casualties and our work set back several days."

"Then let us stay and prevent another such attack. My sharpshooters would put a stop to it, Sir."

Wellington was stunned.

"Your eagerness is as refreshing as it is surprising, Major."

"I am here to see us win this war, Sir."

"A welcome thing to hear after the miserable experience

we have had. Morale is low, Major, horribly low. We need a victory here, for Burgos is the road from France to Madrid, and all of Portugal."

"I understand, Sir."

Wellington rode on to see to other things, and Craven quickly surveyed the scene. Much of the buildings surrounding the old castle were nothing but ruins, the victim of a great fire that engulfed the castle decades before. It gutted it almost entirely, but fire could not destroy the robust stone walls which made the fortress what it was and always had been.

"This way."

Craven retreated several hundred yards where they could make camp in sight of the investment of the castle but were beyond the target of the French guns which continued to fire all day, as if to mock the lack of powder in Wellington's army. They pitched their tents beyond an embankment. It protected them from any cannon balls and acted like an archery butt, whilst that same embankment gave their pickets a good view of the action should it escalate in any way.

It was from this embankment Craven now watched the action unfold as the camp was erected behind him. The heavy rain had given way to drizzle, but that was of little consolation. The ground was already a swamp, and there was little sunshine to help. The hour was late, and the powder they had delivered would do little good this day. They could already see the French filling the breaches that had been re-opened that day.

"Three cannons, Sir, is that all we have?" Paget asked in disbelief at how ill prepared they were to besiege such a robust fortification.

"It will have to do."

"And now, Sir? What do we do?"

"Be ready to fight at a moment's notice, for that is all we can do here."

They settled in for the night as they gathered about their fires. Craven could see the same low morale that infected those working at the castle investment was spreading to his own soldiers, and they had not even been there a day.

"Will the powder make a difference, Sir?"

Craven shrugged.

"Perhaps, but the only thing that will take that place is an assault, and it will have to come soon."

"Yes, I fear it, too, for why would they surrender whilst winter approaches?"

They had not sat about the fires for long when heavy rain began to smatter down upon them. They were forced to retire to the modest shelter of their tents, which they felt lucky to have been able to carry with them, for they had spent many a night under the stars. Craven awoke to a soaking wet ground sheet and water streaming through his tent. He got up in disgust and wrapped his cloak about him in an attempt to get warm as he sprang out into the daylight. The rain was only light now, but it was an even bleaker scene than when they arrived the day before. He climbed atop the mound protecting them to look out across the investments. The heavy rains had washed away the gun battery walls and filled in many of the trenches. The cannons had been pulled back to safety whilst men toiled in the mud to rebuild the defences under sporadic cannon fire. Others bucketed water out from the trenches. It was grim work and yet another setback.

"Well at least the enemy will not sally out now, for there

is nothing for them to take," declared Craven.

They watched as labourers toiled in the mud all day and into the night. The next morning proved dry as the guns were drawn back into place, and once more the bombardment began. Though as before it was a modest one, and yet it was more than enough to clear the breaches once more and sweep away the retrenchments the enemy had made behind them. British, Portuguese, and Spanish troops soon began to gather ready for an assault. It was no secret what was about to occur as there was no way to hide it.

"We attack by day, Sir?" Paget had become quite accustomed to night assaults on such fortifications.

"I hear some of the assault parties got lost upon the last attempt and this ground is awful under darkness."

"What are your orders?" Ferreira asked.

"I want everyone ready. Whatever happens here we will support it as best we can."

"I'll see it done."

He went on and began to bark his orders to several others. Spanish and Portuguese troops were formed up together whilst Foot Guards and King's German Legion soldiers were gathered, too.

"The Guards will make an assault?" Paget asked.

Craven nodded in agreement, for they all knew what that meant. This was a last attempt with the best troops Wellington had to offer. If they could not succeed, nobody could. At thirty minutes past four in the afternoon there was an almighty eruption as a mine placed under the Church on the Southern edge of the castle was ignited. It caused much of the wall to tumble down to the ground and create a rubble ramp. Cheers rang out from the troops before the orders were given for them to advance.

"Come on, boys!" Craven led the Salford Rifles forward to assist wherever they could.

The assaulting troops advanced on the castle from three sides in a simultaneous assault. The mine had boosted morale, and many of the troops were just glad to be doing something more than digging trenches in the face of cannon fire, though the enemy guns kept on firing as they advanced. The Foot Guards were over the first parapet and ditch in no time, as the enemy provided little resistance. The breaches would not allow them to hold the outer line. On they rushed for the second palisade, as many of the King's German Legion soldiers abandoned their own flank and rushed in beside the Foot Guards in a frenzied rush.

Hundreds of redcoats stormed on towards the main breach in the old medieval wall as French infantry poured fire down upon them from the parapets and towers. Moxy and many others paused for a moment to take well aimed shots at the enemy. As they attempted to take their shots, several Frenchmen were struck, but many more took their place and kept up the withering fire. A great many of the KGL and Guards fell as they made their advance, yet still they scrambled up the loose stone.

Craven rushed on up it behind them with sword and pistol in hand. He climbed over the dead and wounded until finally he reached the top of the breach. Only a few dozen men had made it to the top, and a brutal French salvo ignited before them, killing most instantly. A musket ball grazed his cheek, causing him to pivot about and realise how few were behind him as they struggled over the bodies and loose ground. Many fell back to the rear with awful wounds. Paget was almost at the top to join him when an almighty war cry rang out. Craven turned back to see a wall of cold steel approaching as a French counterattack with fixed bayonets stormed towards him.

Paget leapt up enthusiastically behind him with sword and pistol in hand just as he was, but his eagerness fell away upon the horrifying sight as the enemy came at them like a battering ram. He took aim with his pistol and fired instinctively, bracing himself to fight as if somehow, they had some chance of holding. Birback and Caffy climbed up beside them to help.

Craven snapped back to reality as he followed Paget's example and unloaded both barrels of his pistol into the advancing French charge, but they would not be stopped. Bayonet clashed with sword, and Craven and his party had no choice but to give ground as they fiercely countered the enemy bayonets. They were driven back down through the breach. Paget slipped and began to fall, but Craven caught him. He held him up as he beat two bayonets away with his sword. They continued their retreat until they were back where they had started at the base of the ramp, surrounded in the dead and dying.

The French troops gave out a cry of celebration, as they would not risk advancing beyond their walls, but they had thrown out those who had breached it.

"Come on, Sir, let's up and at 'em!" Paget shouted enthusiastically.

Craven shook his head.

"But, Sir?"

"It's over. We must retreat," he lamented.

Paget looked back in frustration at how close they had

come, but then to the horror of how many they had lost as the wounded were picked up and helped on their way. Craven himself turned back to help up a Private who had been shot through the hip and helped him hobble away. Paget was the last one standing as he peered up at the enemy who sneered back at him. It was as humiliating as it was infuriating. He turned away from them and fled with his shoulders slumped like a dog running with its tail between its legs.

CHAPTER 15

Day after day the British guns bombarded the enemy breaches as they attempted to widen them, but mostly just destroyed what the French rebuilt or filled in by night. The status quo was maintained, and that could only mean one thing, another assault would be needed, but few could see how it could be achieved when the last few had not. On the fifth day after the most audacious assault yet, Wellington came out to marvel at the fortress beside Craven. He seemed to be in better spirits, but not because they had achieved victory, for nobody was under such an illusion. Yet the General seemed to be at peace.

"They say Napoleon himself passed through here and ordered these defences to be made, did you know that?"

"I did not, Sir."

"This is one of the last great fortresses before the Pyrenees, for which we might have driven the French over if we had been successful here," declared Wellington as if he had already accepted defeat.

"Sir, we can still overcome this fortress."

"Even if that were true, we could not hold it, and time is now against us."

"Sir? And why is that?"

"Yesterday the enemy pressed upon us to the North, and in far greater number that I had expected. Additionally, I have received word of the French armies to the South. Joseph and Soult make an advance on Madrid as I predicted, but they too are in greater number than I had thought. It seems I was wrong regarding Clauzel, who commands an army far greater than any of us could have imagined possible, and now Souham marches on us, which only confirms it. We face French armies far greater than our own, and Hill has already begun to withdraw from Madrid."

Craven was horrified, as their seemingly strong advanced position was collapsing on all sides.

"What do we do, Sir?"

"The only thing we can do, we withdraw," admitted Wellington with a heavy heart.

"And then, Sir?"

"We will attempt to make a stand when it is convenient to us, but make no mistake, we are in danger. We march for Tordesillas. Perhaps our luck will turn there, and we may turn and fight."

"Yes, Sir," groaned Craven.

"We move under cover of night, withdrawing simultaneously along all roads available to us. For we must put some distance between ourselves and Souham. I know this is not what we wanted. It is not what any of us wanted, but it must be done."

"Yes, Sir," agreed Craven as he walked away.

Withdrawing after such an incredibly successful campaign throughout the year left a bitter taste in the mouth, but few were sorry to see the back of Burgos as they prepared to march. It had become a misery where soldiers only went to die in the most awful of conditions.

"Are we really to abandon the city?"

Paget had been listening from afar.

"For now, but we will be back." Craven gazed upon the castle enviously.

"Sir?"

"What is it?"

Paget gestured to their backs, and Craven turned about. All the Salford Rifles had gathered as a crowd behind them as they awaited news.

"Is that it?" Charlie asked.

Craven nodded in agreement as groans of frustration rang out. They had toiled and sacrificed for nothing. Many were still bandaged from their wounds suffered from the assault, and several were no longer with them being dead and buried. Matthys looked to him to say a few words, though he struggled to find them as it was a disappointing outcome for them all.

"This battle is over, but there are so many more ahead!"

They were silenced but not reconciled.

"We will not see France this year. But let us not forget how far we have come. There was a time not so long ago we were being run into the sea and looking at total defeat. This here feels like a bitter blow, for we have all become accustomed to victory. Salamanca made us feel as though we were unstoppable.

Well, we were! And we will be again!"

Cheers rang out as they realised how much more there was to fight for.

"Can I say a few words?" Vicenta asked.

Craven gestured for her to step up onto the mound beside him, as he was grateful for anyone who would step up and say some words. All eyes were on the former guerrilla fighter.

"What we have done here across my country has been quite remarkable. We have lost in this place, and that is that, but my people lost our whole country. Yet here we are still fighting back. So do not be disheartened, for we still have our lives, and we still have the courage in our hearts to keep on fighting!"

A roar of support followed as Craven looked to Matthys in amazement. She rarely said much, and her words were all the more impactful as a result, and he knew there was nothing he could say better.

"Gather your things but leave the canvas up until it may be taken down in secrecy!"

They went about their work as Craven turned his gaze back to the mighty castle.

"We never had a chance, did we, Sir?"

"I fear not, Mr Paget."

They watched as the soldiers all around them went about their duties as if nothing had changed, for they could not risk letting the enemy know of their intentions. Moxy soon sparked up a fire for the same reason, but it was a welcome reprieve from the rain showers that came nearly every day. They seemed to live in perpetually soaked uniforms.

"Will we ever return?"

"We have to. This is a bitter turn, but it is not the end.

Remember Salamanca and how many times we chased the enemy before it was their turn to chase us, and back and forth we went?"

"Yes, Sir?" replied Paget enthusiastically.

"It is no different now as we march back and forth, not committing to battle unless we can be certain of victory. You see the survival of this army is a victory in itself, but for the enemy, merely surviving is no victory, for they occupy a foreign land which resists them at every turn. No, they will not have victory until they have destroyed all means of resistance."

"And we are that resistance, Sir?"

"Yes, and just one part of it."

Paget perked up as the notion put him in rather better spirits. They watched the day pass as every soldier played their part in the act to not give away their intentions to the enemy. Finally, the sun was going down, and they knew it would be time to move, though leaving their fires to march in the darkness in their wet clothing did not have much appeal. Soon enough it was dark, and they watched as a great many soldiers poured over the two bridges. They marched with their muskets and rifles at the trail as to appear as crowds of locals, and it seemed to work. The evening went on peacefully until a Spanish cavalry regiment began to cross, all riding in the saddle.

"Oh, no," Craven whispered as he watched the foolish horsemen let their pride put their lives and the lives of many more at stake. For there was no mistaking that this was a military force, and the cannons of Napoleon Battery opened a heavy fire upon both bridges. Many horses reared up in panic as shells struck the bridge. Some threw their riders whilst others fled as the cavalrymen desperately held onto their saddles.

"Fools!"

They watched as both bridges were cleared as volley after volley was fired upon them, an easy target for the French guns to zero in on. They only fell silent once the bridges were empty once more, but that was little relief. Both bridges were now out of bounds for those attempting to cross as it would draw further fire. They watched as the final columns turned back North to take a long road around.

"It is about time we followed them," insisted Matthys.

Craven took one last look at the mighty fortress which towered over them defiantly. No matter how he spun it to his friends and comrades, he knew it was a defeat. Not a costly one, but a defeat, nonetheless. He led his horse on as they quietly shuffled on in what would be a long march through the night. But nobody complained, for they knew that if they stopped the French would soon catch up with them. For many hours they went on until finally Craven stopped them to rest with what little remained of the night. A few hours' rest would have to do.

The sun was soon rising once more, not that any of them could see it as a grey bleak sky brought yet more rain. They marched on for rest of the day without seeing any sight of the enemy. As they lit their fires, they imagined soft beds and roofs over their heads when they finally reached wherever would be their winter quarters. They knew that the season of campaigning was over. All they had to do was reach safety and all would be well.

"Major Craven, Sir!"

Craven's eyes shot open as he slept lightly as if expecting trouble all night, but it was first light. He leapt to his feet as Paget led him on to a ridge where Moxy and Ellis were observing enemy cavalry on the hills in the distance.

"That is more than a scouting troop," declared Craven.

"Many more," added Moxy who had clearly witnessed a much larger force.

Craven looked to Ellis, surprised that he carried on his old duties despite his promotion.

"You don't have to do this anymore, you know that?"

"You do," replied Ellis bluntly.

Craven shrugged as he led them back to the camp. They were at the tail end of one of the many snaking columns retreating towards Ciudad Rodrigo in the direction of Portugal.

"On your feet. We are moving out!"

Cries rang out from officers and NCOs alike as they hurried to get them all moving. The danger bearing down upon them now felt very real. They hurried on towards a stone bridge that crossed a streambed, which though dry was deep and impassable at any speed for a body of soldiers. British cavalry awaited them as a final rearguard. It was a welcome sight to know somebody was watching their backs as they hurried over the bridge to safety. But as they got to the other side, they found a trap awaiting the enemy. Guns of the Horse Artillery had been drawn up and ready to fire, and a great mass of British and KGL cavalry waited to counter charge.

"We mean to do battle here?" Paget smiled, imagining they might get a chance at the enemy.

But Craven was too busy surveying the ground to answer him. The bridge lay at the base of a valley with hills rising to the North and South. British infantry had gathered on the Southern hills from where they could watch and threaten any advancing French forces. But they looked more like an audience than active participants in what would come next. Craven hurried on, and it was not long before they were met by the welcome sight of KGL light infantry battalions concealed and ready to pounce. Craven had come to rely on the German infantry just as Wellington had, as they were stalwart and dependable soldiers. They were dug in around the edge of a small village and the woods nearby.

The Salford Rifles had barely gotten to a position of safety when they looked back on down to the bridge. The French cavalry approached and attacked the British cavalry awaiting them. The two forces rushed into one another and clashed with blades back and forth before the French were driven off, as if not expecting such fierce resistance. A subdued cheer rang out from the infantry, perhaps uncertain how significant the small victory was or maybe to keep their presence hidden from the enemy.

Craven took a deep breath as he looked around at the force they had to repel the enemy with. The infantry and cavalry were all dependable soldiers, but he could see a mass of irregular cavalry on a hill to the East. He took out his spyglass to get a better look.

"Who are they, Sir?" Paget asked.

"Mounted Spanish Guerrillas."

Craven gazed upon their ragtag equipment. They wore few uniform items, except that which they had taken from the enemy or stolen from friend or foe. They watched the French cavalry regroup and gain in strength as more came up. In the distance a great army was advancing across the hilltops towards them. This was nothing more than a holding action, and they all knew it. For nothing short of the whole of Wellington's army could hope to stop the vast French army. And they would need Hill and the troops from Madrid if they were to have any chance of success. There was an uneasy wait of several hours as both sides postured and manoeuvred to find the best manner of attack.

Late in the morning, a number of French cavalry managed to find a path across the dry streambed and thought themselves quite lucky, until a volley from the well concealed KGL light infantry sent them reeling and back over to their side.

In the afternoon the French made another advance on the British cavalry holding at the bridge. Once more they were driven away by a clash of sabres as pistol and carbine shots were exchanged. Even though the enemy were beaten back, the British cavalry soon withdrew back over the bridge, not wanting to withstand a third attack. The time had finally come for the battle proper to start, and they all knew it, but in that moment, they heard Lord Wellington's name be called out as several troops pointed towards him. He had taken control of the action personally and was galloping about barking his orders.

The KGL light infantry began a retreat up the road, and Craven led the Salford Rifles along with them. The British cavalry made repeated charges against the French cavalry as a means to prevent them from going after the infantry, but there was no serious action, as both sides merely attempted to intimidate the other. Hours had gone by, but the scene was heating up as the enemy applied further pressure.

"What are we doing here, Sir?" Paget asked wearily.

They were formed up as line infantry just as the KGL light infantry were. In the hills of either side of the shallow valley they could see French troops one side and British on the other. Both watching on as a vast audience whilst the battle went on between them, just as though they were the great mob at the Colosseum in Rome as gladiators battled it out before them. But as the waft of sulphur from the black powder swept by them, they knew for certain it was not the gladiatorial arena. The trap was set, and all they had to do was wait for the enemy to take the bait.

The thundering sound of a great many horses had them all on edge. They could not yet see who was approaching and why, but the sound of pistol fire soon alerted them to danger.

"Form square!"

Craven was stunned by the notion. It was not something they were accustomed to, but his small force of Salford Rifles was not nearly large enough to form the defensive formation that would protect them against cavalry.

"You heard the man!"

Craven pointed to the two KGL battalions forming square. The Salford Rifles raced to join them and bolstered the near two thousand infantrymen as they formed into the defensive formations. Craven and those mounted rushed into the hollow of one of the squares as the order to fix bayonets echoed out. The ring of metal socket bayonets locking into place sounded almost like the clash of cavalry sabres. Craven looked to the KGL colours and senior officers who had gathered at the centre of the square. He could not help but feel the roles had been reversed with the enemy. They were the ones behind walls and surrounded only days before. The square was a daunting place to be, as in spite of its strength, if it were penetrated it was little different to the slaughter that followed the successful assault of a fortress. And they had all witnessed such a horrific event after Salamanca.

They watched on as a mass of cavalry came into view and stormed across the bridge. British dragoons were mixed with mounted Spanish guerrillas as both fled from a great mass of French cavalry. All three were muddled together, battling it out man for man with swords as they came down the road. It was not what anyone had planned for. The cannons of the horse artillery could not fire for risk of hitting their own, and the rest of Wellington's cavalry could not charge for fear of condemning those fleeing to their deaths as they became trapped between the two sides.

The plan was falling apart before their eyes, but the French soon gave up the chase as they formed up upon crossing over the bridge. Soon enough the French had swelled to a great force, and the British horse artillery had limbered their guns and fled. The British cavalry who had fled across the bridge were formed beside three hundred KGL dragoons, and with great bluster both sides charged into one another in a great clash of cavalry. It was a great spectacle to behold, as steel clashed with steel, and a brave effort. But the French cavalry were in such great numbers they pressed on and soon swept Wellington's cavalry aside.

"Make ready!" came the call as the squares prepared to receive the great mass of French cavalry.

Paget readied his rifle, determined not to miss another Frenchman. Craven did the same, for they could fire over the heads of the infantrymen forming the square from their saddles. The mass of French cavalry came at them in a thunderous fashion. Hussars, chasseurs, and even Lancers raced towards them as they looked to finalise their victory after having swept Wellington's cavalry aside with ease.

"Present!"

They brought their weapons down into the firing position.

"Fire!"

A volley burst out from both squares, but only from the sides opposing the cavalry, reducing the volume of fire which both battalions could unleash by nature of their defensive formation, yet providing the all-round protection of a fortification as the French cavalry broke over them like waves. They circled around, poking and prodding to find any weakness, but they only found more lead, as those at the flanks and rears of the square got their chance to unleash fire upon the enemy. Swords clashed with bayonets, and lancers cheekily lunged for the infantrymen. They were met with furious resistance, as those among the square not battling in hand-to-hand combat hurried to load and keep on firing. Round and round the cavalry rode but they could not find an opening. More of them were shot from their saddles until finally they galloped away. The infantry cheered loudly as they would not be broken like the French squares had been by their own KGL cavalry after Salamanca.

"Load!" cried one of the KGL Colonels who was weary of what might come next and refrained from joining in the celebrations.

He was right to be cautious. The masses of French cavalry were already regrouping and reforming to make another attempt against them. Ramrods scraped up and down barrels as the light infantrymen hurried to prepare their weapons, doing their best not to skim their knuckles on their fixed bayonets.

One French cavalry officer rode forward of his lines as if to taunt the squares. He held up his hat in readiness to call for another charge, but a rifle shot cracked out, striking him in the chest. The smoking muzzle that had unleashed the shot was Moxy's. The KGL Colonel looked back at him in disgust for a moment, for no order had been given to fire. But a cheer rang out and he turned back to see the French officer slump over his horse, falling down dead from the saddle. The KGL infantrymen erupted into a great cheer and laughter, the incident serving to bolster their resolve and lift their morale at the incredible shot that had been made at four hundred yards and from the saddle. The Salford Rifles were even louder as they celebrated the shot, but Moxy merely smiled as he began to reload in readiness for the charge.

"Nice shot," declared Craven.

"I was aiming for his hat."

"Truly?" Paget asked.

Moxy smirked and shrugged, and Craven could not help but laugh. His laugh was infectious as the square celebrated Moxy's triumph in defiance of the French cavalry. They came forward still, but what a sight it must have been to a cavalryman to ride against infantry who merely laughed at the danger before them. The soldiers of the two squares stood their ground defiantly, not just because they knew they must in order to withstand cavalry, but because they would not falter in the face of the enemy.

"Fire!" roared the order once more.

A rippling volley downed many of the French cavalrymen, and further shots went out as they encircled the two squares once more. Round and round they rode, trying to find a way in until several fired pistols and cleared the smallest of openings where a lancer tried to force his way through. Craven drew out his sword and pushed on to deal with the interloper. Before he could get there, a KGL infantryman grabbed hold of the lance and pulled the man forward onto the bayonet of one of his comrades. The gap was quickly closed as the enemy were driven back at bayonet point.

The French cavalry could find no way in and continued to be shot from their saddles until finally they gave up the fight and fled. An elated cry rang out from the infantry, for the poor discipline of many of Wellington's cavalry was not what had stopped the French advance, but the stubborn resolve of the light infantry. Many threw their shakos into the air in jubilation as they continued to celebrate. It was not a victory, but they had denied one for the enemy, and that was enough.

Craven looked to Wellington who watched on with some relief as he passed orders for the army to march on.

"We will have to turn and face them again, Sir, and soon, will we not?"

"No doubt, Mr Paget, and we'll be ready."

CHAPTER 16

It was dark as Craven led the Salford Rifles into the bivouacked camp Wellington's army had set up around a village on the road Southeast of where they had opposed the French. He groaned as he leapt from the saddle to stretch his legs. They had been on the road for many hours in a slow slog across more than twelve miles. It was a modest distance compared to the great journeys he had made in the past, but their days in Madrid had made him a little soft, having gotten used to the luxuries of city life. The camp was unusually noisy and rowdy as several men nearby fought with their fists. Others encouraged them, and not a single NCO attempted to stop them. Laughter and loud cries echoed out all around.

"What is wrong with them, Sir?"

Paget would have expected them to be in more sombre spirits after a day of marching and the French army hot on their heels. Craven spotted a soldier passing them by as he drank merrily from his canteen as if it were a pint of ale. He snatched it from the man's hands.

"Hey!" The man said nothing more as he noticed Craven's officer's uniform. Craven took one sniff of the canteen and shook his head.

"They're drunk. This is wine."

"The wine harvest was just completed," announced Vicenta, meaning there would be ample fresh stores in the villages all around.

"Oh, dear," remarked Paget as he marvelled at upon the thousands of drunken soldiers and the complete breakdown of discipline.

"Give that here," insisted Birback to one of the passing drunken soldiers.

"No!" Craven roared angrily.

The drunk clutched onto his canteen and fled for fear of it being taken from him, let alone any disciplinary charges he might face.

"We do not drink tonight."

Matthys was stunned by the revelation as Craven sealed the canteen he had snatched away from the passing soldier before tossing it back into his hands.

"God bless you, Sir," thanked the man as he ran off before Craven changed his mind.

Birback groaned in frustration.

"There'll be time again for drinking. Plenty of it, but I will not be caught out by the French because we are drunk."

Birback shrugged and smiled as he remembered the last time it had happened to him, which was funny, for he was also naked in that instance and remembered it fondly, despite how much danger he had been in.

"Find us some firewood."

Birback groaned but did as he was told as they found a space to settle in for the night. Within moments Moxy arrived with a burning log in one hand and a pile of split logs in the other.

"Who did you steal those from?" Ellis asked mockingly as if they were the same friends they had always been and that his new uniform had changed nothing.

"Whilst they were busy drinking wine beside their fires, we were fighting. I think they owe us," he smiled.

"They do indeed."

"So, was it worth it? Putting on that uniform for a woman?" Moxy asked playfully.

"The thought of being an officer once more is one I had long dismissed, for it was a simple life among the ranks. I never would have thought it possible I would go back, and I never wanted to, but for her, I would do anything."

"Anything?"

"Anything short of joining Napoleon."

"And if that was the condition, you would walk away from her?"

Moxy got their fire going.

"Yes, I can live with a great many things, but I could never side with that maniac, not for anything in this life."

"But you'll throw us all in the dirt?" Craven joined them and thought of the chaos Ellis' situation had created.

"Of course, because I know you can fight your way out," retorted Ellis sharply.

The others soon gathered around as two more fires were

struck up for their party, which seemed like a mighty force in Craven's eyes. Yet among Wellington's army they were but a tiny element.

They could hear several officers ranting and raving at the drunken masses as they tried to get them under control, but to no avail. Most of the officers ignored them, likely because they were indulging themselves in the same wine or had lost all hope of wrangling the drunken soldiers.

"If the French are force marched through the night, they could sweep away the whole of this army," declared Matthys in deep concern as the drunken army would offer little resistance until they were sobered up.

"And if the enemy do attack, Sir, what will we do?" Paget asked.

"Flee and hope to escape with our lives."

Dawn revealed the extent of the drunkenness as officers struggled to get the army moving. Many men had to be kicked awake, and even a large number of the officers remained in their beds. Morale was low, and it could be seen on the faces of many who had seemingly accepted defeat, or at least that their successful campaign had come to an end. Most seemed blind to the threat hanging over them. Craven was astonished to see Birback up on his feet and looking remarkably sober.

"What?"

"You really didn't go looking for wine last night?"

"You were right. If the French march on us I want to be ready."

"That has never stopped you before?"

"I was wrong," he whispered.

"What was that?" Craven smiled.

"You heard me," grunted Birback.

Craven smiled as if he had finally won a long running argument, but Birback was not done.

"I want to survive this war. I never really cared before. Today is all that mattered to me, but now…"

"What has changed?"

"I have."

The army marched on in spite of the sore heads of the great majority of them. Soon enough they took up positions around a riverbank that was an obvious and strong position with which to make a stand against the advancing French force. The army was spread across many villages and bridges with several miles between each. Engineers got to work on each and every bridge, with the intention of destroying them to slow the enemy advance, but it was no easy feat. The robust old stone Spanish bridges required many hours of work to bore holes in the arches so that explosive charges could be placed in a location to be able to bring them down.

It was not long before British artillery bombarded the advancing French forces as they pressed on for the bridges, but it was a half-hearted attempt. They soon gave up and retreated to find the vast wine stores that had plagued Wellington's army the day before. Drunkenness and disorder now overcame the French just as it had the British, who now watched and laughed as the French got their fill, knowing the awful state they would be in the next day.

"What is needed of us here?" Paget looked uncertain of the scene.

"For now, there is nothing, but we must be ready for whatever it is."

"Can we, Sir? Can we hold them?"

Craven shrugged as he honestly had no idea. Another uneasy day passed, and in the morning Major Spring approached with a grim expression on his face.

"What is it?"

"The enemy have advanced on our flank, and we can no longer hold these positions," he admitted as riders galloped past them to bring news to the Brigade Commanders.

"Will we ever stop and put up a proper fight?"

"Only Wellington can know that, and his mind is ever changing as everything around him changes."

It wasn't very reassuring, but Craven knew how that felt. They quickly packed up their encampment and were on the road once more as Spring rode beside Craven.

"Did we reach too far?"

He was referring to the ambitious campaign of that year that had seen them liberate vast amounts of Spanish territory, some of which they were now being forced to concede, which left a bitter taste in all of their mouths.

"I cannot say if it was right or wrong to go as far as we did, but I know what it has meant to the people of Spain, and the great tremors it has sent through all of Europe. That has to be worth it, don't you think?"

"I hope so," admitted Craven.

It was not long before they heard sporadic musket fire up ahead. Craven led their mounted element to scout forwards. They came up over a ridge to find a British division defending a position, which at first appeared strong. They were behind a successfully destroyed bridge leading to a small village, but the enemy had found a way to ford the river and were crossing with infantry and cavalry. They could hear Wellington bark his orders to the British Infantry Division's commander as he ordered a counterattack to stem the tide of French crossing the river.

"Well, what are you waiting for?" Wellington spotted Craven nearby.

"On me!" Craven led the mounted Salfords onward as the British lines began to engage the enemy and exchange volleys with those who had made the crossing whilst many more followed. The few French cavalrymen who had gotten across were galloping about in an attempt to harass the British infantry and force them into square, where their rate of fire would decrease drastically and allow the French infantry to press on without such fierce opposition.

"Sweep them aside!"

Craven drew out his cavalry sabre and galloped in to chase off the enemy cavalry. It was the job of the hussars and light dragoons, but in this moment, they were the closest thing. Craven approached his first target, a French cavalryman who had not even noticed their presence as he probed the flank of a line company. A Sergeant Major tried to fend the man off with his spontoon, the last remnants of the old eighteen and even seventeenth century pole weapons. Craven cleaved the man at the neck and killed him in one, much to the appreciation of the Sergeant Major who hurriedly saluted with the great big spear-like weapon. He then hurried on to engage another of the enemy and protect his boys.

Birback arrived almost as quickly as Paget, and yet as he cut one enemy down, he did not stop to loot the body. He rode on at the Lieutenant's side to watch his back. Craven shook his head in disbelief, realising the Scotsman really meant his recent admission.

Volley after volley cracked out as the French fought hard for a foothold. The British infantry matched them in ferocity. Soon the casualties began to amass on both sides, and yet neither seemed willing to waver. Gamboa led the dismounted Salfords forward to join them, but it was barely enough to replace the casualties the division had suffered. The French had lost even more men killed or wounded, but just as in an assault of a fortress, they kept pushing. They tried to make a breach in the British line as it fought at the edge of the village beside the ruined bridge. Gamboa marched in with the dismounted soldiers of the Salford Rifles as they joined the flank of the British infantry and took aim at the enemy.

Back and forth they duelled until hundreds lay dead or wounded. Finally, the French will was broken, and they retreated back across the ford. The British infantry did not celebrate, for the knowledge of the fordable part of the river could not be undone now. They all knew it would not be long until the French pushed across it once more. This was not a victory, merely a holding action. The division stayed in place until long after dark as the dead and wounded were dealt with. Many had bandaged their wounds in place to stay in their companies in readiness for the next enemy assault.

It looked like they would be settling in for the night. Craven and Paget looked across to the enemy positions on the far bank as they sparked fires.

"Hardly a victory is it, Sir?"

"Hardly indeed." Wellington strode in from shadows behind them as the last of the day's light faded away.

"Sir, my apologies." Paget was mortified that he might

have insulted their Commander, but Wellington shrugged.

"The truth is a painful one, but it is the truth, nonetheless."

"What are your orders, Sir?" Craven asked.

"The Fifth Division here will stay and hold, but the rest of the army marches immediately."

"Through the night, Sir?"

"Indeed, Mr Paget."

That was a grim prospect. The nights were starting to get colder, and the regular rains only made it worse. They had already worked and fought a hard day before the march had even begun. Night marches were also prone to all manner of disaster, as entire columns were displaced by poor navigation among a host of other traps.

"And us, Sir?"

"March with the army, Craven."

"But we can help this rearguard action."

"Indeed, but I am in need of rested and fit men when we make a stand. Continue South-West. Soon enough we will face the enemy and make a decision."

"A decision, Sir?" Paget asked.

"If we will stand and fight them."

"And if we do not, Sir?"

"I will not lose this army for the sake of vanity, Craven. If withdrawing further is the best course of action, it will be the one we take. Get on your way, gentlemen. You have a long night ahead but some days of rest to follow. Recover your strength, for you will need it. Good luck you and to us all, for we shall need it."

Wellington vanished as quickly as he had arrived. There

was fear in his voice and they both knew it, but neither would say so.

"Come on, we have a long night ahead," declared Craven.

They were shortly on the road. Morale was low. It felt like defeat to be fleeing from the enemy once again, and a forced night march was a miserable experience which every soldier dreaded. They marched on under moonlight that mercifully gave them more light than some dim nights, but they had more than forty miles to march to reach safety. They carried on through the rest of the next day, leading to complete and utter exhaustion. They practically fell down into a dead-like state upon arriving at another British-held bridge. It was damaged, though not nearly as severely as the last one they had fought beside.

Many of the men did not even pitch their canvas that night and merely collapsed onto it like a groundsheet. They slept quite easily upon them and beneath the stars. For those who had been mounted for the journey, it was not nearly as debilitating, and yet they were still utterly exhausted. They groaned as they stepped down from the saddles of their horses, which were as exhausted as they were.

"Post pickets," Craven ordered Paget who hurried to see it done.

Nobody bothered with a fire that evening nor even attempted to find food. They collapsed in place and slept for a great many hours until the next morning. Craven awoke beneath a tree to find he had merely wrapped his cloak about him and over his greatcoat. He was covered in morning dew, but he felt as though he had awoken from a dream as they had marched to utter exhaustion. A good night's sleep had done them wonders as he stretched and got up. To their surprise they found the

British soldiers defending the damaged bridge were not in fact British at all. From afar they had appeared as Green jacketed riflemen, but in the light of day it was clear they wore black uniforms, and their hats were adorned with silvered skulls with crossed bones. They were quite an intimidating sight and piqued Paget's interest as he was forever curious. Craven sighed and gave him an explanation as he pre-empted the inevitable question.

"Black Brunswickers."

"Germans, Sir?"

"Prussians."

"Once perhaps, but now they will recruit from anywhere and everywhere," Ferreira said a little scathingly.

"As do we," replied Craven as he studied their position.

They were just one mile from the bridge and only a few hundred yards from the nearest Brunswickers who patrolled the area. They paid no notice of the Salford Rifles, and that suited Craven just fine as he studied the bridge. The stone arch had collapsed in the centre and rendered the bridge completely unusable. Yet he knew a few engineers would make light work of the repairs if they could secure the Brunswickers' side. The Germans had a single company and so slightly more in number than the modest Salford Rifles.

"Come on, I want to see it for myself."

Craven pulled off his greatcoat and tossed it down before marching on towards the bridge. Paget and Ferreira followed close behind as Matthys organised some parties to forage for wood and food, mostly from passing wagons. They had no intention of stealing it from the locals as the enemy did. As Craven approached, he noticed a Brunswick officer smirk when he spotted their party and shot enthusiastically to his feet.

"Who do I have the pleasure of meeting?" His accent was of one of the original Prussian soldiers and not the foreigners they now recruited according to Ferreira.

"Craven, Salford Rifles."

"Captain James Craven?"

"It's Major now," growled Paget.

"Major? One might wonder how you lived long enough to seek such promotion if your exploits are to be believed."

"I fight."

The Prussian officer seemed much amused.

"That is right, a great swordsman, they say!"

He mimicked the positions of a fencer as he took a guard position despite being empty-handed. He leapt back and forth, simulating the actions of attack and defence before laughing out loud.

"A man's fighting exploits are not to be mocked." Paget was most indignant of his behaviour. The Brunswicker stopped and looked at him with a smile before laughing once again.

"I jest of course," he replied, making a small bow which seemed respectful and mocking all at the same time. Craven didn't much appreciate his tone towards Paget.

"What about you, can you use a sword?"

"Why yes, of course!"

"Good, then a little wager?"

"What do you propose?"

"A little friendly swordplay with sticks. Nobody needs to get hurt."

"With you?"

"No, we shall give you a chance. Lieutenant Paget here

will oppose you."

The Brunswicker looked at Paget's small stature and laughed.

"Be careful what you say next, for you will be made to eat your words," said Craven.

The man only laughed further.

"What is your name?" Paget asked politely.

"Why?"

"I should know the name of the man I am about to defeat."

He laughed at Paget who merely walked away.

"We shall return shortly," declared Craven as they headed back to their camp to retrieve the singlesticks which Paget had spent endless hours training and fighting with.

"What a rude fellow."

"Then put him in his place."

"I hate to admit that I will enjoy it, Sir, but I will."

"There is no shame in that."

"I want to hurt him," seethed Paget.

"Many men would have wanted blood for the manner that man spoke to you, I assure you. You are a better man than most."

"I am not sure better than most is enough."

"It most certainly is," added Ferreira.

"These Brunswickers, are they good soldiers?"

Craven smirked. "They can be, but they are a ragged bunch, prone to desertion, and worse. They have been known to fight hard, and sometimes not at all."

"And yet we suffer them?" Paget replied scathingly.

"If Wellington only accepted good men, he would have no

army."

Ferreira meant it as a joke and yet there was plenty of truth to the sentiment. Many of the Salfords watched with curiosity as Paget and Craven retrieved a pair of singlesticks and went on towards the Brunswickers. Dozens of them followed with curiosity, revelling in the beat down they were about to behold. They were surprised to discover it was Paget who would administer it, as he and the Brunswicker squared off beside the damaged old bridge the Germans had been ordered to defend.

"Shall we say the first to five hits?"

Craven managed the bout and used his own sword to keep them apart and see that everything was conducted correctly.

"One, five, ten, it does not matter to me," replied the Brunswicker arrogantly.

His comrades laughed as soldiers from both regiments formed a circle about the two fighters. Salivating at the prospect of a good fight.

"Ready?" Craven demanded of both of them.

"Begin!"

He raised his sword that parted the two singlesticks which crossed at their tips from where they were extended by the two fighters. The Brunswicker pressed forward confidently and stamped with an appel; where the lead foot was beat on the ground to provoke a response from the opponent, but Paget remained firm. The Brunswicker tried again, and this time lurched forward with his body and cried out as if to scare Paget. To his shock the Lieutenant did indeed respond, but not with a flinch, but a lightning-fast timed cut that struck him smartly on the crown of his forehead.

He staggered back a little more in shock than anything else

as it was a quick strike rather than a particularly hard one. The Salford Rifles roared in support of their fighter, but the Brunswicker simply laughed as he got back to the fight. He went on the attack and launched a barrage of blows, but Paget parried them all, traversing out of the way as he landed a blow to the man's lead knee. A cheer echoed out once more as the Brunswickers began to look concerned and a little embarrassed for how easily the modest statured Lieutenant was beating their man.

They crossed singlesticks once more and had a better back and forth exchange. The Brunswicker closed off the space as Paget was backed up against some of the black-clad Germans. He traversed to get away once again against the more physically imposing man, but one of the Germans stuck out his leg, causing him to trip and fall. His opponent was on him in a frenzy, lashing down against him and striking Paget across the back as if it were a whip. Paget cried out from the blow.

Craven stormed forward with his cold steel raised, but Paget looked up. He held out his hand and cried out, "No!"

For he wanted to see this through. He got to his feet and shrugged off the pain as he came to guard once more. The Brunswicker had scored one blow to his two, and he would not let the underhanded German land another. The Brunswicker smirked at him, but Paget rushed forward furiously, and yet with precision. He struck out to draw the man into parries before thrusting to the Brunswicker's chest. The rigid singlesticks did not bend at all like a fencing foil would, and the blow took the wind out of his sails, but Paget was not done. He lashed an upward cut into the man's wrist which caused him to lose grip of his stick. Before it had even hit the ground, Paget wheeled the blade back around and struck an upward cut from the other side. It clipped his opponent's chin and opened a nasty cut there.

The Brunswicker looked furious as he felt for the blood flowing from the wound on his chin, which was as bruised as his ego. He growled angrily and rushed towards one of his associates who carried his live steel blade.

"Don't!" Craven cried out. The officer hesitated for a moment, "Not because I will kill you, but because he will." Craven looked to Paget, having complete confidence in his good friend.

Paget scooped up his adversary's singlestick and walked away without another word. Craven kept a keen eye on the Germans and a firm hand on his sabre should they attempt anything untoward, but they dared not do so. And so he went on to be by Paget's side, who was shaking with adrenaline and anger.

"I am sorry, Sir."

"For what precisely?"

"My conduct."

"Nobody here thinks less of you for it, I can assure you that."

"But I do," he muttered in disappointment with himself.

"You won the contest, and nobody was killed, except for perhaps that Brunswicker's pride," replied Matthys earnestly.

"What are we doing here, Sir?"

Paget was frustrated by their situation and lack of direction of purpose.

"Get in some rest. The enemy will soon be upon us, and we should have our strength."

"Attack? Here?" Paget looked back to the ruined bridge

with doubt.

"Perhaps not here, but the call to arms will arrive soon enough, and we need not wish for it to come sooner."

It was a rare thing for Craven to not want to seek out and relish a fight as soon as he could find it. Paget took note as they returned to their camp and settled in for a quiet day. Soon enough the fires were lit, and they made the most of what rations they had. The sun had not been down for long when many were heading for their beds, and though Paget did not look ready, he was soon convinced by Charlie as they went off together.

"The chap I knew would never sleep with a common soldier," muttered Bunce from where he sat by one of the fires.

It was a badly kept secret that Charlie was a woman in a man's uniform, but that didn't seem to bother him nearly as much as a gentleman mingling with the ranks, and yet he said it out of Paget's earshot.

"Nobody cares what you think." Ferreira sneered. He was looming in the background, his drab uniform not reflecting any of the firelight.

"**Perhaps you should. All of you, for things are done a certain way for good reason. Imagine what Wellington would do if he learned of this,**" replied Bunce arrogantly.

Ferreira strode up beside the Captain and leaned in over his shoulder.

"**If Wellington hears of this, then we shall know from whom he learnt of it. It would be a great betrayal, but Craven would never get his hands on you, and do you know why that is?**"

"Tell me why," he seethed.

"Because I would find you first."

Ferreira lifted a dagger that he had sneakily hung over Bunce's other shoulder and touched the cold steel to the man's throat. Bunce nearly jumped out of his skin but then froze as he felt the razor-sharp blade bite into his flesh.

"What is the meaning of this?"

But Ferreira would not let go. He held him in place with his other hand as a trickle of blood dripped over the bare steel.

"You listen to me, you little shit. There is not a soldier amongst the Salfords who would hesitate to kill you if you do harm to Mr Paget. I would give you a quick death, but I cannot say the same for all of them. He is most precious to us all, do you understand?"

Bunce was quivering.

"Yes, yes I do," he replied in horror.

Ferreira shoved him forward as he took the dagger away. He wiped the blood from it with a handkerchief before sheathing it upon his belt. He looked down on the sheepish Bunce.

"If you cannot fit in here, you should leave before it costs you your life."

Ferreira left without another word. Several of the Salford Rifles had witnessed the incident and now looked upon Bunce with disgust. The newly arrived Captain looked utterly powerless as he got up and left to find some solitude to save himself further humiliation.

Paget awoke after an uneasy sleep to find Charlie was still comfortably enjoying hers. He could not stop thinking about the duel he had partaken in the previous day. It should have been a friendly exchange, and yet it was anything but. He could not stop thinking about it. He was restless and finally climbed out of bed to go for a walk. There was little moonlight with which to see anything. What there was reflected from the river running beneath the ruined bridge and he felt drawn to it. Yet as he approached, he could see the Brunswickers on guard duty. Thirty of them protected the bridge whilst the others slept nearby. He stopped a two hundred yards short of them, for he did not want to create any trouble. He couldn't imagine he would be very welcome amongst the Brunswickers, and he could just make out the officer he had thoroughly beaten.

"You can't sleep either?"

Paget recognised the voice instantly. It was his old friend Bunce, who was sitting on a tree stump nearby.

"There is a lot on my mind."

"What you have done out here, I know of only a small amount of it, but it is quite incredible."

"I have only done my duty as best as I could," replied Paget modestly.

"I don't think anyone believes that is all you have done," smiled Bunce.

The first glimmer of sunlight was rising on the horizon as they gazed out upon it pensively. Bunce looked a little uncomfortable as though he struggled to find the words to apologise, but the courage eluded him, and so an uncomfortable silence followed. Yet after a few moments there was a warbling war cry from down by the river. It was as unsettling as it was surprising, as if some kind of monster was about to climb out from the water. Bunce shot to his feet as the two of them looked out towards the ruins of the bridge. There was a glimmer of movement from the water beside the bridge on the same side as they were before another cry rang out and a flurry of activity followed. The last remnants of moonlight glimmered from fixed bayonets of a mass of soldiers who rose out of the water like sea creatures. Not only did they wear no uniforms, but they wore no clothes at all. They charged stark naked at the Germans with their muskets and bayonets in their hands. It was a mesmerising and terrifying sight, the naked men crying out like demons as they charged against the Brunswickers.

"Come on!"

Paget ripped his sword from its scabbard and charged on to help with the defence. Bunce was most unsettled by the scene of the naked raiders, but he felt compelled to go after his friend. They had gotten halfway when the Brunswickers defence collapsed entirely without a fight. Even the officer Paget had fought with ran without ever having fired a shot nor clashed with the enemy with cold steel. Paget staggered to a halt, realising there was no hope. Along the bridge he could see masses of French infantry crossing with planks, ladders, and tools with which to complete the bridge once more. There would be no stopping them now as hundreds more French troops arrived at the banks on the far side. The naked Frenchmen danced about with glee as several fired shots triumphantly into the air and jeered at the fleeing Brunswickers, and towards Paget, too.

It was several more minutes before Craven arrived with a few others and halted beside Paget as he came to the same realisation. The enemy had captured the bridge, and there was nothing to be done for it. Long ladders were thrown over the collapsed bridge, and French soldiers ran along them to join their naked comrades, ensuring the riverbank was secure. Craven sighed but then smiled.

"What is it, Sir?" Paget was amazed he was not more disappointed.

"You have to admire the balls on them, don't you?"

He drew a few laughs, and the others soon joined in, but Paget looked at the French force with trepidation, knowing what it would mean. They would have to retreat yet again. It felt like all they did now was retreat, and yet there was nothing more for it. The enemy pursued them relentlessly across a vast area which they could most easily be encircled if they did not defend every road and bridge the enemy could approach. For Paget it was exhausting. He found himself yearning for a fight as Craven always had in a most surprising reversal of their roles.

CHAPTER 17

On they marched in another demoralised retreat. Made worse that they all knew they were now on the road to Salamanca and the place where they had routed the French army of Portugal. It felt like a huge step back and a far cry from the triumphant celebrations in Madrid, which was surely now being left to the enemy. For Hill could not hold back the vast French forces descending upon him. The Spanish capitol was only one hundred and twenty miles East of Salamanca. Just a few days' ride, and yet it felt so far from their grasp, despite the weeks they had spent there in triumphant jubilation. Major Spring rode up beside Craven, and it was a welcome arrival, for they were all clambering for news. Or at least news of something other than their retreat.

"What now?" Craven did not expect good news.

"I wish I could tell you, Major, but I do not know any better than any other man."

"You must know something?"

"In these wide-open lands Wellington got a true glimpse of the French army, and it was far greater than any of us could have imagined. The army we defeated at Salamanca is reborn and perhaps stronger than it was before, a remarkable achievement."

"You sound impressed."

"I am, and whilst I am not sure we have the strength to stand and fight, we have done one of the most important things Wellington sort to achieve this year."

"Yes? And what is that?" Craven could not seem to find a positive outlook in the situation. Spring laughed at his grumpy attitude.

"My dear, Craven, the French armies here in Spain coming together might seem a worrying prospect, but I think you have forgotten your instincts and not considered why they have done this. The French are greatly threatened by us, so much so that they have amassed all their grand armies here with which to meet us."

"But how is that any use if we cannot defeat that monster they have created?"

"Because those French armies have been pulled from all across Spain, and every day they spend chasing and opposing Wellington is a day with which the guerrillas act against French-held territory with impunity. Every day our Spanish allies wreak havoc all across this country. We do not need to defeat this grand French army. All we must do is not lose our own."

Craven shrugged as if he had awoken from a slumber. He realised that all was not lost, in fact far from it, very little was truly lost.

"All we must do is survive, so that we may go on next season?"

"Yes!" Spring cried out excitedly.

Craven breathed a sigh of relief.

"I had thought a retreat would spell disaster, that we might march on all the way to England."

"But has there been a defeat? We have withdrawn but we have not been defeated."

"And if we winter after this, what will it do for morale?"

"A humiliating year for France, and Napoleon is most preoccupied in his latest endeavour. As long as this army makes it to winter quarters, then this year will be nothing short of an outstanding victory, the same victory all felt after turning the enemy at Salamanca."

"We march there now. I fear we would not fare so well a second time if the enemy are as strong as you say."

"Four armies now descend upon Salamanca in what could be the largest battle of this war, but it must only be fought if we can be certain of victory."

"And you are not?"

"I am not," he admitted.

Craven could see it was a huge risk. The enemy pursued them relentlessly, eager for revenge and to regain some of the dignity they had lost after their first bitter defeat at Salamanca.

"A lot of blood has been spilled across that ground," Craven mused as he remembered the body of General Le Marchant. He was just one of many soldiers who had fallen during the battle, but none symbolised the losses more than he did, "Survive? That is all we must do?"

"For now, yes indeed. All we must do is reach the safety

of our winter quarters and we shall have our victory. Craven felt an overwhelming relief. It had seemed all was lost, and yet now he realised this was merely all posturing to save the army for the next campaigning season.

"Next year will be a big one, won't it?"

"Was this one not?" Spring replied in surprise.

Craven nodded in agreement as he lifted his head high upon the realisation that this was not defeat. Far from it.

"Keep your men in good spirits and ready to fight, just like the rest of the army. If we must do battle in these coming days and weeks, then by God we will, but the survival of this army is more important than anything else."

"Yes, Sir."

For many days they marched on until finally Wellington and Hill's army combined with much jubilation. For together, they had more than fifty thousand British and Portuguese soldiers and over ten thousand Spanish, too. It was a vast force which Wellington rarely commanded all at once, and yet the question on so many minds. Was it enough? The population of the city welcomed the army once again, but this time hesitantly and with trepidation. Madrid had been abandoned and they feared the same. There was no shortage of wine and other liquor, and no amount of discipline would keep the troops from consuming it as many took up quarters in the city itself. Others erected canvas cantonments beyond the city limits.

Craven sighed as he sat down at the same bar where he had enjoyed some drinks before the assault of the forts in the city, in what felt like a year ago. A dread loomed over them all. They knew the enemy were coming, and it was only a question of how many days it would be until they had to face the French force.

"Sir?" Paget sat down opposite Craven.

"Yes?"

"Sir, some say the French army is twice our number, is that true?"

Craven shrugged.

"But, Sir…"

"I don't know," snapped Craven, "I know only what I have heard the same as you!"

Paget looked like a scolded puppy, and Craven appeared to be mortified that he had caused it, realising what he had done.

"I understand, Sir," added Paget in recognition of his regret, "But what of what Major Spring had to say, Sir? Was that not good news? That we will fight on for next season?"

"Yes, but we have to make it to next season first."

Craven knew how much was at stake and how easily they could lose it all. He turned his attention away from the misery that was the almighty French force bearing down upon them, as he looked to Paget and thought back to the events that had unfolded whilst they had been apart. The bitter loss of Nooth was not so fresh now and so Craven took his chance to pry.

"Why did you go after Bouchard?"

"Because you told us to, Sir," Paget replied without hesitation.

"You know better than any how dangerous that man is, and yet still you went?"

"All of war is dangerous, but we pick our moments to strike whenever we can. Timing is everything. That is what you taught me."

"And you do not regret it?"

Paget shook his head.

"I deeply regret the loss of Nooth, but I did not kill him. That bastard Bouchard did."

Craven was relieved to hear it.

"I should not have put a warrant on Bouchard's head."

"Yes, Sir, yes you should have. Bouchard is not just an enemy soldier, he is a spy, and one who has dealt a great deal of damage to this war effort. Any chance to remove him from this war should be taken," insisted Paget boldly.

"But I didn't do it for the war. I did it for me."

"Can a man not do something for himself and for the war simultaneously, Sir? Is that not Birback in his entirety?"

Craven chuckled, content to have the mood lightened.

"I am only sorry that I could not end him," declared Paget passionately.

"Do you think you could have?"

"I know I could. I let a moment of weakness stop me."

"That moment of weakness has a name, doesn't it?"

Craven gestured towards Bunce. Paget did not look comfortable naming and shaming him, but he could not deny it.

"He is not a weak man, far from it, but he has not seen this war for all that it is. A few years ago, I would have been just the same."

"We have all made mistakes and missed opportunities. Let us just be sure we do not repeat them, hey?"

"Yes, Sir."

Days went by as the anticipation and dread continued to build until finally the orders came just as they expected. The army was soon on the move, but it was not going far. They found themselves forming up in the same positions to the East of the city where they had faced Marmont earlier that year. It had been a such a crushing and decisive victory as few could ever imagine they would have to fight over the same ground again. Yet that is precisely where they were forming up. There was a feeling of dread throughout the army, not just that they might lose, but that it might undo all of the work they had achieved over that ground months before. Craven's thoughts turned to General Le Marchant once more, and he felt sick that his sacrifice could be for nothing if they were defeated on the same ground in which the General had fallen.

A day passed as they slept in place on the hilltops, but the next day Craven was called to Wellington's side. He approached with Paget next to him. They found their Commander looking out from a great vantage point, but as they reached him, they got their first full glimpse of the enemy force and its vastness. Paget felt a little faint at the sight of it.

"My God," he gasped as he looked out upon the vast force.

"Indeed," agreed Wellington.

"You called for me, Sir?" Craven asked.

"I did."

"What can I do for you, Sir?"

"The enemy are ninety thousand or more to our fifty thousand and a little over ten thousand Spanish. The enemy are more than a match for us."

"Yes, Sir."

"What would you do, Major?"

Craven took a deep breath. It was a lot of pressure on his shoulders, and yet he already knew his answer.

"I would not fight a battle I could not win, not if I had any other choice."

Wellington nodded in agreement, as Paget looked back and forth at the massive armies which were formed on either side. He could see only a small part of their own army. They were spread out over hills and through woods, whereas he could see a great deal of the enormous French force assembled below them. They had a great advantage in position, but it seemed like it would not be nearly enough to make a difference against the French.

"Sir, a defeat will achieve nothing, but the survival of this army could mean everything," added Paget without having been asked.

But down below them the enemy was already assembling to do battle.

"We may not have a choice," replied Wellington.

But just as he finished, a drop of rain hit the General's face, and then more followed before a torrential rainfall began. They stayed out in it for a few moments before it worsened further, and Wellington led them to a canvas shelter that had been erected from which they could watch the enemy. The rain lashed the enemy army, but more than that, it hammered down upon the ground before the two armies for hour after hour.

"Just like Agincourt," smiled Paget.

That was a great victory which every Briton would so very much wish to relive as the ground before them turned to a quagmire; just as it had done on that fateful day where French knights had been shot and beaten down into the thick mud and thoroughly defeated by a far smaller force. Paget let himself dream for a moment that they might relive that experience and utterly demolish a French army just as King Henry had. But the enemy made no attempt to advance as the rain continued relentlessly all day. Both armies spent a miserable day and night in place as they waited to do battle, or at least for the other side to initiate it. Just as it had been the last time, they were on the heights East of Salamanca. The French would have to make the first move, for Wellington would not advance out of his strong position until the enemy was spread thin and weakened.

Campfires provided little relief that night as the rain did not let up, and everyone was soaked through and covered in mud. Bunce took a seat beside Paget as they both shivered in the horrible conditions. It was November and winter was fast approaching. It was not the time to be out at night in such weather, and yet they had no choice.

"I am sorry," declared Bunce.

Paget shrugged as if he did not know what his old friend was referring to.

"I am sorry that I made you doubt yourself. I cannot condone what you were going to do to Major Bouchard, and nothing will change my mind, but it was wrong to interrupt you in that moment. I should have made my objections before the enemy were in sight or held my tongue until long after."

"Yes, you should have. Bouchard is a monster, and he must die, by any means that are necessary. You didn't know what he had done, what he is capable of," reflected Paget unapologetically.

"I know more now than I did, for I have spoken with many about him."

Paget's anger faded a little as he became curious.

"You asked the men?"

"I did. You and the Major trust these common soldiers as

if they were gentlemen. I do not understand it, but I am trying to."

Paget nodded in agreement.

"I did not understand it either, not until I lived it. But the common soldier and the officer is not so different. We might speak differently, but in our hearts, there is little difference. There are good and bad ones wherever you look, and these soldiers Major Craven has assembled are the very best of men, many of them far braver, more honest and more decent than many a Lord," Paget went on in defence of his companions.

"Would you have shot him dead if I had not delayed it?"

"Yes, and if I had another chance there is not a thing you or anyone could say that would make me hesitate for a second. I trusted my gut to pursue Bouchard, and I should have seen it through."

"If you get another chance, I will stand with you."

"You would? And what of your conscience?"

"There are things in war and in this service which we do not understand. When Lord Wellington makes an order, we do not question it, for we have faith in his command. I have not seen all the things you have, and it pains me to say that I have but a tiny amount of the experience you have, BP. It made me feel small and I am ashamed to say it, but there it is."

"There is no shame in an apology."

Bunce nodded in agreement.

"I know it must have been a lot for you to accept, but the next time something happens like that with Bouchard, I need you to trust me."

"And I will."

"But don't stop holding me to a higher standard. Come to

me, and tell me your thoughts, whether you think I will like them or not. Not one of us should be above reproach, not even Major Craven."

"You would speak out against the Major?"

"Certainly, and I have many times, as have many others, and he would listen to your concerns, too, once you have the Major's respect."

"And how do I get it?"

"Fight for us. Not just for the King and Wellington. Show the Major you fight for each and every one of those who stand and fight beside you. Be the soldier you would want to have by your side."

Bunce nodded in agreement as he snivelled at the prospect, for he felt most out of place and out of sorts, and the cold and damp weather was only making it worse.

"Will we fight tomorrow, do you think?" he finally asked as he tried to move on and do as Paget suggested.

"I should hope not, for I do not believe we can win."

"No? I never would have thought you would doubt in Lord Wellington."

"I do not, but that does not mean he can achieve the impossible."

"Is our situation so dire, do you think?"

"I know it is. I have seen the French army. It is almost twice the size of our own."

Bunce looked horrified.

"I had heard rumours, but…" he gasped.

"It does not matter. All that matters is that this army lives to see the next season."

Bunce looked stunned.

"What?"

"It is true."

"I thought we were fighting to win this war."

"Yes, but it will not be done this year. The army is exhausted, soldiers and horses alike. We have campaigned all year. We began early in the harshest of conditions through the snow and ice, and now men and animals alike are exhausted and malnourished. We must reach safety and rebuild through this winter, or all that we achieved this year will have been for nothing."

"Is it not for nothing now? For we give up all the ground that we gained."

"It might seem it, but so much of Spain is free. Lands to the South which you have not seen. We dreamed for so much this year, and we should not be disheartened to only have achieved some of those dreams."

Bunce smiled.

"What is it?"

"Nothing. Just that I do not recognise the boy I once knew. You have changed so much, and yet the optimism remains. Remarkable after all you have seen."

"That is what we fight for."

"I do not begin to understand many things that you have done, and I know I do not agree with much of it, but the fact you stand so strongly for what you believe is something to admire."

"My father would not think so," sighed Paget.

"He is not the one here fighting this war, is he?"

"He is not," smiled Paget.

They made themselves as comfortable as they could in the

constant drizzle and sodden ground. The next day was little better, as the sun could not be seen through the dense cloud cover and the ground had not dried at all. Any hope of a French advance had been lost as there would be no overcoming the swampy ground, but they could hear the clatter of Wellington's baggage train move on towards Ciudad Rodrigo. The two young officers went out to a vantage point where they could see Craven and Matthys gazing out into the distance. The enemy beyond had a lazy start to the morning with little enthusiasm for an advance.

"They will not come, Sir, will they?" Bunce asked of Craven.

"No. They fear a repeat of the last encounter and the defeat it would be if they fought up these muddy slopes."

"Then we are saved."

Craven turned in surprise, but then looked to Paget to realise how the new Captain had come to the conclusion with help.

"It is a blessing in disguise. For this dreadful weather has saved us from a battle we could not win."

"What will we do now, Sir?"

"Make our way for Rodrigo and regain our strength."

"A shame to give up this ground."

Craven shrugged.

"It matters not. If we do not make battle here, then this meeting of these two armies will be forgotten to history, for it does not matter. All that matters is the next battle, not one that could have been."

"Sir?"

"What is it?"

"Sir, Mr Paget went after Major Bouchard on your orders, and I truly believe he would have been successful were it not for my interference. My sincerest apologies."

Craven nodded in agreement, as he looked into the Captain's eyes to see that he genuinely meant it.

"I once had a chance to kill Bouchard. I had but to lunge forward and plunge my sword into that man, and it would all have been over, and yet I too hesitated. The reasons for which do not matter, but I regret it, and I think of it often. But the truth is I cannot change it, and neither can you. All that matters now is what you do going forward."

"Yes, Sir," replied Bunce appreciatively.

"I will say this, though. Trust in Paget, for I do not know a man who thinks and worries more about each and every action he makes than Mr Paget. If you are to trust the instinct of any man first and foremost, it must be him."

"I will, Sir, I will," promised Bunce.

"He is out there somewhere, isn't he, Sir?" Paget asked as he thought of Bouchard.

"Yes, waiting and looking for his moment to strike."

"We shall be ready for him," declared Bunce.

Craven smiled.

"Nobody is ready for Bouchard. He is a shadow."

"Then we shall be your lamp, Sir."

"You will?" Craven asked in surprise.

"Yes, Sir. You say I should trust in Mr Paget, and I do, and he believes in you as much as he does Lord Wellington. I admit that I did not understand why, but I am starting to see it, and any doubts will be set aside by my trust in Paget. I am here for you, Major, to hell and back and through anything."

"I'll hold you to it, as will every other man in this unit."

"Yes, Sir, and I to them," agreed Bunce.

"Then there is hope for you yet," smiled Craven.

Paget punched his old friend lightly on the arm in a friendly gesture of appreciation.

Orders echoed out along the lines. Orders to march and retreat as they had all been waiting for. There was a sense of relief but also sadness, for many wanted to fight even knowing they could not win.

"It is over, then. The Campaign of the year is done," declared Bunce.

"Not until we have marched to safety. It is more than fifty miles to the safety of Rodrigo, across difficult terrain, and with an army this size it will be no easy thing. And the enemy will harass us at every turn. A great battle may not have come, but now we must battle for the survival of this army all the way. We must run the gauntlet," declared Craven.

CHAPTER 18

"Get on, you wretch!" Wellington roared at a junior officer sitting at the side of the road, being without a horse and having to march on foot with the common soldiers.

It was a humiliating scene for the disgruntled young man who picked himself up and went on. Wellington continued to rave about him as Craven approached.

"The greatest knaves and worst soldiers I have ever encountered or read of!" Wellington cried.

But many of the soldiers passing by felt the same animosity towards their commander for not letting them have a chance at the enemy. Wellington growled loudly before riding on and crying out his derision and fury to many more along the way. Major Spring rode up beside Craven as he noticed the concern on his face.

"He rages at loyal men who have marched many hundreds of miles and overcome battle after battle," declared Craven.

"Yes."

Craven was surprised by the admission.

"He would break the morale of the soldiers who have followed him throughout?"

Spring looked concerned as he peaked about to see who was listening before going on quietly.

"Wellington's anger masks his anxiety. For there is much to fear."

"More than the enemy giving chase to us now?"

"Moscow has fallen, and some rumours and reports say that the Czar might capitulate. If it is true, then Wellington commands the only army in all of Europe still capable of defeating the French. This hungry and bedraggled bunch are all that stands between Napoleon and complete domination, and Wellington is responsible for it all. For this is the only army of Britain, and its loss would not just end the war here in Spain, it would bring down our government and mark the end of it all."

Craven gasped in horror as it was a lot to place on their shoulders.

"I had no idea the situation was so dire."

"It could be, and we hang on a knife's edge."

"I told my men we were running a gauntlet here to get back to Rodrigo, but I had no idea how true that was."

"We must survive this march. We cannot lose this army. We cannot turn and fight, and we cannot afford any mistakes. The future of the world depends on the survival of this army now. The army retreats across multiple roads, scattered and vulnerable. French cavalry pursue us and harass us at every turn. They must not be let to hinder us, do you understand?"

"I do," agreed Craven.

"Wellington will not admit it, but he needs assistance, and your methods are just what is needed. Give them hell, Major."

"Yes, Sir."

Spring rode on.

"On me!" Craven pulled his mounted troops out of the column. Gamboa approached at the head of the rest.

"Stay with the army, and ensure they get to Rodrigo."

"Yes, Sir!" Gamboa ordered them out of the line to assist with a rearguard action on foot.

"Is the situation so dire?" Paget had been listening in throughout.

"Pray it is not, but go on as if it is," replied Craven as he led them on.

He had just thirty mounted infantry by his side, but they rode on to the rear as they sought out the enemy. It was not long before they could hear the crack of pistol and carbine fire as the British cavalry did what they could to slow down the French advance.

"What are our intentions, Sir?"

Craven sighed as he rode on a little further before drawing them to a halt so that he could address them.

"Listen to me very carefully," he declared solemnly, "The situation across Europe is perhaps the most dire it has ever been. The survival of this army is the most important thing in the world now. We must stop the enemy from reaching our boys. It is a four-to-five-day march to Rodrigo. If this army survives, then hope remains, but if it is lost, then the war may be lost with it. We must do everything in our power to stop the French inflicting damage or slowing down this march."

"Point us at 'em!" Charlie yelled.

"Yeah!" Birback roared in support.

Similar sentiments followed as the whole party cried out in agreement.

"Follow me!"

Craven turned his horse about and rode on towards the sound of gunfire. It did not take long to find a skirmish ongoing between French and British cavalry amongst a wood where they could not easily manoeuvre. Craven rode up to within a hundred yards before bringing them to a halt and took out his rifle.

"Pick your shots well! Fire at will!"

Rifle fire cracked out and powder smoke filled the wood. A dozen French cavalrymen were down in a rippling volley, and as the mounted riflemen began to reload, the Frenchmen turned and fled. For they would not stand against another volley of accurate fire, but Craven hurried to reload. The British cavalry officer saluted in appreciation towards them as they rode on to give chase to the enemy.

Musket and pistol fire rippled out in all directions as enemy cavalry squadrons looked for any opening or weakness amongst the British rearguard. Craven slung his loaded rifle onto his back and rode on as they hunted their next target. He led them on to a ridge line where they paused and looked out in astonishment at the vast French army winding its way towards them like four giant dragons.

"Craven!"

He turned to see Bouchard himself atop a horse as it reared up in the distance. He had twenty other mounted men by his side, and for once they wore their military uniforms and were not hiding in the shadows. Though that was more likely so as to not be shot by their own side as guerrillas than through any sense of pride and decency. Bouchard rode forward across the two hundred yards between the two as he came to do battle.

"Make ready!"

Craven formed his mounted riflemen up and had them prepare their weapons.

"Present!"

Bouchard looked in horror at the bristling line of rifles. He had expected a single combat, but Craven had no time or care for it as he was done playing games.

"Fire!"

The line of rifles erupted into a cloud of powder smoke. Paget had been aiming for Bouchard himself as he was determined to not miss a second time, but as he squeezed the trigger, he noticed Bouchard pull back on his reins. He grabbed one of his comrades which he pulled in front of him to use as a shield. The cloud of black powder smoke obscured any sight between the two sides as Craven ripped his double-barrelled pistol from its holster in readiness to shootdown any Frenchman who made it through the smoke. But they could hear the coughs, splutters, and cries of the wounded, and as the cloud lifted, they saw the devastation of their accurate rifle fire. Half of the Frenchman's men had been blasted from their saddles. Several lay dead and many were wounded and looked worse for wear. Bouchard was unharmed. For the man he had pulled in front of him had been struck by three balls which were meant for him. He looked in disgust and despair as Craven went on to reload his rifle to take another shot. It was clear that if he remained, he would be shot dead, and so as they gathered up their wounded and fled.

Paget cried out in triumph, for it felt like a great victory to see Bouchard's back as he ran from them. Cheering and laughter echoed out at his expense.

"You better run!" Craven roared as he finished loading his rifle before slinging it over his back ready for the next engagement.

"What was he expecting?" Bunce asked in surprise at the French charge against superior numbers.

"He expected us to run," replied Paget.

"Why?"

"Because if you knew more about him, you would have run," admitted Paget, for the fear of the formidable French officer remained.

"It is not the last we shall see of him I fear," added Matthys.

"Let him come," seethed Craven.

All the fear he had felt towards the terrifying French officer had faded away. Bouchard was a wonderfully skilled fighter, and yet the hold he had over men from the fear he struck to their hearts and stomachs was the secret weapon that made him so magnificent. Craven could see it now as he watched Bouchard flee in fear for his life.

"His time will come," insisted Matthys.

But pistol fire soon drew their attention to action off to their flank as cavalry squadrons battled it out just five hundred yards away in open ground.

"On me!"

Craven drew out his sabre and led them on. Paget raced to be by his side, and yet Bunce got ahead of him, even whilst riding Augustus. The young Captain weas eager to gain the respect and trust of both of them. He rode in parallel with

Craven as they darted in against a unit of French cavalry. Bunce did not even slow down as he galloped with the point of his sword out in front like a lance. He buried it in the chest of one of the enemy before letting his arm swing back as he galloped on. The speed and motion retrieved his blade and left his opponent to collapse dead in the saddle and slumping down to the ground. Paget looked impressed but had no time to celebrate as a sabre swung for his head. He slowed Augustus down and parried the blow in the hanging guard position before reaching for his opponent's sword arm. He took a hold of it and brought his own sword about, thrusting through the man's shoulder. He cried out but slumped down with the sword still in his body, causing Paget to lose hold of it. At the same time the Frenchman's heavy sabre fell into his lap, and so he took it in hand ready to defend himself and fight on.

A cut was swung for him, and he lifted the sabre instinctively. It felt twice the weight of his sword, and it probably wasn't far shy of that figure. He barely got it in place and flinched as the swords made contact. Such a quick and feeble parry with his own sword would have been blown through by a heavy cut, but to his amazement the strike stopped dead as if it had struck a stone wall. The heavy sabre in his hands had taken all the weight of the blow with little effort from his own body, and he marvelled as the experience. But another blow came from the same man, and he was forced to move his sword to the other side to parry that. He tried to counter with a cut after it, but the huge blade was slow and clumsy in his hands and was easily parried.

The exchange went on with slow and predictable blows that both men parried until Paget remembered the point and plunged it into the man's chest, finding it almost as quick as his lighter blade. He gasped with relief as his little contest was over, and he looked around for his sword. He could see no sign of the man whose body it was embedded in. There was a glimmer of movement he noticed out of the corner of his eye, and he looked up at a sabre swinging for his head as if to take it off. He struggled to lift the heavy French sabre to protect himself, but it was unbearably slow in his hands. Yet another sword slashed down against his attacker's and knocked it aside just in time. That sword was in the hands of Bunce who engaged Paget's attacker for him. Paget looked relieved as he watched on, but soon noticed his old friend was struggling against the weight of the blows being lashed down against him.

"Oy!" Paget cried angrily as he spurred Augustus forward to help his old friend who had saved him from certain death. He lashed down heavy if clumsy blows on the Frenchman. They had little chance of finding an opening, but the pressure opened one for Bunce who thrust his sword home against the Frenchman. Cries echoed out as the French cavalry parted from them and fled. They looked for a weakness in the British lines, and yet they found only strength as they were resisted at every turn.

"Thank you," said Paget to his old friend.

"No need, for you would do the same."

They watched as the French cavalry fled, but Paget leapt from his horse and frantically looked around for any sign of his sword or the man who it had been left in.

"What are you doing?"

To Craven it looked as though he were attempting to loot the bodies, and he was the last one they would expect it from.

"My sword, Sir, my sword."

"Where did you leave it?"

"In one of the enemy, Sir."

Craven knew how much the sword meant to him as it was a bond he had felt throughout his life. He leapt from his horse to help in the search, but it was not long before they had scoured through all of the bodies to no avail. Paget looked out to the fleeing Frenchman as he realised the man had ridden off with it still in his body. He looked distraught as he looked at the heavy French sabre in his hands and cast it to the ground in disgust.

Craven did not hesitate for a moment. He went to his horse and took out his beloved Andrea Ferrara, paced over to the Lieutenant, and thrust it into his hands. Paget was stunned, for he had the pleasure of using the beautiful sword only once before and did not imagine himself so lucky to do so again.

"But, Sir?" Paget felt uncomfortable being the guardian of such a sword.

"You cannot ride with us without a sword, and I won't have you struggle with that French rubbish."

Paget smiled as his protests were half-hearted as he very much wanted to wield the blade. He drew it just a few inches from its scabbard to marvel at the broad hollow ground diamond section blade. It was near twice the breadth of his own but barely any heavier. The hollow grind had removed so much mass from the blade without compromising any rigidity.

"Thank you, Sir."

He hooked it onto his sword belt and tucked his own sword's scabbard into his saddle in the hope that he might one day retrieve it and re-unite them. He patted Augustus gently before leaping back into the saddle and looked across to notice Birback was still in the saddle, despite there being bodies he could have looted.

"You do not look for booty?"

"There is a time for it, but it is not now. If we cannot save this army, then it is all over," he lamented.

Paget was not sure if he was genuinely concerned for the war effort or just that an end to the war might mean an end to the looting he enjoyed so much. Paget smiled as he liked to think it as the former, and yet knew there was a good chance it was the latter.

Craven led them on to a vantage point from where they could see across a broad valley. The French pressed across a great front looking for any weakness as Wellington's army continued to march in the gruelling conditions. It was a miserable time, and few of the soldiers they came across looked particularly happy with their fate. Yet Craven could not blame them, for they did not know all that he knew. To most of the British army it felt worse than a defeat, having not even been given a chance to seek victory.

Back and forth they chased the French cavalry whilst giving ground to larger forces in a cat and mouse game day after day. On the third day the fatigue was truly setting in for both sides, as the horses were exhausted and went on at a leisurely pace. Ciudad Rodrigo was in sight now, and the French efforts to pursue and harass them became half-hearted at best. There were no more charges nor darting gallops to look for some advantage as cavalrymen on both sides exchanged pistol and carbine fire, but little came of it.

Fires were soon lit, as Craven and his party made camp for what they knew would be the last night before reaching the safety of the fortified city of Ciudad Rodrigo. It was an anxious night, as all knew that if the French were to make one final great effort against them it would have to be now. They sat quietly about a single fire, fearing what might come. Eight remained on duty as pickets at all times, out in the darkness on their own in the cold.

Birback coughed as he got to his feet, deliberately drawing attention to himself.

"Sometime to say?" Craven asked.

"Aye."

"Well go on, spit it out."

As much as he didn't imagine the Scotsman had anything useful to say, he welcomed the end of the uneasy silence.

Birback groaned as he got up and looked a little sheepish as if he were uncomfortable or embarrassed, which was a most unusual sight for Craven and anyone else who knew him well.

"I…I…" he stuttered.

"Spit it out, man."

"Okay." He took a deep breath before letting it all out, "I didn't come here to Spain or put on this uniform for the best of reasons. Truth is, I don't know why I did, probably because I couldn't think of anything else to do. Running from the enemy to hide through the winter might not feel good to many of you, but think of the year ahead, and the years now behind us. There is not a place I would rather be. So long as we still live and fight together, the French are losing this war, and we are winning at life."

Matthys shook his head and was almost in tears in shock at the poetic words of the ruffian. A few others grumbled in agreement whilst many were just as stunned and speechless as Matthys. Charlie shot up and patted the Scotsman on the back.

She took over before anyone could find their words and went on with a smile.

"My life here in Portugal and Spain was a miserable one before I put on this uniform. Not many officers would have allowed it, but here we are, thriving."

A cheer rang out as she sat down, but Amyn now stepped up to speak, which drew particular attention. For he was never one to speak many words at all, let alone willingly address them.

"I lost my home, my land, my people. I lost everything. But I found something new here amongst all of you, and I thank you for guiding me on a new path."

Ellis shot up to take over.

"I thought I joined Craven to run and hide from what I was." He looked down at his officer's uniform, which he had long given up until recent events, "I thought I joined Craven and the Salfords so that I could be invisible, and for a time that was true. But the truth is, this time here amongst you has allowed me to be whatever I needed to be, and now it has led me to the love of my life. I never thought I would put on this tunic ever again, but for her, and for all of you, I do."

Paget led an enthusiastic cheer as Ferreira was next up.

"I hated this job, and I certainly never signed up to fight, but the times we live in are quite exceptional. You helped me find my courage, and in turn have given me the skills and strength to fight for my country. We might now fight across Spain, but my country will not be safe until the French are driven not just from Portugal but also Spain, and so this is still my fight and a fight for my country. Thank you for dragging me kicking and screaming in the right direction."

He drew a great many laughs as he sat down. "Go on, get

up there," insisted Charlie as she poked at Craven.

He begrudgingly got to his feet and looked around. The misery and sadness that had been on their faces had faded away, and he was now gazing upon gleaming smiles amid a great boost to morale.

"You have all said it so well, and I do not want to repeat what has already been said better than I can do it, so I will just say this. I could not hope for better friends to be by my side. I could not even dream of it, for I never thought it possible, and I would run any gauntlet with you, because I know we would come out the other side of it stronger than ever before."

A cheer rang out as they settled down in good spirits. Not even the miserable weather and threat of ninety thousand Frenchmen pursuing them could ruin the mood.

The next morning, they were on the road once more, but in far greater spirits than they had been, which could not be said for much of Wellington's army. Discipline and order had broken down completely as much of the army wandered on with no drill nor formation. Drunkenness was rife, a large number continuing to drink as they plodded on, and even many of the officers amongst them had no will left to instil discipline. The army was broken, and they could only hope that it could reach safety and rebuild.

"Sir, Sir, General Paget, Sir!" cried out a junior officer who had a deep cut on his face and rode an exhausted horse up to Craven.

"What has happened?" demanded Craven, for he knew how grave a situation this was, for the man spoke of General Edward Paget, one of Wellington's senior commanders.

"He was caught unsuspecting by French cavalry, Sir."

"Where was his escort?"

"He had none, Sir."

Craven growled angrily for the carelessness of the situation.

"Where was this? Show me!"

"That way, Sir," pointed the officer.

"Come on!" Craven led his party on to attempt a rescue. They rode on with the bleeding officer leading them.

Craven looked to Lieutenant Paget.

"Any relation?"

"No, Sir, same as the first time you asked me some years back," insisted Paget.

They rode on as fast as their weary horses would take them.

"There!" cried the bloodied officer.

Fifty French dragoons rode on ahead with the General under guard. He had only one arm just like Nelson, which must have made it near impossible to put up much of a fight, and yet it would not have mattered when he was so severely outnumbered. Moxy took up his rifle.

"No, you could hit the General!" Matthys growled.

Moxy was disgruntled, but even he knew it was a risk shooting at mounted troops on the move when there was one of their own amongst them. Craven drew out his sabre in readiness to make a charge.

"Are we doing this, Sir?" Paget asked in amazement.

"We must do everything to save the General!" Bunce insisted without any care for the risks.

But they watched in horror as another fifty French dragoons rode up over the crest ahead of them to join with the first party. Craven shrugged it off as if it mattered not.

"We can't do this." Matthys rode in and took the reins of Craven's horse.

"Unhand me," growled Craven.

"It is done, and nothing can change that. Throwing away our lives will not improve matters."

"Come on, what are you waiting for!"

Bunce went forward, wheeling about several times as he swung his sword about in the air, trying to rally some support for a charge, but nobody would move without Craven's say-so.

"The General cannot be saved."

"Matthys is right. I hate to say it, but he is right," added Paget.

Craven growled angrily as the General was led away in what felt like a painful reflection on the campaign. For so much was being lost before their eyes, and there was nothing that they could do to change it.

"Will you do nothing?" Bunce demanded angrily.

Craven looked to his friends. Many were still bandaged from their wounds and exhausted from a long campaign. He had to let this go and he knew it.

"I wish that I could."

"He is right there!"

"Wellington is trying to save this army, and that is what we must do now, too."

Accepting defeat was a heart wrenching feeling. It made him feel sick to his stomach, but it was the best of a bad set of choices. He imagined it was just how Wellington felt having to retreat over so much of the ground they had fought so hard to secure. He turned his horse about and led them away, knowing many would be as angry and disappointed in him as the army was of Wellington.

"But…" began Bunce.

"Not another word," snarled Paget.

They turned about and rode on, leaving the General to his fate just as they were leaving Northern Spain to the French. They rode on without any more signs of the enemy who had given up their pursuit as they drew nearer to Ciudad Rodrigo, the old walled fortress city which had put up such a fight against them earlier in the year. Much of the scars had been repaired since then as the fortification was repaired to serve against any French threat. Not only was it a formidable fortress, but it remained one of the two keys between Portugal and Spain.

They rode into a tented camp to find the disgruntled army looking somewhat relieved to be off the road and within the safety of the city, though the exhaustion was plain to see. Uniforms were faded and ragged. Shoes were worn through and falling apart. For many it had been a ten-month continuous season of campaigning over many hundreds of miles and some of the most challenging battles that one could imagine. Major Spring was waiting to greet them as they made their way for the city.

"I am sorry to say you will find no space. You will have to make camp here," he declared as the huge army had invaded the city.

Craven groaned as he gestured towards Matthys to see to it.

"General Paget, the enemy have him."

"You know for certain?"

"I saw it with my own eyes. If there was anything I could

have done, I would have."

"A dark day all around," Spring said quietly.

"Indeed, but we will be back."

"I must deliver this news to Wellington, though I wish I could save him from it."

"Major?"

"Yes?" he sighed.

"We live to fight another day, and fight we shall," insisted Craven.

Spring nodded in appreciation as he went on.

Craven followed his comrades on as Matthys found them some flat ground at the edge of the camp which looked peaceful and within easy reach of firewood. They began to assemble the camp as fires were started, though it was a miserable experience to imagine spending a winter under canvas.

"We will find better quarters soon," insisted Craven as he sat down beside a fire that Moxy had got going. Hours passed into the evening, and they began to settle as they made the most of the last hour of sunlight.

"James Craven!"

Whoever had shouted was so loud it brought hundreds of soldiers to silence. There was such anger in the voice that it drew all eyes. Craven's face turned to stone for a moment as he recognised it instantly. He shot up to see a lone cloaked and hooded figure in the field between their camp and the wood which fuelled their fire. Nobody could see the man's face, but Craven knew who it was, for he would recognise Bouchard's sinister tone anywhere and anytime. He pulled back his hood for the rest of them to see with many gasping in horror. Moxy and Paget both reached for their rifles.

"No," Craven ordered.

"But, Sir?"

"I said no, Mr Paget."

Craven stepped out in front of his comrades. Bouchard was standing defiantly before several hundred soldiers who would gladly see him dead and had the weapons to do so, and yet he showed no fear.

"You sent an assassin to shoot me dead, didn't you?"

"I did," replied Craven unapologetically.

"Because you are a coward who would not face me!"

But Craven did not rise to the occasion and remained calm.

"No, because you mean nothing to me. I do not care how you die, only that you do."

"Then come and see to it by your own hand!" Bouchard cried angrily.

It was the most emotional they had ever seen the Frenchman who was typically so stoic and methodical, even sadistic in how calm he was whilst dishing out death and destruction. Yet he sounded unhinged and desperate now, unlike Craven who was as calm as he could be.

"Are you not man enough to face me in single combat!"

Craven took a deep breath before storming forward.

"Sir!" Paget yelled.

"Do not try to stop me!" He looked back at the Lieutenant.

"No, Sir."

Paget had no intention of doing so as he drew out the Andrea Ferrara blade from his sword belt and presented it in both hands to Craven, who marvelled at the blade that was like an old friend. He took it as he unhooked his sabre belt and passed it to Paget before going on. Bouchard smirked as he cast off his cloak to reveal he still wore his French officer's tunic beneath. Both took off their tunics and cast them aside. Bouchard drew out his sword, an agile and straight cut and thrust blade not unlike Craven's.

The two men faced off at twenty yards, both with their swords hanging low by their sides, as if to show no fear of the other. Yet the dynamic was different than every other time they had met. For Craven no longer feared him. Bouchard's aurora which he so carefully fostered had fallen away, and now they would fight as equals with skill being all that mattered.

Bouchard raised his sword and pointed it forward at Craven with full extension and walked forward calmly and boldly. It was the walking pressure of a Spanish Destreza fencer and that made Craven smile. A few years ago, it would have been alien to him, but he had seen it all now as he remembered the lessons of De Rosas.

Craven engaged on the Frenchman's blade but traversed to break his advance. He was prepared to parry what came next as he stopped Bouchard's blade and delivered a quick beat. It knocked the tip aside and almost disarmed him. Bouchard looked surprised, but he tried to hide it as he came to guard in a more typical French fashion. His sword hilt raised just above the shoulder and his tip directed to Craven's chest, his knees bent and supple like a foil or smallsword fencer. He launched a snappy cut over the top, which Craven parried and countered with his own. Another thrust came back, but he disengaged and reacquired Bouchard's blade on the other side, launching a rapid counter thrust that passed within a hair of Bouchard's eyes. His eyes opened wide in horror, but he seized his opportunity by grabbing hold of Craven's blade close to the hilt with the intention of disarming or locking his weapon. Yet before he could take advantage of the hold, Craven leapt forward and crashed a thunderous left hook into the Major's temple.

Bouchard lost his hold on Craven's blade as he staggered back stunned from the blow that disorientated him. He looked disgusted as if he wanted to protest at the ungentlemanly conduct. And yet he had no leg to stand on based on his past indiscretions, and there was not one man there who would listen even if he tried. For there was not a man in sight who did not want to see him dead.

He came back to guard as they closed again. Bouchard threw a flurry of sharp and accurate cuts one after the other, but Craven parried each and every one. Bouchard feinted towards Craven's leg, but he snapped a quick cut across the back of his hand. It made him wince as it opened a long if shallow cut, but this blood flow seemed to focus the French Major as he came at Craven with more precision.

Attack after attack was made, and Craven struggled to parry each of them. He could barely get a strike in when Bouchard slashed across his upper right arm and opened a cut, which caused blood to flow and soak into his shirt. Craven ignored the pain as it did not matter to him. Again, they clashed, and as Craven slashed towards Bouchard's face, the Frenchman ducked under and drew a long cut across Craven's torso. Craven's shirt was now soaked in blood, but he was so hyper focused on the fight he did not care. Bouchard was his equal if not better, but there was a determination in Craven's eyes that was unwavering. Bouchard's hold over him was over.

"The arrogance, to ever think you could have defeated me. It will be your downfall," Bouchard seethed with anger as he tried to reassert himself.

"I was a fool to ever think you were to be feared. You are nothing, and you came here because you know it!" Craven threw back at him.

Once more they exchanged attack and parry before Craven slid up Bouchard's blade and smashed him in the face with the ward iron, which sent him tumbling back. The rough tactics were most unsettling to him, for he was accustomed to striking fear into the hearts of his adversaries, and yet Craven remained unwavering. Bouchard made a flurry of feints and thrusts. He even landed one quick cut on Craven's left shoulder, but Craven cut away, knocking him back despite making a parry, for the force knocked him away.

Bouchard thrust for Craven's belly, but he voided away and took hold of Bouchard's blade in his left, even though the keen edge bit into his palm and blood trickled out from his clenched fist over the blade. He pulled Bouchard in close and smashed the pommel of his sword into the Frenchman's head. He staggered back even more stunned than the blow to his temple as blood trickled down his face.

Bouchard put on a brave face, but it was anger and desperation that had led him here, and he was beginning to despair. It seemed that no matter what damage he inflicted on Craven, it was returned two-fold. It was as if Craven was unkillable. He rushed forward and swung a hooking thrust without opposing Craven's blade. It was a very dangerous blow to attempt, as he had no protection whilst he did so. Even so it was also very difficult for Craven to stop as it hooked about his own. He backed away and parried as best he could, and the Frenchman's blade skimmed his shirt. It had come close, for the blade came within an inch of Craven's heart. Bouchard smirked as he knew how close he had come.

They closed and cut and thrust back and forth once again before a brief pause. Bouchard smirked once more as he came forward and delivered three appels, strong beats on the ground with his foot as he hopped forward to intimidate Craven and force him to overreact.

Craven backed away as if he was flummoxed, but in truth he was reading Bouchard like a book. He could see the Frenchman setting up the same dangerous thrust that had almost worked just moments before. Bouchard cried out in an attempt to sell his deception completely, as he reached in with his wide hooking thrust, one against reaching around Craven's sword without any protection to himself. Craven was ready for it. He cast his rear leg backward and dropped into a low and deep lunge, not a lunge to gain reach, but to drop his entire body far below Bouchard's point which sailed over his head. He simultaneously drove his own sword into Bouchard's chest. The Frenchman had been advancing with such speed and aggression that he ran himself halfway up Craven's blade before he came to a stop. Craven got back up to his feet and held Bouchard up with his sword in his left hand.

"Your reign of terror is over, and know this, I am coming for Napoleon, and I am coming for France, and you couldn't stop me," seethed Craven.

He ripped his sword from Bouchard's chest and let him fall to the ground, as a mad cry of elation erupted from the audience.

Craven pulled off his cut and bloodied shirt. He wiped the blood from his blade before tossing the wet rag down onto Bouchard who lay bleeding out from the gaping wound. He breathed a sigh of relief that it was finally over and turned back to join his friends. But he noticed a look of horror on many faces and quickly turned back.

Bouchard was running at him, having used the last of his life energy in one furious charge, his sword directed forward like a lance. The tip of his sword was almost upon Craven's body when a rifle shot cracked out and struck Bouchard in the heart. He collapsed at Craven's feet, and his sword fell from his hands as smoke bellowed from Paget's long rifle. Craven kicked the Frenchman over to see him draw his last breath. It was over.

"That bounty, Sir?" Paget asked playfully.

Craven took the purse from his belt and tossed it to Paget without any protest. Paget smiled as he felt the hefty weight of the bag before tossing it to Matthys.

"Purchase all the food and wine it will buy and let us celebrate."

"Yes!" The crowd roared with joy as Birback and Moxy lifted him into the air and placed him on their shoulders. They paraded him about with gratitude as Ferreira went to Craven, and they watched the Salford Rifles erupt with joy.

"You didn't need to take the fight," declared the Portuguese rifleman.

"Yes, I did, not just for me, but for them," he replied as they watched the jubilant scenes.

"A hard year," he reflected.

Craven nodded in agreement as he thought back on the gruelling campaign.

"This year we took back half of Spain. Next year we will take the rest. We ran the gauntlet, and we came out the other side."

Paget revelled in the celebrations until he was finally put down, but as he spun about and laughed and leapt with joy, he caught a glimpse of a figure in the woods. It was Joachim, and he was certain of it. He looked about for Craven and then back to the same spot. The mysterious man was gone.

"What is it?" Charlie asked as she looked at the worry and dread about his face.

"Nothing, it's nothing," he smiled.

"Come on, it's time to celebrate!"

"Yes, yes, it is," admitted Paget. He tried to put it to the back of his mind as Charlie rushed on to help Matthys find some supplies.

Paget went to Craven and Ferreira looking mortified.

"Sir, I fear what the new year will bring."

"Don't, for we shall deal with the next year when it comes. Enjoy this moment, enjoy this victory, and every victory after it."

"But, Sir, the…" began Paget.

"No, this time if for us. It is for Nooth and so many more who fell before him. And for those still here fighting on. Today we celebrate our victories!

THE END

Printed in Great Britain
by Amazon